MCNALLY'S GAMBLE

Lawrence Sanders

McNally's Gamble

WHEELER
PUBLISHING, INC.
ROCKLAND, MA

★ AN AMERICAN COMPANY ★

Published in Large Print by arrangement with G.P. Putnam's Sons in the United States and Canada.

Wheeler Large Print Book Series.

Set in 16 pt Plantin.

Library of Congress Cataloging-in-Publication Data

Sanders, Lawrence.
  McNally's gamble / Lawrence Sanders.
    p. (large print) cm.(Wheeler large print book series)
  ISBN 1-56895-487-5 (hardcover)
  1. McNally, Archy (Fictitious character)—Fiction. 2. Private investiga-
tors—Florida—Palm Beach—Fiction. 3. Palm Beach (Fla.)—Fiction.
4. Large type books.   I. Title. II. Series
[PS3569.A5125M345 1997b]
813'.54—dc21   97-34313
                                                            CIP

MCNALLY'S GAMBLE

CHAPTER 1

HERE'S AN ANECDOTE you may find difficult to believe. Even I can scarcely give it credence although I was witness to what occurred.

Early in December two Boston villains decided to jaunt to South Florida to escape the rigors of winter and enjoy the sunshine and thong bikinis of Miami Beach. It wasn't long before they were tapped out, a rapid decline of their operating funds accelerated by a visit to the casinos in the Bahamas.

Determined to avoid an ignominious and cash-poor return to their hometown, they decided a criminal enterprise in Florida was the answer to their financial problems. The two wetbrains resolved to kidnap the young child of a wealthy Palm Beach resident, hold him or her just long enough to collect a sizable ransom, and then skedaddle northward.

With no more planning they immediately launched their caper. They slowly toured the boulevards and back roads of the Town of Palm Beach, marveling at the endless rows of mansions they passed. I'm sure visions of sugarplums danced through their tiny, tiny minds, each sweetmeat printed with a dollar sign.

On the second day of exploration they espied a young lad trudging along by himself

1

on the verge of South County Road. No cars or witnesses being nearby, the two improper Bostonians brought their rental car to a screeching halt, grabbed the startled kid, and hustled him into the back seat, where he was threatened with instant annihilation if he uttered a single word or attempted to attract the attention of anyone to his plight.

I imagine the moronic thugs figured if the boy lived in Palm Beach his parents must have a gazillion bucks. Wrong! The boy's father, Maurice Franklin, was moderately well-to-do but a Croesus he was not. He owned a medium-sized pest control business and earned a steady annual profit, but nothing to justify a front-page article in *The Wall Street Journal*. His wife had died of cancer the previous year. His son, the kidnapped Timmy, was his only child.

I knew these details because Maurice Franklin was a client of McNally & Son. When Timmy did not return from school, Franklin's Haitian housekeeper called him at work. In turn he called Timmy's school, his friends, and then, becoming increasingly worried, phoned the police and my father, Prescott McNally, sovereign of our law firm. The pater ordered me to liaise with the Palm Beach Police Department and keep him informed. I do not believe anyone was unduly concerned at that stage of the affair.

Things took a more somber turn the following morning. Timmy had not appeared. The case was assigned to Sgt. Al Rogoff of the PBPD,

2

which heartened me since Al is an old confrere and I trust his professional expertise. I knew he would attempt to trace Timmy's movements after the boy left school, check hospitals, accident reports, and shelters for runaway children. Finally, I learned later, the FBI was informed about noon that a possible kidnapping might be in progress.

I thought I better put in a personal appearance to show the McNally & Son flag, so to speak, and offer what help I could. I arrived at the Franklin home to find the Feds in command and I was allowed entry only after Sgt. Rogoff vouched for my bona fides.

FBI techs were busily installing a variety of electronic devices. One would amplify all telephone conversations so everyone could hear clearly both sides of a phoned dialogue. A voice-activated deck would make a taped record of all calls. A third dingus was designed to trace the source of incoming calls within minutes, obviating the need of searching phone company logs.

While this work was in progress I went over to a couch where our client, Maurice Franklin, was sitting upright, gripping his knees with white knuckles. I identified myself, expressed my sympathy and that of McNally & Son. I assured him we stood ready to offer whatever assistance we could.

He was a bulky man, massive through the neck and shoulders, with an indoor complexion made paler by stress. "If Timmy's been kidnapped," he said, his voice thick, "and I get to them, I'll kill them. I swear it. Putting their hands on my son. I'll destroy them. I don't care what happens to me afterward."

"Understandable, Mr. Franklin," I said as soothingly as I could. "But we don't yet know for certain he has been kidnapped."

"They'll probably want a lot of money," he went on, not listening to me. "Maybe a million. Maybe more. How can I come up with that?"

"Don't even think about it," I urged. "If a ransom demand is made, believe me, sufficient funds will be available."

I was still trying to comfort him and the technicians were still at work wiring their black boxes when the telephone rang. There must have been a dozen men in the room at that time and I think we all froze and stared at the shrilling phone. The FBI special agent in charge beckoned to Maurice Franklin.

"Answer it," he commanded. "If it's a ransom demand, keep them talking as long as possible. Follow the script we suggested."

Our client nodded and staggered to his feet. I assisted him. The amplifier had been connected and we all heard the ensuing conversation.

Franklin: "Hello?"

Boston-accented masculine voice: "You Morry Franklin?"

"Maurice Franklin. Yes, I am Maurice Franklin."

"You got a son named Timmy?"

"Yes."

4

"We got him."

"What!?"

"Let's not play games, Morry. This is a snatch. You want to see your kid alive again? Home and happy?"

"How do I know what you're saying is true?"

"Bosco, bring him over here. Timmy, say hello to your pop."

"Hi, dad!"

"Timmy, are you all right? They haven't hurt you?"

"I'm okay. They gave me a Twinkie."

"Don't be frightened, son."

"I'm not scared but I do want to come home, dad."

"Of course you do and I want you home. Put the man back on the phone."

"See? We got the kid and he ain't hurt. Satisfied?"

"How much do you want?"

"Whoa! Wait a minute. This is just the first call. You bring in the cops and your kid is gone. You understand?"

"Yes."

"You'll be hearing from us again. About how much it will cost and how to deliver it. Meanwhile sweat a little."

Click!

The phone went dead. It was then I believe we all became aware of incredible good fortune. Maurice Franklin had Caller ID. In Florida this is a small device attached to your personal phone which, on an illuminated

5

screen, reveals the name and telephone number of the most recent caller. In this case the screen displayed the name and phone number of a well-known West Palm Beach motel, one of a national chain.

There was a great hoot of triumph and relieved laughter. Apparently the Beantown lamebrains were not aware of Caller ID and had made their threatening call from their current residence. I remember Sgt. Rogoff once told me ninety percent of successful law enforcement is not due to clever investigation but to the rank stupidity of the criminals. For every Professor Moriarty there are many galoots who rob a bank and attempt to make their getaway on a bicycle.

Within twenty minutes a plan was devised and all the officers, Feds and locals, rushed outside to their cars. I was ordered to stay with the father. We were assured we would be informed as soon as possible of the result of the rescue attempt.

I saw Maurice Franklin had a severe attack of the shakes and asked him if any strong spirits were available. He pointed to a sideboard, where I found a modest collection of bottles including a liter of Sterling vodka. Mother's milk! I scouted about, discovered the kitchen, and poured two tumblers of iced vodka. I brought our distraught client his drink and he took a ferocious gulp, shuddered, drew a deep breath.

"They'll find Timmy?" he asked me, pleading.

"Of course they shall," I said firmly. "Tell me about the boy."

For the next hour or so he talked nonstop, relating what a wonderful son he had, how fortunate he was to be blessed with a child like that, how teachers and friends adored him, how intelligent and talented he was, what a wonderful future lay in store for him. Meanwhile I sipped my drink and just listened, nodding and smiling, not speaking but praying silently this affair would end happily.

It did. The front door was flung open, Sgt. Rogoff entered. His beefy arm was about the shoulders of a handsome, fair-haired lad, and Al's face was cracked in a grin from here to there.

"Timmy!" Maurice Franklin shouted, lurched to his feet, rushed to his son, weeping. He flopped to his knees, gathered the boy into his arms. They embraced tightly. Bliss on a stick.

"Are you all right?" the father asked, his voice choky.

"I'm hungry, dad," I heard Timmy say.

I laughed and pulled Rogoff into the kitchen. I poured him a small vodka and another for myself. I deserved it; I had endured an hour without talking.

"Any problems?" I asked the sergeant.

"Nope," he said. "We got the key from the manager and waltzed in. The kid was watching TV and the two master criminals were playing high-card for nickels."

"Beautiful. Did they say anything?"

"Yeah. One of the imbeciles asked me, 'How did you know where we was?' I told him we employed a Gypsy fortune-teller who used a crystal ball. She saw everything, knew everything, told us everything."

"What did he say to that?"

"He said, 'No shit?' "

We finished our drinks. I left Sgt. Rogoff with the Franklins. Before I departed I phoned Mrs. Trelawney, my father's private secretary, and asked her to inform the seignior Timmy had been rescued from his inept abductors and all was well.

I told you the entire incident was incredible and so it was. But it did happen and I know you have the utmost faith in my veracity. Thank you.

The thwarted offense reinforced my belief that kidnapping is one of the most despicable misdeeds in the sad gamut of human transgressions. But the events of the next few weeks were to prove there are more heinous crimes.

CHAPTER 2

ARE YOU FAMILIAR with the name William Claude Dukenfield? No? Then perhaps you know him under the name of W.C. Fields, the author of almost as many bons mots as Oscar Wilde. During a period of dreadful inflation in the 1920's Fields remarked, "I can't see how the human race is going to survive now

8

that the cost of living has gone up two dollars a quart."

I was reminded of Fields's quip on the December afternoon after leaving the Franklin home. I was seeking a birthday gift for my father at a Palm Beach liquor store. Prescott McNally was not only mein papa but he was also urboss of the legal firm of which I am a loyal if habitually tardy employee. I am the son, Archibald McNally.

Although I do not possess a degree, having been ejected from Yale Law for an escapade too outrageous to retell, I had been granted gainful employment and assigned the task of making Discreet Inquiries when our clients' problems required investigation before their distress came to the attention of the gendarmes or a supermarket tabloid which might feature the matter next to an article entitled "Extraterrestrial Accused of Flashing!"

I finally chose a graceful decanter of XO Courvoisier cognac for the sire's seventy-something year, consoling myself for the cost with the hope I might be granted a sip on special occasions.

I had it gift-wrapped and enclosed a card stating, "Happy Birthday and many of them." I knew my father would be offended by any greeting more affectionate. He is an austere man who values reason over emotion. I, on the other hand, believe the heart commands and the mind obeys. (The glands may cast their vote as well.)

I drove my fire engine–red Miata back to our

ersatz-Tudor manse on Ocean Boulevard. I pulled into my slot in the three-car garage, disembarked, and started for the back door leading to the kitchen. But then Hobo, our crossbred terrier, came bouncing from his gabled house to greet me. I gave him an expected pat and ear tweaks and assured him he was the doughtiest dog who ever lived. I believed it; family and friends concurred: Hobo was one fearless canine. But modest. Praise him and he yawned.

I found Ursi Olson working in the kitchen. She is the distaff side of the Scandinavian couple who keep the McNally ship afloat. Her husband, Jamie, is our factotum, a taciturn character with a fondness for aquavit and pipe tobacco with an odor distressingly similar to asafetida.

Ursi was in an understandably peckish mood. My father had refused to approve a celebratory birthday dinner party with several close friends as guests. And when Ursi began to plan a scrumptious family-only feast, the lord of the manor informed her he would much prefer a simple meal of pot roast with potato pancakes and dilled green beans— hardly a challenge to Ursi's culinary skills.

However, she declared triumphantly, he hadn't mentioned dessert, and she had constructed a confection known in New York as seven-layer cake although I think it is rightfully called Dobos Torte. It consists of fifteen thin alternating layers of cake and milk chocolate creme, the whole covered with dark chocolate icing. One taste is enough to make you roll your eyes and swear to begin dieting—tomorrow.

The guv's birthday dinner went delightfully. The crew always takes its cue from the captain and that evening the skipper was in a genial mood and we responded. He even consumed two slender slices of the torte (I had three) and expressed hearty thanks for his gifts: a James Upshall pipe from the Olsons, my cognac, and from my mother, Madeleine, a V-necked sweater she had knitted in an argyle pattern. Pops was especially pleased with her present and forbore to mention one sleeve appeared to be two inches longer than the other.

Dinner concluded, my parents and I moved into his study and I hoped it might be for a postprandial birthday toast with the XO Courvoisier I had given him. No such luck. Father seated himself in the leather throne behind his monumental desk, motioned mother and me to club chairs, and posed a question that was to ignite a devilish Discreet Inquiry testing the sagacity and deviousness of yrs. truly. What a doozy it was!

"Archy," he said, "are you acquainted with Mrs. Edythe Westmore?"

"I've met the lady once, sir, at a charity bash at The Breakers."

"Oh?" he said, and elevated one of his gnarly eyebrows, a display of legerdemain I've never been able to master. "And how did you happen to meet?"

"Her necklace of garnets broke and I helped her retrieve them."

"Do you also know her son and daughter?"

"No, father, I do not."

"Are you aware Mrs. Westmore, a widow, is on our client list?"

"No, I didn't know that." I turned to mother. "She is a close friend of yours, is she not?"

The mater smiled. She is a rather large woman who succeeds in being simultaneously imposing and soft. Her complexion is a bit florid (the poor dear suffers from high blood pressure) but I think her uncommonly attractive. When I was a mere whelp and became addicted to attending revivals of old movies I was amazed at how mother resembled Mary Boland: same good looks, more pleasing than striking, and a similar ditsy manner.

"Perhaps not a *close* friend, Archy," she replied. "But we do see each other frequently. Edythe belongs to both my bridge and garden clubs. Her African violets are simply unpareil. Is that the right word?"

"Nonpareil," I corrected gently.

Father stirred restlessly and I knew he was becoming impatient with our gibble-gabble. "Maddie," he said, "suppose you repeat to Archy what you told me last night concerning Mrs. Westmore."

"Well, our bridge club met at Suzy Longhorne's two days ago and after we finished playing, refreshments were served: cucumber sandwiches and some lovely petits fours Suzy bought at a new bakery in Boca.

They were *so* good, especially the ones with mint icing."

A sigh from behind the desk. "Mother, please get on with it."

"Anyway," she continued, "we started talking about the stock market and real estate, and Edythe Westmore said she had recently consulted an investment adviser who is a real expert and is making her a lot of money in unusual things."

"Oh?" I said. "Such as?"

"Stocks that aren't even listed in the paper. And a tin mine in Bolivia and oil wells in Texas."

Mon père and I exchanged a quick glance.

"And now," she went on, "Edythe said he has a wonderful deal for her. He says she could make a small fortune."

I knew the retort to that: "If she starts with a large fortune." But all I said was, "Did Mrs. Westmore give any details about this wonderful deal?"

"Yes, he wants her to buy a Fabergé egg from a man in Paris. This man needs cash and is willing to sell the egg for half a million dollars. Edythe's financial adviser says she could easily get more than a million for it at auction, even two or three million."

"Then why," I asked, "doesn't the man in Paris put it up for auction?"

"Edythe didn't say. I don't think it occurred to her to ask."

Then father and I stared at each other. "Is Mrs. Westmore wealthy, sir?" I inquired.

He lapsed into his mulling mode: a long period of silence during which he undoubtedly held an internal debate on the ethics, necessity, and possible unwelcome repercussions of answering my question. He'd go through the same process if he was invited to put Colman's mustard on his broiled calves' liver.

"Moderately wealthy," he pronounced finally. "But not to the extent that a single investment of half a million dollars would be considered prudent."

"A Fabergé egg," I repeated. "What an odd investment. I have heard them described as the world's costliest tchotchkes."

Father straightened in his chair, not at all amused. "Do you have anything on your plate at the moment?" he demanded.

"No, sir. Not since the Franklin kidnapping is resolved."

"Then I suggest you institute Discreet Inquiries anent this so-called investment adviser Mrs. Westmore is consulting and particularly his recommendation she purchase a Fabergé egg. You must tread carefully here, Archy. The lady has not requested our assistance and McNally and Son has no right or duty to go prying into her personal money matters. But she is a valued client and I would not care to see her defrauded by a common swindler. From what mother has told us, I fear it is exactly what may happen."

"I concur," I told him. "It has a whiff of flimflam."

"Then look into it," he said sharply. "But be circumspect. The client must not be aware of your investigation. Is that clear?"

"Yes, father."

He rose and I knew I was dismissed. I wished him a final "Happy Birthday," which he accepted with a wan smile. Then I left my parents alone. I suspected they had private memories to exchange. Birthdays are a time for fond remembrances, are they not?

I climbed the stairs to my third-floor mini-suite: sitting room, bedroom, bath. It was small, cramped, and under a leaky roof but I cherished it. It was my sanctuary and the rent was zilch.

I lighted only my third English Oval of the day and poured myself a small marc. This is a brandy made from the residue of wine grapes after they have been pressed. It is possibly the world's most powerful sludge.

Thus equipped, I sat at my grungy desk, put up my feet, and phoned Consuela Garcia, the young woman with whom I am intimate and, regrettably, sometimes unfaithful. As I explained to my pal Binky Watrous, my infidelity is due to a mild but persistent case of satyriasis caused by seeing Jane Russell in *The Outlaw* at an impressionable age.

CHAPTER 3

SHE PICKED UP the phone.

"Martha?" I said.

"I'll Martha you, goofball," Connie said. "Have you been behaving yourself?"

"Don't I always?"

"No," she said. "Why haven't you called?"

"I am calling," I said. "Right this very minute. It is I, Archibald McNally, famed epicure, bon vivant, dilettante, and lout-about-town. How are you, hon?"

"Okay, I guess. Tired. Lady C. has been working my fanny to a nubbin. She's planning a sit-down dinner for local pols and so far she's changed the time twice, the menu three times, and the guest list is revised every hour on the hour. She's been a world-class pain."

Connie is employed as social secretary to Lady Cynthia Horowitz, possibly the wealthiest doyenne in Palm Beach, proud of six ex-husbands, and possessing the personal warmth and social graces of a pit viper. I happen to admire the Lady and consider her prickliness more amusing than offensive. She does have many local detractors but I suspect their enmity springs from envy. They have never been invited to dine at her table and enjoy the *risotto*

16

alla champagne e foie gras prepared by her French chef.

"Suffer in silence," I advised Connie. "Christmas is right around the corner and with it comes your annual bonus."

"Good thinking on your part," Connie said.

"Listen, hon," I said. "How about dinner on Saturday?"

"I may work. If I do, dinner will have to be late and informal. I'll let you know."

"Whatever," I said. "Your wish is my command."

"Since when?" she scoffed. "Now I'm going to crash. I'm exhausted."

"Sleep well, luv," I said.

That was the extent of our conversation. Please note the teasing tone and absence of vows of love and/or passion. I enjoyed our casual relationship and—fearing a closer alliance: the dreaded M-word—hoped it would continue. Sheer cowardice on my part, of course.

Despite her zealous investigation and occasional confirmation of my extracurricular activities, Connie endured. She was suspicious, jealous, and had every right to be. But she endured. What a marvelous woman she was! And what a cur I was.

I resolutely turned my thoughts away from my own behavior to a more immediate problem: the conduct of an "investment adviser" who sought to persuade a financially naive widow to purchase a Fabergé egg. Why that particular bijou, I wondered, and not a bag of diamonds, a Rembrandt, or even the jaw-bone of a dinosaur?

What exactly did I know about Fabergé eggs? Not a great deal. The treasures were designed and created by the world-famous House of Fabergé, jewelers and goldsmiths, headquartered in St. Petersburg. They were commissioned by the Russian czars Alexander III and his son Nicholas II. Two of the opulent fantasies were made each year from 1885 to 1917 and given by the reigning czar to his wife and mother to celebrate the Russian Easter.

At the moment that was the extent of my knowledge and I realized I'd have to learn more. One final personal note: Several years previously I had seen four Fabergé eggs exhibited at a Manhattan art gallery. I was surprised by their size—or lack of thereof. I had envisioned towering wonders of gold and diamonds. What I saw were glittering masterpieces no higher than six inches. It made their artfully detailed craftsmanship all the more impressive.

I keep a journal in which I record accounts of my Discreet Inquiries. I try to make entries every day or so during the course of an investigation. I include everything: facts, rumors, surmises, even scraps of conversation and descriptions of the physical appearance, personality, dress, and habits of the people involved.

Donning my reading specs, I flipped to a fresh page and began scribbling notes on Mrs. Edythe Westmore, her investment adviser, and the Fabergé *objets de luxe.* I thought of heading the page "The Case of the Rotten Egg" but discarded the notion. A few weeks later I was happy I had.

Labors completed, I had one more marc, a final coffin nail, and listened to a tape of Ella Fitzgerald singing "I Didn't Know What Time It Was." She finished and I knew what time it was. So I went to bed.

I have a lifelong habit of oversleeping (I refuse to be a slave to an alarm clock) but on Friday morning I managed to wake in time to breakfast with my parents in the dining room. I was glad I wasn't still snoozing for Ursi had whipped up a batch of blueberry pancakes she served with little turkey sausages. What a great way to start a new day!

Father had his nose deep in his morning newspaper, so mother and I did all the chatting, mostly about a shopping trip she and Ursi were planning to replenish the McNally larder and Hobo's supply of Alpo and kibble. I was on my second cup of black coffee when I remembered what I wanted to ask her.

"By the way, moms," I said, "there's something I need to know. When Mrs. Westmore was telling your bridge club about her investment adviser, did she happen to mention his name?"

"Oh, Archy, I'm sure she must have. Now let me think..." She pressed the tip of a forefinger against a soft cheek. "Of course!" she cried, brightening. "A very unusual name. Twain. I distinctly remember because it was just like the writer Mark Twain. But his name is Frederick Twain."

"Thank you, dear," I said. "You've been a big help."

Breakfast concluded, the family separated. I returned to my aerie to don a sport jacket I had recently purchased: a tweed blazer with bone toggles instead of buttons. Natty is the word. Then I dallied at my bedroom window. It overlooks the graveled turnaround fronting our garage.

I waited patiently and finally saw father leave for the office in his black Lexus. A few moments later Ursi and mother departed on their shopping trip in Mrs. McNally's ancient wood-bodied Ford station wagon. I trotted downstairs and went directly to papa's study. I sat behind his desk in his high-backed swivel chair feeling like a czarevitch eager to ascend the throne.

Really all I wanted to do was use the old man's telephone directories stacked in the lower drawer. I pulled out the thickest with listings for the entire West Palm Beach area and searched for Frederick Twain. Nothing. Then I tried the Boca Raton book. Nothing again.

Of course it was possible he had recently moved to our region or had an unlisted number. But both seemed unlikely for a man in his business desirous of being easily available to clients and potential clients. Perhaps his surname was spelled differently: Twayne or Twane. But mother had been definite about the name being the same as that of the author of *Huckleberry Finn*.

I was trying to puzzle it out when suddenly a light bulb flashed on in the air above my head—just as in the comic strips—and I laughed aloud. My solution of the problem was due to my knowledge of the giddy way my mother's mind works. I grabbed the telephone directories again and began looking for the name Frederick Clemens.

I found him. He was a resident of West Palm Beach but was not listed in the Yellow Pages in the investment adviser category. Incidentally, the title means diddly-squat. You or I or anyone can anoint ourself an investment adviser, financial consultant, or money manager.

My first thought was to phone him immediately, use a false name, and attempt to set up an appointment. My second thought was better because I remembered the Caller ID that had solved the Franklin kidnapping. If Frederick Clemens's phone was similarly equipped he'd know at once I was calling from the residence of Prescott McNally. It would hardly honor my father's injunction to conduct the inquiry with the utmost discretion.

But I knew how to finesse the problem. I phoned Binky Watrous.

"You're home?" I greeted him. "I thought you might be with Bridget Houlihan." I was referring to his light-o'-love.

"She's gone," he said gloomily.

"Gone? You mean she's given you the old heave-ho?"

21

"No, no," he protested. "She left yesterday for Ireland to spend some time with her family. I miss her already."

"Of course you do. And so you will welcome an opportunity to alleviate your sorrow by assisting me in a spot of sleuthing,"

"Great!" he said, coming alive. "Will I be paid? Even a modest stipend?"

"Afraid not, old buddy. The boss wouldn't approve. We'll have to continue considering it on-the-job training. However, there will be fringe benefits. For instance, I'll be happy to stand you lunch today at the Pelican Club at noon."

"Okay," he said cheerfully. "At least it will get me out of the house. The Duchess keeps nagging me about seeking gainful employment. She doesn't seem to realize I am, by virtue of my unique talents, destined to be an entrepreneur rather than an employee."

"Duchess" was the Palm Beach sobriquet bestowed on Binky's formidable maiden aunt who has supported her ne'er-do-well nephew since the accidental death of his parents when he was just a tad. As for his "unique talents," the only one I was aware of was his proficiency at birdcalls, hardly a marketable skill. But he did have a Ph.D. in fatuity. He once asked me what I thought it might cost to have his three-year collection of Victoria's Secret catalogues bound in vellum.

"This assignment you have for me," Binky said. "Does it involve, ah, danger?"

"Oh, I doubt it. It really requires mental agility rather than physical action."

"Good-oh! If eventually I'm to become an independent private eye, I think I'm more the Philo Vance type than Mike Hammer, don't you?"

"Undoubtedly."

"Outwit the baddies," he burbled on, "instead of shooting them in the brisket. That's the way to go!"

Binky couldn't outwit Mortimer Snerd, and I began to wonder if I was making a horrible error in recruiting him. But it was a simple task I wanted him to perform. I couldn't see how he might possibly foul it up. I learned.

"One more thing," I said. "This is a very hush-hush operation and I must have your solemn pledge you will reveal nothing of it to anyone—including Bridget when she returns."

"Wouldn't think of blabbing, old boy. My lips are sealed."

I could have made a ribald reply to that but resisted the temptation and merely said, "The Pelican at noon," and hung up. I scrawled a quick note of Frederick Clemens's name, address, and phone number, then left the study and went out to the garage. I swung aboard my chariot, pulled onto Ocean Boulevard, and headed north.

I had absolutely no intention of putting in even a *pro forma* appearance at the McNally Building on Royal Palm Way. My private office there is so small most visitors enter sideways. Instead I headed for Worth Avenue, which rivals Rodeo Drive as a sparkling carnival midway in which the concessions lure well-heeled patrons and browsers with more dreams than dollars.

CHAPTER 4

AMIDST THE PLUSHY stores offering precious merchandise in even more precious surroundings, Windsor Antiques looked like a dusty sparrow lost in a flock of preening peacocks. The front was a drab grayish beige. The single show window had held the same display as long as I could remember: a hand-carved mahogany tea caddy, probably Victorian, of surpassing ugliness.

The shop was owned and operated solely by Mr. Sydney Smythe, an aged gentleman whose establishment, I often thought, was more thrift shop than a gallery of tempting antiques. The interior was crowded with old things—furniture, lamps, bric-a-brac—but most of them were so ordinary and unattractive it was hard to imagine an interior decorator or collector bothering to visit. I mean, who would be eager to acquire a dilapidated wooden butter churn or ache to put a scarred oak sideboard with a stained marble top in the living room of a shiny Florida condo?

Over the years I had purchased a few small oddities from Windsor Antiques, including a porcelain ashtray made in Paris and imprinted with a full-length portrait of Josephine Baker clad in bananas. Mr. Smythe and I had become easy with each other and occasionally I stopped at his shop for a chat and a look at any campy knickknacks he had added to his stock of junk.

The proprietor was a geriatric dandy, one of the few men I've known who carried a handkerchief (soiled) tucked up the cuff of a jacket sleeve. The jacket Mr. Smythe favored was a purple velveteen (shiny elbows) with a nipped-in waist. Add a waistcoat of petit point (threads dangling) depicting a hunting scene. Add fawn slacks (unpressed). Add patent-leather loafers (scratched) on his small feet. Add a billowing silk ascot (hems opened). And add a wire-framed pince-nez (bent) with oversized lens that gave him the look of an emaciated owl.

"Archy!" he said, offering a limp hand-clasp. "How nice to see you again. Your health?"

"No complaints, sir," I said. "And yours?"

"I survive, dear boy. And at my age—considering the sins of my youth—that is a triumph. Your father is keeping you busy and out of mischief?"

"He's certainly keeping me busy—which is one reason I dropped by. Mr. Smythe, I need your help."

"Delighted to be of assistance if I'm able. What do you require?"

I improvised a cover story on the spot. I'm quite good at spur-of-the-moment lying.

"I've been assigned to evaluate an estate. No

trouble with the stocks and bonds; their value is readily available. But the personal effects of the deceased are a problem, and one in particular: a Fabergé egg. I hoped you might provide some information on its history and current monetary worth."

I thought my request startled him. He blinked several times and grabbed for the pince-nez before it slid from his bony nose.

"A Fabergé egg?" he repeated. "Have you seen it?"

"Yes, sir."

"How large?"

"Perhaps five inches high excluding its stand."

"Jeweled?" he asked.

"Lavishly," I replied.

"Ah," he said, "then it's apparent you're dealing with a Fabergé Imperial egg—the name given to those created for the czars. You must realize, dear boy, the House of Fabergé created an enormous volume and variety of products, including such things as cigarette cases, figurines, picture frames, and clocks. Certainly one of their most popular items was egg-shaped bijous since eggs symbolized rebirth and resurrection and there was a huge demand for them as gifts during the Russian Easter. Some Fabergé eggs, made of precious or semiprecious stones, are no larger than jelly beans. But it is the Imperial eggs that have caught and held the world's fascination. This egg you are attempting to evaluate—did you open it?"

"Open it? No, sir, I didn't touch it."

"Pity. You see, Archy, every Imperial egg contained a 'surprise,' revealed when the egg was opened. It might be a clockwork bird, a model coach or yacht, or even diminutive oil portraits of the czar's family. Some of the surprises, being smaller than the egg itself, are miniature marvels. The perfection of design and craftsmanship is simply awesome."

"How many of these masterpieces were made, Mr. Smythe?"

"It is generally accepted a total of fifty-three Imperial eggs were created, including two made in 1917 that were never delivered to Nicholas the Second due to a slight obstacle called the Russian Revolution. Those two eggs have never been identified. It is not even definitely known if they were completed."

I wanted to keep him talking. For a dealer in grungy antiques he seemed to know a great deal about Fabergé eggs and I wondered how he had come by his expertise. Perhaps in the past he had owned a shop featuring such rare, beautiful, and expensive treasures.

"I suppose," I said, "all the Fabergé Imperial eggs are in museums or in the hands of private collectors like our late client."

The comment seemed to displease him. He made a grimace almost of distaste. I could not understand his reaction; it was an innocent remark.

"Debatable," he said finally. "The whereabouts of perhaps eight Imperial eggs are unknown. They may have been destroyed or stolen and hidden to this day. Those were violent, lawless times in St. Petersburg when the Bolsheviks took over. Much of the gold and silver jewelry belonging to royalty was seized and melted down. Oil paintings were vandalized, palaces ransacked, priceless antiques carted off to the hovels of the rabble, and libraries of rare books burned to heat those hovels. So it's understandable how several Imperial eggs disappeared. Peter Carl Fabergé was lucky to escape alive. Nicholas and Alexandra were not as fortunate."

The old man seemed genuinely moved by this recital of history. He removed his pincenez, took the handkerchief from his cuff, and wiped the glasses slowly. The Russian Revolution was as ancient to me as the Punic Wars but Mr. Smythe acted as if the execution of the Romanovs happened yesterday.

"Fascinating stuff," I said, to let him know I appreciated his efforts. "Could you give me a rough idea of what you think the Fabergé egg in our late client's estate might be worth? Just a ballpark figure."

He shook his head. "I cannot do that, dear boy. It depends on the provenance and authenticity of the egg as well as its design, the surprise within, and its physical condition. I suggest you have an appraisal made by someone more expert than I. If you wish I can recommend several reputable and knowledgeable people."

Something he had said alerted me. "Its authenticity?" I repeated. "Are you implying it might be a fake? A forgery?"

"The possibility does exist," he said, nodding. "There have been a few attempts to sell a fraudulent Fabergé Imperial egg. All have failed. No one has been able to reproduce the exquisite workmanship of Carl Fabergé's artisans. And you know, most of them were quite young—in their early twenties."

"Amazing," I said, tried to think of more questions to ask and couldn't. "Mr. Smythe, I want to thank you for giving me so much of your time."

"Do I seem busy?" he said with a faint smile. "I enjoy talking about antiques and their history."

"Well, you've been a big help, sir. If my father approves of having the egg appraised I may return to ask for your recommendations. Or, I warn you, I may come in just to learn more about the House of Fabergé and their marvelous eggs."

"Anytime," he said genially, and we shook hands.

I exited into the steely December sunlight, slid into my barouche, and sat a few moments reviewing what I had just heard. Interesting. Top-notch grist, one might even say. The salient fact, I decided, was the attempts to sell counterfeit Imperial eggs. If it had been tried before, it was quite possibly being tried again— with Mrs. Edythe Westmore the intended victim of the forgery. She didn't seem to me worldly-wise enough to insist on an expert's appraisal before purchase.

I headed for West Palm Beach wondering

how I might finagle a tête-à-tête with Mrs. Westmore or, better yet, a kaffeeklatsch with the entire Westmore family. I like to know the people I'm defending. Sometimes they reveal strengths or weaknesses, or even just predilections that make my job easier. Besides, I'm a sociable bloke. I can endure solitude but I much prefer companionship, chatter, and perhaps a wee bit of malicious gossip.

I pulled into the parking area of the Pelican Club, happy to see it almost deserted. It meant the luncheon crowd had not yet arrived, and Binky and I would be able to snag a table in the dining room.

I was one of the founders of the Pelican, a private club, and it remains my favorite South Florida rendezvous. It provides food, drink, a dartboard, and on most nights enough wassail to satisfy the most demanding roisterer, female or male.

Management is in the capable hands of the Pettibones, a family of color. Father Simon is bartender and majordomo, mother Jasmine serves as den mother, son Leroy is our chef, and daughter Priscilla does her own take on how a waitress should behave. They are a merry crew and had rescued the Pelican from the shoals of Chapter 7. (That's total bankruptcy, not the seventh section of this tome.)

The rear dining area was vacant and I grabbed the relatively secluded corner table Connie Garcia and I customarily select. Priscilla was nowhere to be seen but I was hardly seated before Binky Watrous came bustling in. He always arrives promptly for a free meal. Not that he's a moocher; he's just continually tapped out.

"You saved my life," he told me, flopping into a chair. "The Duchess wanted me to escort her to a flute recital. But I told her I had an important business meeting with you. She wanted to know when I start drawing a salary. When, Archy?"

"Binky," I said, "I thought after a period of on-the-job training you intended to go into business as a private investigator, the Philip Marlowe of Palm Beach."

"Well, yes, that's my plan. Do you think I'm ready?"

I didn't say, "Never!" I said, "Almost but not quite."

I was saved from dashing more balder when Priscilla came sashaying from the kitchen. She was wearing what appeared to be a denim muumuu painted with signs of the zodiac.

"Very fetching, Pris," I said. "Where did you get it—army surplus?"

"Keep it up, kiddo," she said, "and you'll need a stomach pump after lunch. You two nits want a drink?"

"Splendid idea," I said. "Vodka rocks for me. Binky?"

"I'll have a Jameson straight, no ice. And please, Priscilla, would you ask Simon to add three drops of Irish Mist."

"I think his dropper is broken," she said, "but I'll try." And she bopped away.

31

"His dropper is broken?" Binky said, bewildered.

"Forget it," I advised. "It was just sass. So you've switched to Irish whiskey, have you? Thinking about Bridget?"

"Oh, yes," he said dreamily. "She's probably wandering through the shamrocks right now, wishing I was there."

"Or quaffing a pint of Guinness Stout and trying to remember your name. Why don't you marry the girl, Binky?"

"Why don't you marry Connie?" he countered.

We glowered at each other, a nice pair of poltroons.

Binky is a palish lad with fair hair and a wispy blond mustache in need of a good dose of Miracle-Gro. He is of short stature and small-boned, so there is not much to him physically. Or mentally, I might add. I recall he once tasted the vichyssoise he had ordered and complained indignantly to the waiter, "My soup is cold!"

But he's a good-hearted chap, no malice in him, and the fact that his gears may have slipped a notch or two doesn't diminish my affection for him. I mean, he's really an innocent with a limited comprehension of the brute world. Some women react to his naïveté with a desire to mother him. Binky is not so ingenuous as to let those opportunities for a more intimate relationship slip by.

Priscilla returned with our drinks. "What's on the menu?" I asked her.

"Stains," she said. "But if it's food you want, Leroy is pushing knockwurst, sauerkraut, and baked beans."

"Sounds good to me," I said. "Binky?"

"All right," he said doubtfully. "But will it give me gas?"

"It might," Pris admitted. "If it does, please wait until you're out in the parking lot."

And she went into the kitchen cackling.

CHAPTER 5

WE NURSED OUR drinks while I gave my Dr. Watson a rundown on the role he was to play in the new Discreet Inquiry.

"There's a man in West Palm," I started, "who claims to be an investment adviser, financial consultant, money manager—whatever. Apparently he makes his living by handling other people's money."

"I'd like a job like that," Binky said.

"And you may be as well qualified as he. Anyway, I have his name, address, and phone number. What I'd like you to do is call him, try to set up an appointment, and if you succeed, go see him."

"Won't he ask where I got his name?"

"Sure he will. Tell him you were at a cocktail party and heard one of the guests singing his praises and so you decided to look him up. I think he'll buy it."

"But why am I looking him up?"

"Because you have some money to invest."

"Cool," Binky said happily. "How much do I have—a million?"

"Let's start small. Tell him you have about fifty thousand dollars in CD's and money-market funds but you're looking for higher yields."

"But I haven't got fifty thousand, Archy."

I sighed. "I'm aware of that, Binky. But tell him you have to get his reaction."

"And that's all you want—his reaction?"

"Of course not. I want a physical description of the man himself. Is his address a home, or an office? Is it a shabby joint, or impressive? Does he have an assistant or a secretary? How is he dressed? In other words I want to learn as much as possible about him and his business."

Binky took a deep gulp of his drink and was pleasantly surprised. "Simon did add the Irish Mist," he said. "Archy, is this man a criminal or even a suspect?"

"That's what I'm trying to determine."

"Why don't you go see him yourself?"

"This is a very complex inquiry, Binky," I said earnestly (I can do earnest), "and there are many other leads I must follow. I'm depending on you to investigate Clemens. That's his name: Frederick Clemens."

"Should I tell him my name?"

I thought a moment, sipping my own plasma. "I don't see why not," I said finally. "If he runs a trace he'll find you're the closest relative of a wealthy dowager. It will help convince him you really do have fifty thousand bucks to invest."

Priscilla brought our platters and, with Binky's approval, I ordered two steins of draft beer. Lunch looked enormous and we attacked it vigorously.

"What if he asks for the money?" Binky said. "I have eighteen dollars in my bank account."

"Don't talk with your mouth full," I pleaded. "You're splattering me. I don't think he'll want the cash immediately. He'll probably check you out first. He may suggest some investments he thinks are suitable for you. If he does, remember what they are. I'd like to know."

"Archy, what is sauerkraut?"

"Cabbage."

"It is?" he said, astounded. "I hate cabbage—it's so smelly—but this is delicious."

"Binky, stop talking about cabbage and listen to me. When you visit Clemens, dress conservatively—no T-shirt or sandals. And be careful of what you say. You're supposed to be a well-to-do young man, possibly heir to a fortune, who is serious about increasing his income. Do you think you can play the part?"

"A piece of cake," he said. "I'm an excellent actor. I once went to a reception for the president of France and pretended I was the American ambassador."

"Did you get in?"

"No. But only because the ambassador was already there—a woman."

"Good preparation on your part," I remarked. "Try to do better with Frederick Clemens. And

I suggest after you leave him, you make notes of the meeting so you don't forget anything you heard or observed."

"I don't have to make notes; I have an excellent memory."

"Do you? What day is this?"

"Thursday."

"Binky, it's Friday."

"What happened to Thursday?" he said, much aggrieved.

I gave up, convinced now I was committing a horrible blunder in assigning this simp to make the first contact with Clemens. But then I consoled myself with the hope Binky's nuttiness might make him attractive to the financial consultant. If he was a professional con man he'd recognize Binky as a perfect pigeon, ready for plucking.

We finished lunch, too stuffed for dessert, and I signed the tab. I gave my goofy henchman the scrap of paper with Clemens's name, address, and phone number.

"Why don't you call him today, Binky," I said, "and try to set up a meet for early next week. Please let me know how you make out."

"Sure thing, boss," he said. "Thanks for the feed."

We parted in the parking lot and went our separate ways. I drove toward the McNally Building. But I changed my mind before I arrived and headed home instead, hoping mother had returned from her shopping trip.

She had. I found her in our little greenhouse talking to her begonias, as usual. Mother's plants have won several awards at flower shows and she is convinced speaking frequently to the begonias is the reason for their health and beauty. "They are *happy* plants," she once told me—and I believe it. What living things could resist her TLC? Not me.

Hobo was curled up on the floor in a patch of sunlight. He raised his head when I entered, gave me one tail thump, and resumed his snooze.

"Mother," I said, "could you spare a few minutes? I need your help again."

"Of course, Archy. What is it?"

"You know father is concerned about Mrs. Edythe Westmore's dealings with her investment adviser. You heard him telling me to look into the matter but very discreetly. Mrs. Westmore is not to know of the inquiry."

"Well, I certainly won't tell her," mother said firmly. "If that's what worries you."

"Not at all," I assured her. "I know you don't tattle. But I find myself temporarily stymied because I know so little about the Westmore family. I was hoping you could fill me in."

She continued watering the plants lightly with a bulb spray and I followed her down the narrow passages between rough wooden tables and racks.

"As you know," she started, "Edythe is a widow. Her husband died about five years ago, I think it was. I never met him but everyone says he was a very nice man. Always smiling. He fell out of a tree, broke his hip, and died of pneumonia. Isn't that odd?"

"Exceedingly," I said. "What was he doing up a tree?"

"Edythe says he just liked to climb trees. And of course he wasn't a young man when he fell. I've heard gossip he was a heavy drinker and that might have had something to do with it."

"Quite possibly," I said, making a silent vow never to climb a tree. "But I gather he left his widow well-off."

"Oh, yes. She has a beautiful home just south of us and drives a white Cadillac she trades in for the new model every year."

"What kind of a woman is she?"

"Very outgoing. I do think she's put on too much weight in the last few years but I must say it hasn't slowed her down. She's quite active in local charities, a little theater and music recitals."

"No shortcomings at all?"

Mother paused to consider. "Well, sometimes I think she does brag too much."

"What does she brag about?"

"All kinds of things. How much she paid for a new evening gown, the sale of one of her daughter's paintings, a grant her son won—just a lot of different things."

"All relating to money," I observed.

Mother turned to look at me. "You know, Archy, I never thought of it. But you're right; she does talk about money a good deal."

"What about her children? She has a son and daughter?"

"Correct. I've only met them a few times,

so I can't tell you much. The daughter, Natalie, is in her middle twenties and single. She's a strange young woman, very quiet and withdrawn. She does watercolors."

"Of what?"

"Mostly flowers. But they're not real flowers. They're imaginary flowers, if you know what I mean. I saw a few of them. Some are pretty and some are just blah. In my opinion anyway."

"And Natalie—is she pretty or blah?"

"Oh, Archy," mother said reprovingly, "you shouldn't talk that way. I wouldn't call Natalie pretty but she has an interesting face. Almost foreign-looking. It's hard to describe. I'm sorry I can't be more exact."

"You're doing fine, dear. Now how about the son?"

"His first name is Walter and he's about ten years older than his sister. Around your age I'd guess. I only met him once, more than a year ago. He won a grant to go to Africa. I think he's due to come back any day now."

"What is he doing in Africa?"

"Edythe said he's searching for bones. Old bones."

"An anthropologist," I ventured. "Or perhaps a paleontologist."

"What is that?"

"A scientist who searches for old bones. Did he look like a scientist to you?"

"Oh, yes," mother said, giggling. "I mean he was wearing these horn-rimmed glasses with very thick lenses and he had four ballpoint pens sticking out of his shirt pocket. Also there were food stains on his necktie."

"Definitely a scientist," I declared.

"He's married, you know," she went on. "His wife's name is Helen and she lives in Edythe's home. She refused to go to Africa with Walter."

"And what can you tell me about Helen?"

"Well, perhaps I shouldn't say it but I do think she wears her skirts too short. But then she's younger than Walter, maybe even younger than Natalie. Helen is very attractive."

Something in her tone prompted me to ask, "But... ?"

The mater hates to speak ill of anyone. She was silent a long moment, considering her answer.

Finally she said, "But I do think she's more attractive to men than to women."

And I knew that was all she'd say about Helen Westmore.

"Mrs. McNally, you've been of enormous assistance. I've been jostling my brain trying to devise a way to meet the Westmores without revealing my true purpose. I've got to get inside the Westmore home on some pretext or other so I can make the acquaintance of everyone."

"Why, Archy," mother said, sounding astonished, "why don't you just phone Edythe, identify yourself, remind her the two of you met at The Breakers, and tell her I mentioned her speaking of her investment adviser at the bridge club. Say you are interested because you have some money to invest and would like to

40

learn more about the man handling her financial affairs. I'm sure she'll be happy to invite you to visit. You said yourself she likes to talk about money."

I stared at her in amazement. "The soul of practicality!" I almost shouted. "Darling, you're a wonder! I've been trying to connive a devious plot but your plan is simple, easy, and certain to succeed. I love you!"

And I leaped to hug and kiss her smooth cheek, not once but thrice. Her complexion became rosier and she pushed me away, laughing.

"Go along and make your phone call," she commanded. "I have some private things to say to my plants."

CHAPTER 6

I TRUDGED UP to my den reflecting I have occasionally referred to my mother's daftness in this chronicle. But I do assure you she has a goodly store of common sense, practical and realistic. More than once her mundane advice has rescued me from awkward situations caused by my own flights of fancy—such as the time I developed a mad crush on a female Korean contortionist.

With the aid of Directory Assistance I was able to obtain Mrs. Westmore's telephone number and immediately called. But the line was busy and I began to disrobe, planning to change to swimming trunks for my almost daily dunk in the Atlantic Ocean. The air was coolish but I reckoned the water still held enough summer warmth so I wouldn't emerge a goose-bumped blue.

I donned my cerise Speedos, added sandals and a terry cover-up printed with a portrait of Donald Duck. I then phoned again, and this time a melancholy male voice answered, "The Westmore residence."

"May I speak to Mrs. Westmore, please," I said.

"Which Mrs. Westmore?" he asked.

"Mrs. Edythe Westmore," I said hastily. "This is Archy McNally calling. You might tell Mrs. Westmore I am the son of Madeleine."

"A moment, please, sir," he said, and I wondered why he was so sad. He sounded as if he had just won the Florida lottery and had lost the ticket.

It didn't take a moment; she came on the line almost at once. "Archy McNally!" she cried. "It's so nice to speak to you again! How long has it been since you gallantly picked up my beads at The Breakers?"

"At least two years."

"No! Surely not that long?"

"*Tempus* does *fugit*," I said lightly, and then I went into my spiel. I told her mother had mentioned she, Mrs. Westmore, consulted a very successful investment adviser, and since I had a modest sum to invest I wondered if she would be good enough to grant me a few moments of her time so I might learn more about this money manager, his personality, and how he operated.

And you know, while I was delivering this song and dance I had a sudden attack of déjà voodoo and was convinced I had uttered this pitch before. And of course I had—to Binky Watrous when I was instructing him how to handle Frederick Clemens. I am ashamed to admit it but the similarity between the two ploys had not previously occurred to me. Oh doctor, is the McNally brain turning to mashed squash?

I hoped Binky would achieve the success I did, for Mrs. Westmore said, "Of course, Archy. I'll be happy to tell you what I know about Fred. He's such a marvelous man and I was so smart to consult him. Would you like to come over here?"

"I would indeed, Mrs. Westmore. Perhaps early next week? At your convenience."

"Just let me take a peek at my engagement book. Uh-huh. Monday is the only time I have free. How does that strike you?"

"Monday would be fine."

"Listen, Archy, you've never seen my beautiful home, have you?"

"No, ma'am, I have not."

"I have a wonderful idea. Why don't you come for lunch on Monday, say about noon. That will give me time to take you on the grand tour and then at lunch we can talk about Fred and investments."

"I'd like that," I said. "You're very kind to invite me."

There was a short pause. Then she said, "And by all means bring your wife if she'd care to come."

"Impossible," I said with a laugh sounding tinny even to me. "I'm not married, Mrs. Westmore."

"Well, we'll have to do something about *that*!" she said heartily. I cringed, wondering if matrons consider matchmaking a hobby, a sport, or a divine calling.

"See you Monday," she said briskly, and hung up.

I went down for my swim, delighted with the outcome of my plan—or rather mother's plan. I hoped Natalie and Helen Westmore would be present at the Monday lunch. But then I imagined it might be the unmarried daughter Mrs. Westmore had in mind when she vowed to "do something about" my bachelorhood.

The ocean seemed awfully chill.

During the family cocktail hour on Friday evening I informed mother I had called Edythe Westmore and had been invited to lunch.

"She wants me to see her, quote, beautiful home, unquote," I said. "Her investment adviser is a, quote, marvelous man, unquote, and she was, quote, smart, unquote, to consult him. Mrs. Westmore is not exactly a paradigm of modesty, is she?"

Father had been mixing the traditional dry martinis he favors, listening to our conversation. He turned with the crystal pitcher to fill our glasses.

"She spoke of her investment adviser, did she, Archy?" he asked.

"Yes, sir," I answered. "His name is Frederick Clemens but she twice referred to him as

Fred. I would say it implies a certain degree of intimacy, wouldn't you?"

"Not necessarily intimacy," he said in his lawyerly way. "A close friendly relationship perhaps."

"His name is Clemens?" mother said, perplexed. "I thought it was Twain."

"Same man," I assured her. "You were using the pseudonym."

And that confused the poor dear even more.

After dinner I went up to my snuggery and worked on my journal. I jotted notes on the conversations with Sydney Smythe, my lunch with Binky, mother's description of the Westmore family, and the dialogue with Edythe. It may not sound like much to you and at the time I would have agreed. Later I learned those entries contained the seeds of a solution to the most puzzling inquiry I have ever undertaken, other than why scones always fall to the floor butter side down.

I was still scribbling away when Binky phoned. He was in a euphoric mood.

"She called!" he shouted. "Bridget! Ireland!"

"Brava," I said. "Did you talk about the weather?"

"And other things," he said smugly. "She misses me, Archy; I can tell."

"How can you tell? Did she say so?"

"Not in so many words but she kept sighing."

"Maybe she just had a cup of poteen."

"What's poteen?"

"Irish moonshine. Enough of this blather; did you call Frederick Clemens?"

"I did. A man answered but it wasn't him."

"How did you know?"

"Because he said, 'Clemens Investments,' and I asked, 'Mr. Clemens?' and he said, 'May I ask who is calling?' I gave him my name and said I wanted to talk to Mr. Clemens about investing. And he said, 'Just a moment, please,' and then a second man came on the phone and said, 'Frederick Clemens speaking. How may I help you?' "

"So the first man was probably a receptionist, secretary, or assistant. How did Clemens sound?"

"How did he sound?"

"His voice, Binky. Loud, soft, deep, high-pitched, thin, resonant?"

"A mellow voice. Very smooth. The gift of gab, you know. A real salesman."

"Did he ask any questions?"

"How much I was thinking of investing. That's all he asked. I told him fifty thousand."

"What was his reaction?"

"He suggested I come talk to him. He said he wanted to get an idea of my tolerance for risk. What did he mean, Archy?"

"He wants to find out if you're a fuddy-duddy or a cowboy. Did you make an appointment?"

"Yep. Monday afternoon at three o'clock."

"Well done, Binky. Remember what I told you about how to dress. And no birdcalls. You're to impress him with your couth."

"Easy. I've got couth I haven't even used yet."

"I can vouch for that. Call me after your meeting. Perhaps we can get together Monday night. Good luck."

I hung up, pleased with the way things were going. Who wrote of possible slippage twixt the cup and the lip? No matter. I should have taken heed of the warning.

I know it was Homer who said, "There is a time for many words, and there is a time for sleep." I slept.

I awoke the next day full of p&v and feeling not at all guilty for oversleeping on a Saturday morn. I peered out the window and saw a sunlit world with all the trimmings. I spotted Hobo wandering about, waiting for someone or something to entertain him.

The only planned activity on my calendar was a croquet tourney scheduled for noon at the North Palm Beach home of a Pelican Club habitué who fancied himself a Master of the Mallet. You may think croquet an effete game but I assure you it can be vicious when practiced by muscular young men and women, all firmly convinced that nice guys finish last. Needless to say, wagering was one of the reasons for the fierce competition.

I went through the usual morning drill and then pulled on white ducks with a brass-buttoned navy blazer. I bounced downstairs to a deserted kitchen and prepared a toasted muffin sandwich of sharp cheddar, plus a glass of cran juice and a cup of steaming black caffeine. And a second muffin sandwich of sharp cheddar. Croquet demands strength and stamina.

I exited from the back door and found Jamie Olson repainting Hobo's doghouse. The hero himself sat happily nearby watching a man work—always a pleasurable sight. He spotted me, gave a short bark of welcome, and came scampering for a pat and ear scratch. I wandered over to Jamie and exchanged good-mornings.

"Getting shabby, was it?" I asked.

His dentures were clamped down on the stem of his old briar and he spoke around it.

"Yep," he said. "And leaking. I caulked yesterday."

"On behalf of Hobo," I said, "I thank you. Jamie, you know anyone who labors for Mrs. Edythe Westmore?"

It was not an idle question. There is an informal network of butlers, maids, housemen, cooks, chauffeurs, and other servants of Palm Beach residents able to afford a domestic staff. These personal employees frequently exchange job tips and even more frequently exchange gossip about the habits and foibles of their employers, intimacies rarely revealed to the tabloids but so juicy they demand an appreciative audience. Everyone likes a good laugh.

Olson was my source of backstairs rumors and occasionally his inside skinny proved invaluable. I usually gave him a fin or two for his assistance—a practice that would infuriate my father if he learned of it.

Jamie paused in his painting, set the brush atop the bucket, and removed the pipe from his mouth. "Mrs. Westmore?" he repeated. "Got a place south of here?"

"Right."

"Two live-ins," he reported. "Cook is Mary Stebbins. Skinny as a rail. Cooks mostly got heft but Mary don't. Houseman is Al Canfield. Rightful name is Algernon but he likes Al better."

"I know exactly how he feels," I said. "Who does the cleaning and donkeywork?"

"Commercial crew. Comes in three times a week."

"About Al, the houseman... I spoke to him on the phone and he sounded down in the mouth."

"Got a lot on his mind. Looking for a new place."

"Oh? Do you know why?"

"Can't please the missus. Do this, do that, you're not doing it right, what's taking you so long. Like that. Al calls her Madam Nag."

"Uh-huh," I said. "Understandable."

I slipped Jamie his usual pourboire, gave Hobo a final back pat, and started for North Palm Beach. I felt confident I would triumph and perhaps pick up a nice piece of change.

CHAPTER 7

I LOST. I cannot blame it on bad luck although there was plenty of that. But I played like the duffiest of duffers, and the merry hoots of my opponents were crushing. I also managed to lose almost fifty simoleons and was thankful payday was less than a week away. Otherwise I'd have to hit mama for a small loan since my bank account was inching toward the panic level.

The only thing that saved the afternoon from being a complete disaster was the bar and buffet provided by our generous host. A fine selection of cold meats and seafood was available and I partook of everything. But my maladroitness drove me to visit the do-it-yourself bar several times and I put quite a dent in the vodka supply. It didn't improve my skill with a mallet but it deadened the pain of failure.

I arrived back home late in the afternoon driving slowly and carefully. I was in no mood for an ocean swim, feeling a nap would be more beneficial. I was sleepy—all the fresh air, you know. So I shucked my duds, flopped into bed, woke about an hour later and, *mirabile dictu*, felt bright-eyed and bushy-tailed.

I phoned Connie Garcia at her office, figuring she'd probably still be at work. She was and in no mood for casual banter.

"Lady C. is driving me right up the wall," she complained. "I think I'm ready for Intensive Care."

"I can provide it," I promised. "How about our dinner date tonight?"

"It's on," she said. "But it'll be latish and I won't have time to go home and change."

"How late?"

"About eight o'clock. Okay?"

"Of course," I said. "Where?"

"Let's go to Rinaldo's. All I want is a small fettuccine Alfredo and a big Caesar salad."

"No wine?"

"Silly boy!"

"See you at Rinaldo's at eight," I said, and we disconnected.

We shall now fast-forward to a small, comfortable, and garlicky Italian restaurant on South County Road. It is eight o'clock on the dot, and I am standing just inside the entrance awaiting Connie's arrival. I am also stoutly resisting an urge to have a vodka rocks at Rinaldo's little bar. We'd probably be drinking Chianti Classico shortly and I am aware of the perils of mixing grain and the grape.

Connie came bustling in about ten minutes later and if she was exhausted one would never have known it from her manner. She gave me a bright smile and a warm *abrazo*. Also, she smelled nice.

"Wine me and dine me," she commanded.

"At once, m'lady," I said, and found us a corner banquette backed by a garish oil painting of Vesuvius erupting. An apron-clad waiter hustled over to take our order, starting with a bottle of vino. It turned out to be softer and fruiter than I had anticipated but I had no objection and neither did Connie.

In case you have unaccountably missed my previous encomiums, let me tell you about Connie Garcia. She is a Latin femme fatale. She is a Marielita and I think her a maze of contradictions, at once soft, loving, blithe-spirited and jealous, distrustful, vengeful.

51

The latter three characteristics are much in evidence when she suspects or has evidence of my infidelity. More than once she has launched a physical assault upon the McNally carcass when my perfidiousness became obvious. How well I recall inviting a young centerfold to a Friday night dinner at an obscure English pub in Boca Raton. I was certain I would be safe from Connie's intrusion or observation by one of the many spies who delight in informing her of my shenanigans.

But fate was unkind. Ms. Garcia entered with a female friend and immediately spotted me with my nubile dining companion. She marched over to our table and dumped in my lap the entire contents of my bowl of cock-a-leekie. Then she and her pal stalked out. I wasn't scalded but my plan for a lubricious evening had been effectively dampened.

Connie had said all she wanted at Rinaldo's was pasta and a salad. But when the antipasto trolley was wheeled up she could not resist and neither could I. We heaped our plates high with Tuscan hors d'oeuvres but had the strength of character to decline second helpings.

Connie began telling me of her current tribulations in organizing Lady Horowitz's sit-down dinner.

"Everyone in town has been phoning. The word has spread and you know how rumors are exaggerated. People think she's having a banquet for hundreds instead of an intimate dinner for a dozen pols."

"Surely the callers aren't so gauche as to ask to be invited."

"Not in so many words, but very casually they remind me they're in residence, they haven't seen Lady C. in ages and would love to visit her again. What a mob of social climbers!"

"Ever get a call from Mrs. Edythe Westmore?" I inquired offhandedly, not really expecting to learn anything.

"Do I ever!" Connie said. "She's absolutely the worst! Three calls at least. She's so pushy. The woman is in a sweat to mix with the upper echelons of Palm Beach society. Why do you ask, Archy?"

"She's a client and I have to deliver some legal documents to her on Monday. I wondered what to expect since I've never met the lady." I lied just to keep in practice.

"She's a battleship," Connie said, finishing the baby shrimp in garlic and olive oil. "Very hefty."

"Fat?"

"Not so much fat as just big. Tall, wide shoulders, wider hips. Makes her daughter look anorexic."

"She has a daughter?"

"And a son. He's married but not Natalie."

"Natalie?" I said. "Do you know her then?"

"Not really. Just talked to her a few times. She joined my aerobics class for a while but dropped out after three or four sessions. A strange gal."

53

We were silent a few moments while our fettuccine Alfredo was served and the Caesar salad mixed alongside our table in a wooden bowl large enough to hold a medicine ball. The salad was divided into two enormous portions and we dug into our hi-calorie feast. If you wish to subsist on tofu, bran, and bean sprouts you are shunning one of life's greatest pleasures: delicious, aromatic, and fattening foods. And may I suggest a fitting epitaph to be engraved on your tombstone? "Remember me and all my ilk/And drink a toast—perhaps skimmed milk."

As we scarfed I made what I hoped would sound like an innocent query: "Connie, you said Natalie Westmore is a strange gal. Strange as in spooky or as in off-the-wall?"

She paused briefly to consider. "A little of both," she said finally. "For instance, at aerobics we all wore spandex leotards in neon colors. Except Natalie. She wore old-fashioned gym bloomers with a middy."

"Wild," I said.

"Kooky," she said. "There was something else but I won't tell you unless you promise never to repeat it. To anyone."

"Of course I promise. You know I'm the soul of discretion."

"You're the soul of deception, that's what you are. Well, I think Natalie is a thief!"

"Aw, come on!"

"No, really. Every time she came to a session someone lost something. Little things: a comb, a plastic compact, a headband—per-

54

sonal things of no great value. But after Natalie quit, things stopped disappearing. We think she was filching them."

"Whatever for?"

Connie shrugged. "Who knows? Maybe she's a klepto. Or maybe she's just a nut. Hey, this salad is super. Any left in the bowl?"

I beckoned the waiter. I didn't think it smart to pursue the subject of Natalie Westmore. If I did, my Consenting Other would undoubtedly demand to know why I was so interested in a young woman I had never met, particularly one who wore gym bloomers and a middy. I would be accused of possessing a hidden motive of unspeakable depravity. I counseled myself: Go into the roundhouse, Archy; she'll never corner you there.

So I limited my conversation to inconsequential chitchat about the weather, local politics, and the puzzle of why today's tomatoes have lost tomatoey taste. We finished dinner with no further mention of the Westmore clan. We voted to forgo dessert and settled for espresso and ponies of grappa which will numb your adenoids.

"Want to make a night of it?" I asked Connie. "Dancing, perhaps, or finding a good jazz trio and just listening?"

"Some other time," she said. "All I want to do is go home and hit the sack. What do you want to do, sweetie?"

"Go home and hit the sack."

"Whose home and whose sack?" she asked. I looked at her.

"Oh, yes," she said.

Connie has long black hair and a lusty body that doesn't end. She is surprisingly strong and a ferocious lover. Carnivorous one might even say. She does enjoy the horizontal mambo, and if our lovemaking that night had had an orchestral accompaniment, the musicians would have been playing with frenzied *brio,* I assure you.

"Thank you, Escamillo," Connie murmured before I left.

"Thank *you,* Carmen," I replied, but she was already asleep.

I drove home full of *haricots verts* (*anyone* can be full of plain beans), in such an exuberant mood I sang one of my favorite old-timey tunes: "I'm Sitting on Top of the World." I have a tape of Jolson singing that and it's a corker. My own rendition inspired me to wonder why an imaginative automaker couldn't produce a luxury model called a Fettle. Then I could drive home in a fine Fettle. (Tell me, doctor, is my condition terminal?)

When I was safely ensconced in my hideout I flopped in the creaky swivel chair behind the desk and made a lazy attempt to analyze the reasons for my bloomy spirits. The wine of course. And the grappa. And the satisfying grub.

But most of all my ebullience was due to the joyous joust with Connie. What a marvelous woman she was! I resolved then and there never again to cast a covetous eye on any other person of the female faith. Why should

I since Ms. Garcia was all women: complete and total?

I worked on my journal a few moments, jotting notes on the curious proclivities of Natalie Westmore. Then, my eyelids beginning to droop, I went to bed and dreamed of making a romantic trip through a tunnel of love with Thelma Todd. I awoke Sunday morn saddened my pledge of allegiance to Connie had been so quickly betrayed in my sleep. I prayed it did not presage infidelities I might commit while fully awake.

I accompanied my parents to church, feeling my moral fiber needed a bit of starching. But the sermon was devoted to the biblical dictum "The race is not to the swift, nor the battle to the strong," and I spent the remainder of the service trying to recall the name of the sportswriter who commented, "Maybe not but that's the way to bet."

CHAPTER 8

I DRESSED WITH special care on Monday morning, wishing to impress Mrs. Edythe Westmore with my sincerity. I admit the black tropical worsted suit and white shirt I donned gave me the look of a mortician at work but I compensated for my sober appearance by wearing silk briefs decorated with gamboling rabbits. By their underwear ye shall know them.

My first destination was the McNally Building, merely to see if any correspondence or messages had been placed in my office during my absence. I expected nothing of import but found a note from the McNally & Son receptionist stating Mr. Sydney Smythe of Windsor Antiques had phoned late Friday afternoon and requested I return his call. I stuffed the message into my jacket pocket, deciding to phone the moldering fop after lunch. Then I reclaimed the Miata from our underground garage and headed back to Ocean Boulevard.

Mrs. Westmore's enthusiasm for her "beautiful home" was not entirely braggadocio. At least I found the exterior attractive and the landscaping impressive. The house and three-car garage, designed in what is called "Bermuda style," were set on a closely shaven lawn divided by a brick driveway and slated walks. In the background, framing the estate, was a ficus hedge so high it would require a ladder to trim the top.

I parked at one side of the turnaround, disembarked, and took a second look around. The selection of trees was striking: orchid, royal poinciana and royal palm, sea grape, and one magnificent banyan that must have been a zillion years old. All showy, you'll note. Mrs. Westmore was obviously not a woman who would be content with a few scraggly palmettos.

I spotted another structure away from the main residence and almost hidden in the foliage. It was too small for a guest house and too large for a storage shed. It appeared to be constructed of weathered planks from old barns, in sharp contrast to the gleaming white of the other buildings. I couldn't even guess its purpose and resolved to ask during the "grand tour" the hostess had promised.

The front door bell was set in the umbilicus of a half-naked brass Venus—apparently the owner's attempt at whimsy. I thought it barbarous but forced myself to press the belly button. The door was opened immediately by a scrawny, stoop-shouldered gent wearing a gray alpaca jacket and shiny navy serge trousers. His features had such a lugubrious cast I knew he had to be Algernon Canfield, the houseman desperately seeking another job.

"I'm Archy McNally," I started. "Mrs. Westmore is—"

"Expecting you," he completed my statement in his lachrymose voice. "This way please, sir."

I followed him down a hallway covered with flocked wallpaper in a cabbage rose pattern that wasn't as garish as it may sound. We came to opened double doors of what was obviously the Florida room. The houseman departed speedily as Mrs. Edythe Westmore came forward, holding out both hands, fleshy face creased in a welcoming smile. Connie had been right; she *was* a battleship.

"Archy McNally!" she boomed. "How *nice* to see you again!"

"My pleasure, Mrs. Westmore," I said, and

found my two hands grasped separately in hers. Even worse, she drew me near, tilted her massive head, and offered a slack cheek and waited. I obediently bestowed the lightest and briefest of light, brief kisses. It was like bussing a down pillow.

"Oh, do call me Edythe," she said with what I'm sure she intended as a girlish pout. "Why, your mother and I have been friends for ages and you and I needn't stand on ceremony."

Still clutching my hands, she backed off a step to examine me.

"You *are* a handsome lad," she said with a throaty laugh. "I imagine you've broken many a girl's heart."

"Not me," I protested. "I follow the Comedians' Law: Always leave them laughing when you say good-bye."

She granted me a hearty guffaw and exclaimed, "You devil!" She released my paws and I suspect if we had been closer she might have dug an elbow into my ribs.

She was a weighty woman and her voice was even weightier. Stentorian is the word. I imagined if she shouted "Hello!" to a neighbor in Palm Beach, pedestrians in Boca Raton would whirl around to see who was calling. I could understand why Al Canfield hoped to leave her employ as soon as possible. Who could live an easy life with that voice? It would be like attempting to meditate in the midst of a brass band oompahing at the max.

"Archy," she said, "there's been a slight

change of plans. Some kind of a money crisis is brewing at the little theater I help support and they want me to chair a board of directors' meeting at two o'clock. So I thought you and I might eat first and then my daughter will show you around after I leave. Satisfactory?"

"Of course," I said. "I hope I'm not discommoding you, Edythe."

Her laugh was a roar. "I don't let anyone do that," she assured me. "Now come along."

She took my arm firmly and tugged me down the hall to the dining room. I felt like a villain being muscled along by a gendarme. I also wondered why Natalie wasn't joining us for lunch. Perhaps the "slight change of plans" was Mrs. Westmore's ploy to arrange a tête-à-tête between her daughter and yrs. truly. Bachelors do have dark suspicions like that, you know.

A few moments later we were seated at one corner of a table large enough to accommodate ten. The hostess vigorously shook a small crystal bell and after a moment the melancholy houseman shuffled in with our first course: a shrimp and crabmeat cocktail with a nothing sauce. This was followed by a chef's salad (again with a dressing that lacked zing), and concluded with a raspberry sorbet.

It was a decent enough meal but hardly memorable. It would have required little to improve it: freshly ground black pepper in the appetizer sauce, a touch of garlic in the salad dressing, and a drier (and colder) white wine than the chardonnay served. I don't wish to be hypercritical but I am saddened when good food is prepared in a lackluster manner. A bit of culinary artistry can convert grub to a feast.

But if the lunch was uninspiring I found much of interest in Edythe's monologue, interrupted occasionally by my questions and comments.

She had been introduced to Frederick Clemens by a mutual friend during the intermission of a "really creative" performance of *Three Men on a Horse* produced at the little theater to which she gave an annual contribution.

"I do love drama, don't you, Archy? My favorite is *Hello, Dolly!*"

Clemens had invited her to have a drink after the show at which they met. She had been fascinated to learn he was an investment adviser, since it offered a solution to a problem troubling her. Most of the money her late husband had bequeathed was in Treasury bonds: safe enough, she knew, but with a puny yield that didn't allow her to live in the style she wished and make donations to local charities and cultural activities.

"I simply need more income," she told me. "I know one should live off the interest and never touch the principal. But I find that extremely difficult what with inflation and all."

She had finally persuaded Fred to recommend a modest investment and he had suggested she sell some of her T-bonds and buy the common stock of one of the thirty Dow Jones industrials. She did and, sure enough, three months later the stock split two for one. She now had twice as many shares as she originally purchased.

"Isn't that wonderful, Archy!"

I forbore to mention she might have twice as many shares but hadn't doubled her investment since each new share was now worth half the original. Nor did I inform her stock splits are usually announced months before they actually occur. I doubted if Edythe was aware of it—I couldn't see her as an avid reader of *The Wall Street Journal*—but I reckoned Clemens knew of the coming split.

"Surely the stock investment didn't increase your income," I said.

She admitted the dividend from her common stock was less than the yield from her Treasury bonds. But then Fred had urged her to buy a very inexpensive stock not listed on any of the exchanges. It was issued by a new company with a unique product: a palm-sized vacuum cleaner, battery-powered, to be used for removing loose hair from cats and dogs. Less than a month after her purchase of 25,000 shares at a cost of about $30,000 (it was a *very* cheap stock) Fred told her he had sold the shares for more than $50,000, almost doubling her investment.

"I was absolutely stunned! I had no idea there was so much money to be made so easily. Then Fred put my investment funds in shares of a Bolivian tin mine and two oil well projects in Texas. The wells haven't been drilled yet but last week Fred told me the shares of the tin mine were up forty percent. He wants me to hold them. He's convinced their value will continue to increase. He estimated I may be able to double or even triple my money by the end of the year. Isn't that wonderful?"

"Incredible," I said. "Mr. Clemens certainly seems to have the Midas touch."

"Oh, he does! Definitely. Did your mother tell you about the Fabergé egg Fred wants me to buy?"

"I believe she mentioned something about it but didn't go into detail."

"Well, right now it's owned by this man in France who needs money desperately to pay off a note that's coming due. Otherwise he wouldn't sell it because it's very rare and very valuable. Fred says it was one of the last two eggs made by Fabergé for Czar Nicholas in 1917. But it was never delivered because of the Bolshevik Revolution, you know."

Clemens had told her the egg was smuggled out of Russia in a diplomatic pouch carried by a courier from the French embassy in St. Petersburg. The bijou ended up in Paris but then, during the chaos at the end of World War I, the Fabergé Imperial egg had unaccountably disappeared. Whether it was mislaid, stolen, or destroyed, no one knew. Now, suddenly, it had reappeared in the art collection of a former banker who had made some rash investments and was cash-poor.

"Isn't that an amazing story, Archy?"

"It is indeed, but no more amazing than some of the other happenings during those turbulent times. Tell me, Edythe, has Mr. Clemens actually seen the egg?"

"Oh yes. He flew to Paris immediately when his agent over there told him about it. Fred says it is an exquisite piece studded with diamonds. He gave me a color photo and it's just gorgeous! How I'd love to own it. I'd be tempted to keep it and not put it up for auction. Of course it would mean sacrificing an enormous profit, and I'll have to cash in some of my Treasury bonds to pay for it. Fred is very understanding and says it's my decision to make."

"Edythe, I've seen a few Fabergé Imperial eggs in art galleries and museums, and they all open up to reveal a 'surprise'—like a party favor. Or a very expensive prize in a box of Cracker Jack! Did Mr. Clemens happen to mention what this egg contains?"

"Why, no, Archy, he didn't. I must remember to ask him."

"Do that—just for the fun of it."

She glanced at her jeweled wristwatch. "Oh dear, it's getting late and I must run. I'll call Natalie to show you around my beautiful estate."

"Before you do that, Edythe, may I ask if you'd have any objection if I contacted Mr. Clemens and used you as a reference?"

"I'd have no objection whatsoever. But I should warn you Fred is very particular about the clients he takes on. I mean he doesn't just accept everyone. Why, I had to talk a long time to persuade him to invest my money."

"Well, all I can do is try. Thank you for a delightful luncheon and answering all my questions. I do appreciate it."

"It has been fun, hasn't it? And you're a very charming young man. I must tell Madeleine how fortunate she is to have a son like you. Now come and meet my lovely daughter, Natalie."

She pulled me out to the hallway. Standing at the foot of a graceful staircase, she tilted her head back and bellowed, "Nettie! Come down this instant!"

There isn't a hog caller in Iowa who could have equaled her decibel level.

CHAPTER 9

WE WAITED A moment on the portico steps until Mrs. Westmore drove out in her new white Caddy. She waved to us and I lifted a hand in response. But Natalie just stood there stolidly, head lowered.

I turned to her. "Well..." I said and gave her my Supercharmer smile—100 watts. I thought it best to save the Jumbocharmer (150 watts) for emergencies. "Well, Nettie, shall we take a look around? I may address you as Nettie, mayn't I?"

"If you like," she said indifferently.

Her apathy didn't disturb me because I was delighted with her voice: low, soft, almost timorous. What a welcome relief from her mama's manic bray.

We wandered out onto the grounds and passed the open garage. There was still one car within: a six-year-old Toyota Corolla that looked as if it had been cruelly mistreated.

"Yours?" I asked idly.

She nodded. "I inherited it from my sister-in-law," she said, and I heard the bitterness in her tone. "Helen has a new Buick Riviera in a special color. Lavender."

"Nice," I said. "Nettie, would you mind if I smoked a cigarette?"

"Yes, I would," she said. "You shouldn't smoke. You'll get lung cancer."

"I know. I also drink, which will give me cirrhosis. And I breathe even though the air is horribly polluted."

She made a small noise and I turned to look at her. I hoped she might have laughed. It would be gratifying from such a somber young woman. I paused a moment to glance around. "Wonderful trees," I commented. "The old banyan is magnificent."

"Yes," she said. "It's the tree daddy fell out of and then he died. Should we go back to the house now?"

She was hurrying me and I resented it. "In a moment," I said. "The small structure back there in the foliage... What is that used for?"

"You wouldn't be interested."

I stared at her. "Nettie, we seem to be having a slight problem communicating. I *am* interested."

"Well, it's my studio. Where I paint."

"May I see it?"

"If you like," she said, totally impassive again.

She walked a step or two ahead of me. She was wearing a long bleached denim skirt, almost to her ankles. And above was a knitted sweater in a heathery green. It was sleeveless but the cool breeze didn't seem a bother. Her bare arms were muscled and I couldn't decide if she had a deep suntan or if her skin was naturally tawny.

She had her mother's height but, fortunately, not her girth. In fact she was quite slender. And flat. Boardlike would be a fitting adjective. But she moved gracefully with a floating stride. Her blondish hair was cut short and so ragged I wondered if she barbered herself.

As for her features, my mother's verdict, "not pretty but interesting, almost foreign-looking," was close to the mark. I had seen her narrow face before in Modigliani portraits. Natalie had the same curious mixture of mystery and passivity Amedeo had caught on canvas.

The door to the studio was closed with a padlock so old and rusty it looked as if a strong yank might spring the shackle. Natalie fished a key from her skirt pocket and, after several ineffective tries, succeeded in opening the lock and then the planked door. She stood aside and motioned me in.

"It isn't much," she said.

Correct; it wasn't. I stepped into a square room scantily furnished. I saw none of the scattered paraphernalia usually found in an artist's workshop. Instead of an easel there was a wooden drafting table, tilted upward, and a high stool with a rattan seat. A tall cupboard with closed doors sagged crazily. I assumed it held brushes, watercolors, and supplies.

A cot was planted in the center of the floor. It was covered with a single sheet and light cotton blanket. The small pillow was soiled. I could see no plumbing, not even a faucet. The most attractive feature was a skylight: two big hinged windows opened by hanging chains.

"Plenty of light for your painting," I observed.

She suddenly became talkative. "And for two or three hours a day I get the direct sun. I can suntan naked on the cot. After locking the door from the inside of course. See the bolt? I've slept here a few nights when the weather is nice. Then I look up and see the stars."

She stopped talking as abruptly as she had started and bowed her head as if embarrassed by her outburst. I turned my attention to the walls. The interior of the cabin was lined with cheap wallboard which bore a number of Natalie's watercolors of imaginary flowers. A few were framed and hung. The others were simply pushpinned to the wall. Again mother had been right: "Some are pretty and some are just blah."

I stepped closer to examine her work and sensed her coming up behind me, possibly to observe my reactions. I thought her brushwork was merely serviceable but her sense of color was admirable. The subject matter turned me off—all those buds, blooms, and leaves that never existed in nature but were products of her imagination or dreams. What surprised me were the blossoms with an undeniable resemblance to sexual organs, male and female.

"Well?" Nettie said at my shoulder. "What do you think?"

"Striking," I said. "Unique. Are you familiar with the work of Georgia O'Keeffe?"

"No."

"Take a look," I advised. "I think you'll be amazed at what she did."

"I don't want to study other people's work. I want to be me. Original."

"Surely you went to art school to learn technique, perspective, composition. Didn't you study the work of other artists then?"

"I never went to art class. I bought a book and taught myself."

"Remarkable," I said.

"A lot of hard work but I enjoy it. It's my escape."

"From what?"

"Oh…" she said vaguely. "Things. People."

"All people? Surely you have friends."

She lifted her chin. "A few," she said defensively, and I guessed she was lying.

Perhaps I looked at her pityingly—I didn't mean to, I swear I didn't—but what happened next astounded me. She looped her bare arms about my neck, careened into me, thrust her head forward and attempted to kiss my lips. But in her frantic haste her aim was bad and she kissed my chin. She tried again and this time succeeded. Her mouth was hot.

She pulled away and gasped, "Archy?" It was an entreaty and the first time she had used my name. Then she kissed me again, her assault so ravenous I staggered back a step. But she would not let me escape and in the blink of a gnat's eye I found myself clutching her as tightly as she embraced me. I am not made of cedar shingles, you know.

It was I who had the sense to close the inside bolt on the door before we fumbled away our clothes. We then attempted to determine if a folding cot could bear the weight of two bodies and the demented thumping of our naked pas de deux. It couldn't but fortunately it collapsed slowly and I do not believe either of us was aware of our descent to the floor.

Lordy, her body was magnificent and I recant all those snide comments made previously about its boardlike appearance. Spring steel was more like it; the overall suntan was bronzy rather than tawny. But I wasted little time taking inventory, set to work, and elicited a series of low sounds: sighs, moans, and one muffled sob. Of bliss I hoped. I was, I admit, more vocal than Nettie but I do not believe she was affrighted by my repertoire of yelps, whinnies, and yodels.

Eventually the game ended of course. Score tied: 1 to 1. We lay there on the ruins of the cot, both of us breathing as if we had just completed the sixty-meter hurdles. She raised her eyes, coughed a short laugh, the corners of her mouth went up. But it was a trompe l'oeil smile given, I guessed, because she thought I expected it.

"Wonderful," she said.

"Ecstasy," I said. "From the movie of the same name."

Then she glowered. "Can't you be serious?" she demanded.

"No, I cannot," I told her. "I am a frivolous scatterbrain. I want you to know that from the start."

"The start of what?"

I shrugged. "Whatever may ensue from our delightful introduction. But if you desire a solemn, profound bloke, I am not he. If you can be satisfied with an ardent nincompoop I shall do my best to oblige."

She sat up, hugged her bare knees, regarded me gravely. "I don't think you're as dizzy as you say, Archy." Then, suddenly: "What did you and mother talk about at lunch?"

"This and that."

"I'll bet you talked about money."

"The subject may have come up," I acknowledged.

"She wants to spend a mint on a stupid Fabergé egg," she said wrathfully. "There goes my inheritance."

I grinned. "Selfish," I said, "but honest. Are you acquainted with Frederick Clemens, her financial adviser?"

"I've met the creep. I can't stand oily men like him."

"Oily?"

"You know what I mean. He puts on the smoothy act and both mama and Helen think he's God's gift to women. I think he's a fake."

"Why do you think that?"

"He insisted on buying one of my paintings. He said it was a masterpiece, which was a lot of hooey. He just wanted me on his side so I wouldn't object to mama giving him money for the Fabergé egg."

"I gather from what you say that your sister-in-law is already on his side."

"Wait'll my brother gets back," she said. "He's supposed to arrive this week. I'm going to tell Walter what his dear wifey has been up to."

"And what has she been up to?"

"That's for me to know and you to find out."

"Natalie," I said, laughing, "I haven't heard that expression since nursery school."

"I know what I know," she said darkly, then abruptly switched gears on me. Very mercurial, our Nettie. "Do you want to see me again, Archy?"

It was a challenge and stopped me. Did I want to see her again? Well... yes. I knew I was risking Connie's wrath if she learned I was playing ring-around-a-rosy with a certified ding-a-ling who performed aerobics in gym bloomers. But when lust comes in the door prudence goes out the window—or something like that.

Also I sensed Natalie might prove a valuable source of skinny relating to the internal conflicts of the Westmore family. She had already revealed much and hinted at more. Surely I would be a fool to reject such assistance. But the specter of Ms. Garcia lurked, my very own avenging angel. And so I dithered.

"I don't mean to go out," Natalie said. "I'm uncomfortable in restaurants and bars. I'm not a social creature. But I thought you might like to come by occasionally and we could just, you know... talk."

"I'd enjoy that," I said at once, happy with her suggestion. Connie would never in a million years discover me engaged in extracurricular activities within a ramshackle shed on an Ocean Boulevard estate. "But I don't want to be a nuisance. Suppose I give you my unlisted home phone number and when you feel like company give me a call and I'll come running. How does that sound?"

"Yes," she said, "I think it's the best way."

I had felt certain she would approve. It gave her control of our liaison, y'see—exactly what she wanted.

I stood up (with some effort) and began dressing. "Then let's do it that way. Why, we might even have a picnic in here. That would be fun."

"Fun?" she said, seemingly surprised by the word. "I'm not sure I know how to have fun."

"Yes you do. You just proved it."

Her smile was a revelation. She positively beamed for one brief instant.

I jotted my phone number on a scrap of discarded drawing paper. Then I leaned down to kiss her upturned face. "Thank you, Nettie," I said. "Please, do give me a call when you're in the mood."

"Yes," she said, "I shall. What's that cologne you're wearing?"

"Not cologne. Aftershave. 'Obsession.' Like it or hate it?"

"Like it," she said, and repeated "Obsession" as if it had a special meaning for her.

I lifted a hand in farewell, unbolted the door, and stepped outside. I paused to light a cigarette and heard her close the inside bolt on her secret place.

I was preparing to remount the Miata when a lavender Buick Riviera came purring up the driveway and halted in front of the garage. I waited until the driver alighted and slammed the door. She spotted me and came sauntering. Something insolent in her jouncy walk.

"And who might you be?" she asked.

"I might be Ludwig the Second, the Mad King of Bavaria," I said. "But actually I am Archibald McNally. I have just lunched with Mrs. Edythe Westmore and have been given a tour of the premises by Natalie."

"Ah," she said. "A new friend of the family?"

"I hope to be. And I presume you are Mrs. Helen Westmore?"

"You presume correctly," she said with a smile so scintillant it made my Jumbocharmer look like a night-light. "But friends of the family call me Helen. And may I call you Archy?"

"It would please me," I assured her.

But she wasn't listening. She was staring at me, up and down, with a look I can only define as appraising. What a bold, almost brazen look it was! I feared she might step forward to examine my teeth and squeeze my biceps to judge their bulk.

She was a zaftig woman who carried herself with impudent self-confidence. Her manner was more than forward, it was fast-forward, and I reckoned there were few pleasures she denied herself. Women who have a taste for instant gratification scare me. I always think of female arachnids who select an amorous mate, copulate, and then devour the poor chap.

"I hope to see more of you, Archy," she said, her voice almost a purr.

"I'd like that," I said. I may have stuttered.

"Ta-ta, luv," she caroled, gave me a wink and a flip of her hand, and danced up the steps into the house.

I thought of those spiders again. I'm too young to die.

CHAPTER 10

IT WAS THEN pushing four o'clock, obviously too late to return to my orifice. (I wish I could stop spelling it that way.) So I tooled the Miata homeward, musing on my eventful afternoon with the Westmore women. They were not exactly the three witches from

Macbeth but they were not the three Graces either. An odd and intriguing triumvirate I decided.

When I was seated behind the spavined desk in my very own sitting room, shoes off and tie loosened, I remembered to phone Sydney Smythe at Windsor Antiques. We exchanged cordial greetings and he then explained the reason for his original call.

"You know, dear boy," he said, "I have been thinking about the Fabergé egg you told me about—the one included in the estate of a deceased client."

"Ah, yes."

"You wished to learn something of its provenance and current market value. I fear I was unable to provide much information, not having examined the egg. But I do possess several excellent illustrated volumes on the art of Peter Carl Fabergé. It occurred to me that if you would open the egg and describe to me the 'surprise' it contains, I might be able to identify it in one of my reference books and answer your questions in more detail."

"That would certainly be a help, sir," I said, wondering where my fabricated story was leading me and how I could finesse the dealer's request. "I'll certainly open the egg at the first available opportunity and report to you what, if anything, I find inside."

"Excellent!" he said with more enthusiasm than I thought my reply warranted. "I love investigations into the history of beautiful antiques, and I've become quite consumed with curiosity about this particular Imperial egg. Do keep me informed, dear boy."

He rang off and I replaced my phone thoughtfully. His interest in the Fabergé egg I had invented did seem to me excessive but that wasn't the only oddity I found fascinating. Mr. Smythe had asked me to describe the surprise in *my* egg, and a few hours previously I had asked Mrs. Westmore to describe the surprise in *her* egg.

Of course mine was imaginary and I still had to determine if the Fabergé egg being hawked by investment adviser Frederick Clemens was also whole cloth or actually existed. And if it did exist, was it authentic or a counterfeit being peddled by one or more villains who had selected Mrs. Edythe Westmore as their mark?

I noted these puzzles in my journal along with a description of the Westmore estate and Mrs. Edythe's comments anent Frederick Clemens. I interrupted my scribbling a few times to phone Binky but was informed by the Duchess's houseman that Master Watrous had not yet returned home. I thought it strange. I could not believe his meeting with Clemens was still in progress. Unless the goof was regaling the investment adviser with a recital of birdcalls, including the peep of a titmouse.

I showered and changed into casual duds before descending for the family cocktail hour. As we were sipping our traditional dry martinis I casually mentioned I had lunched with Mrs. Edythe Westmore and had met both her daughter and daughter-in-law.

"Did you, Archy?" mother said, much interested. "Tell me, what did you think of Helen Westmore?"

I was glad she hadn't asked my reaction to Natalie! "Why, I think Helen is a very attractive woman in a flamboyant sort of way."

"Flamboyant," the mater repeated. "Yes, it's a good word for her."

"Do you know anything of her antecedents, mother?"

"Oh, it's a very romantic story. She was on the stage you know and played a role in a road company that gave a week of shows at the little theater Edythe helps support. Walter Westmore saw her in one of the performances and fell head over heels in love. The road company moved on but Helen remained, staying with the Westmores. She and Walter were married about a month later. It was love at first sight."

"Apparently so," I said. "Do you happen to recall the play Helen was in when Walter was smitten?"

She thought a moment, head tilted. "I think it was *The Odd Couple,*" she said finally.

I thought I heard a muffled snort from father but I may have been mistaken.

Dinner that night was Brunswick stew, a tasty concoction which usually contains the meat of game animals—squirrel, raccoon, boar, venison, etc. Ursi Olson's version had only chicken and rabbit but to give it a little zip she had added small dumplings spiced with cracked black pepper. They did the trick; the stew was ready to erupt.

I climbed slowly back to my aerie after dinner, happy the meal had been more than adequate compensation for Mrs. Westmore's insipid lunch. I collapsed at my desk and had a wee brandy to soothe my inflamed uvula. I phoned Binky Watrous again and this time the wannabe sleuthhound was home. I thought his greeting was giggled.

"Binky, are you potted?" I demanded.

"Not quite, old boy," he said, his words slushy. "Still upright. Still vertical."

"But not for long," I predicted. "What on earth prompted this disgraceful descent into blottoland?"

"He took me to dinner."

"Who took you to dinner?"

"Frederick Clemens."

"You josh."

"I do *not* josh. We were sitting around discussing heavy financial matters and Fred looked at his Rolex and said it was nearing time for a c-tail—that's what he calls them: c-tails—and would I care to join him for a glass or two and a spot of dinner. Naturally I said I would be delighted and so we did. A funky little Italian place. I had brains."

"Too late," I said.

"With eggs," he added. "Plus lots and lots of vino. It was a very jolly din-din."

"Binky," I said desperately, "before you

become totally unglued I am going to ask you a number of questions. Please try to be as concise and accurate as is possible for one in your benumbed condition. Primo, does Clemens work out of his home or does he have an office?"

"Both. He inhabits this very posh condo—acres of space—and one big room is the office. Lots of glass, chrome, black wood. Elegant, y'know. Computer with all the bells and whistles. Three telephones on his desk: red, white, and blue."

"A Yankee Doodle dandy. And the assistant you spoke to on the phone—was he present?"

"Yep. Name is Felix. No last name mentioned. Tall, skinny guy. I mean really tall and really skinny. Never smiles. Wearing a white suit, black shirt, white tie."

"The return of George Raft," I said. "Did he go to dinner with you and Clemens?"

"No. He chauffeured us to the restaurant in a maroon Bentley and then picked us up later. I don't much like Felix."

"Why not?"

"He scares me. I think he's a wrongo."

"Because of the way he dresses?"

"And he stared at me. Not a nice stare. Cold. Also he uses a fruity cologne. Also one of his fingers is missing."

"Which finger?"

"Index on his right hand."

"At least he can't pull a trigger," I said. "Unless he's sinistral."

"Archy, I'm getting sleepy. Can I go to bed now?"

"No, you cannot," I said. "You're doing fine and I need to know more. Especially about Clemens. How old a man is he?"

"Fortyish. Hard to tell exactly. I think he does facials and manicures. I mean he shines."

"Not oily?"

"Oily? No way. A splendid chap. Sort of Spencer Tracyish. A fast man when it comes to picking up a tab. And tips like a zillionaire."

"Sharp dresser?"

"Not sharp but rich. Wearing a flannel suit you'd kill for. Had on cuff links like miniature gold ingots. Archy, you should see the way he was shaved. I wish I could shave like that. I always seem to leave patches."

"I gather you approve of the man."

"I do, I really do. Sterling character. No front to him. True-blue."

"Uh-huh," I said. "Did he offer any suggestions on how to invest your fifty grand?"

"He says I should buy three-month Treasury bills."

"Oh," I said, disappointed. "No oil wells or tin mines?"

"Nope. He said I'll sleep better at night with T-bills. And he offered me a job."

"A job?"

"Well, not a regular nine-to-fiver. He wants me to recommend people I know who might be interested in investment advice. If he lands anyone as a client, I get a hundred bucks as a finder's fee. A soft touch, huh, Archy?"

"You're going to do it?"

"Sure I am. I already gave him a short list. You're at the top."

"What! You actually gave him my name?"

"I couldn't see any harm. If he calls, you can turn him down or go see him."

I was about to scream at him but then I thought he might have stumbled into a seemingly clever way for me to meet Clemens. I wouldn't seek him out; let him come to me. It would surely be as circumspect an introduction as my father required.

I recalled Mrs. Westmore telling me how difficult it was to persuade the investment adviser to enroll her as a client. "He doesn't just accept everyone." But here he was paying Binky to lasso new customers. I began to appreciate the thespian talents of Frederick Clemens.

"Sleep," Binky said pleadingly. "I beg you, Archy, let me sleep now."

"All right," I said. "Off you go. It was a stellar performance, old boy, and I thank you."

I hung up, pleased with the background info Binky had provided. Not earthshaking, you understand, but basic stuff that would help me limn an accurate picture of Clemens and his operation. Nothing I had learned so far proved the man a legitimate investment counselor or a charlatan eager to make a big score.

I had intended to scrawl an immediate journal précis of Binky's report but found I was brooding on a completely different subject. All afternoon and evening I had held it at bay, feeling there were more important tasks to be accomplished, more important thoughts to be thunk. But now I simply *had* to recollect and try to find meaning in that incredible escapade with Natalie.

If I saw Mrs. Edythe Westmore as a Percheron of a woman and Mrs. Helen Westmore as a lustful soubrette, how was I to characterize Nettie, encapsulate her personality in a phrase? I could not. The conflicting clues in her behavior perplexed me.

Did the spells of apathy spring from weltschmerz or was she indifferent to everyone and everything about her because she was so intensely self-centered? She had certainly proved herself capable of physical passion but had regained control by setting the terms of an encore—if there was to be one.

At times she had seemed to me perpetually angry, carrying chips on both shoulders and atop her head. Yet she had also displayed loving tenderness and a puppy's desire to please. As for her outlandish flower paintings—some sexually explicit—I had absolutely no idea what they might signify.

No doubt about it: she was a fey young woman, and I went to bed with the conviction that a continued relationship with her could only mean trouble for yrs. truly. But such a foreboding had never dissuaded me from previous romantic gambles. As a matter of fact, I have found the presentiment of danger frequently acts as a stimulant, just as pleasure is heightened by a sense of guilt.

Of course it could be this is all folderol and I merely suffer from a chronic case of swollen glands.

CHAPTER 11

THE SUMMONS ARRIVED sooner than expected. On Tuesday morning I was seated in my cubbyhole in the McNally Building, doodling on my desk blotter and imagining with some amusement the reaction of Mrs. Edythe Westmore if I gifted her daughter with a new folding cot. When my phone rang I picked it up idly, guessing it might be Connie Garcia eager to relay the latest Palm Beach gossip.

But it was a masculine voice: deep, resonant, with a smooth texture.

"Mr. Archy McNally?" he inquired.

"This is he," I said. "Or him if you prefer the vernacular."

I was rewarded with a small chuckle. "My name is Frederick Clemens," he started. "I am an investment adviser located in West Palm Beach although I have several clients in the Town of Palm Beach whose names I would be happy to furnish—with their permission of course. Mr. McNally, a mutual friend has suggested you may be interested in diversifying your portfolio to take advantage of special situations with a higher yield or tax benefits not offered by conventional investments. If I am mistaken or if you would prefer to continue dealing with your present brokers and/or financial counselors, then I apologize for this intrusion and shall not contact you again."

I admired that speech. Somewhat verbose, I admit, but it flowed suavely in his rich baritone with nary a hesitation or change of tempo or volume. I thought it quite possible he was reading from a script. Telemarketers frequently do.

"What is the name of our mutual friend?" I asked.

"Mr. Binky Watrous."

"Oh yes, I know Watrous," I said. "An amiable chap. Life of the party and all that. And what exactly is the nature of the special situations you mentioned?"

"There is a variety available," he answered, not missing a beat. "Ranging from those as risk-free as any investment can be to those offering higher returns but definitely on the chancy side. I always try to tailor my advice to clients in accordance with their desire for growth, income, or both, and with their tolerance for risk."

Oh lordy, he was good. Being no stranger to glibness myself, I can recognize a spielmeister when I hear one, and Clemens was a world-class champ.

"What I would like to do," he continued in his mellifluous voice, "is to meet with you personally to explain my investment philosophy and methodology in greater detail. No obligation on your part of course. But if we find ourselves compatible and sharing the same financial goals perhaps we can initiate an association of benefit to both of us."

"I don't suppose it would do any harm to discuss what you have to offer," I said cautiously, playing the role of a wary investor. "Naturally I would like to increase my investment income without the danger of heavy losses."

"Very understandable," he said soothingly. "That is my aim for all my clients. Now then, where and when can we meet?"

I had no desire to invite him to visit the cramped locker in which I toiled. Nor did I think it wise to reveal I was the son of McNally & Son, with our own imposing building on Royal Palm Way. Clemens would learn my identity soon enough—it would be impossible to fake it—but I wanted to remain incognito as long as possible, especially during our first meeting when I hoped he would be unaware of my vocation: conducting Discreet Inquiries for a firm of attorneys.

After a short discussion it was decided I would come to his office at two o'clock that afternoon. He gave me his address and directions on how to get there with a minimum of traffic tie-ups.

By the time we concluded our conversation we were on a first-name basis, Archy and Fred—at his suggestion. He really was a dynamite salesman, wasting no time in establishing a warm, personal rapport with a potential customer. I do believe before he hung up he could have convinced me I was in desperate need of an encyclopedia or a vacuum cleaner.

I spent the next hour phoning buddies who worked at banks and stock brokerages in the Palm Beach area. I asked each the same question: "Ever hear of a guy named Frederick Clemens? Claims to be an investment adviser."

The replies were negative; none of the maîtres d'gelt I called had heard of my quarry. But all promised to consult their client lists and make inquiries at local professional associations. I had a feeling the results would be zilch. Señor Clemens seemed to be a newcomer who had appeared out of nowhere and was working hard to earn a reputation as a financial whiz.

I headed for the Pelican Club hoping an injection of calories, liquid and solid, might provide inspiration in my pursuit of the *real* Frederick Clemens. So far I had only the contradictory judgments of Edythe and Natalie Westmore and Binky Watrous. Their opinions left me with a blurry portrait of this enigmatic man.

I was early; the club's bar area was empty except for Simon Pettibone behind the mahogany. He was watching a stock tape flicker swiftly across the screen of a portable TV set. Mr. Pettibone never plays the Florida lottery or goes to Las Vegas, claiming Wall Street is the biggest casino in the world. I do not believe his portfolio is plump but he is a keen market maven with enough sense never to offer recommendations. Ask him how to make money in common stocks and invariably he replies, "Buy low; sell high." And prithee, who can argue with that?

"Good news, Mr. Pettibone?" I asked him, climbing aboard a barstool. "The market is alive and well?"

He flipped a hand back and forth. "Some up, some down," he said. "As usual. What can I do for you, Mr. McNally?"

I ordered a vodka gimlet, happy fresh lime was still available as a garnish. As I watched our mixologist work his wonders it suddenly occurred to me he might be able to suggest a solution to the problem bedeviling me.

"Mr. Pettibone," I said, "I need your help. You are a man of erudition and experience, especially in the world of investing, and I would welcome any assistance you can provide."

He set the gimlet before me. "Buy low; sell high," he advised.

"No, no. It is not a stock tip I seek; it is an equine of a different hue." I paused to sip my drink. Elixir! I took a gulp and continued more briskly. "This afternoon I am to meet with a gent who claims to be an expert investment adviser or financial counselor—whatever. But I have reasons to question his competence and trustworthiness. To put it baldly he may be a felonious hustler out to make a quick buck and then skedaddle. As I'm sure you're aware, I am the most naive of tyros when it comes to matters financial and particularly the arcane techniques of sophisticated investing. I was hoping you might suggest some questions I could ask this fellow to test his bona fides as a skilled manager of other people's money."

Mr. Pettibone came a step closer and leaned forward across the bar. He was a handsome man with a sculpted face and a skullcap of tight gray curls. "That's what he does for a living—invests for other people?"

"Correct. I presume he charges his clients a set fee or perhaps a percentage of their income. I haven't yet determined how he works."

"And you want to find out if he's on the up-and-up?"

"Exactly. I hope to start by trying to discover just how learned he is when it comes to what he calls the methodology of investing."

"Where does he put his clients' money—stocks and bonds?"

"Those certainly, including securities not listed on any exchange. Plus oil wells in Texas and a tin mine in Bolivia."

Mr. Pettibone straightened up and stared at me. "Uh-oh," he said.

I nodded and pushed my empty glass across the bar for a refill. "Are there any words or phrases I might use to help determine if he's truly a financial expert or simply a con man?"

Mr. Pettibone was silent until he had finished constructing my second gimlet and slid it in front of me.

"There are questions you could ask," he said. "Is this man in commodities? Currency trading? Futures? Options?"

90

"I have no idea."

"Then there's no point in quizzing him about hedges, straddles, butterflies, and shorting against the box. Besides, it would take too long to explain to you what those terms mean."

"How right you are. Can you suggest something simpler?"

"What about bringing up the subjects of buying on margin or selling short? Splits? Stock dividends?"

"Too simple," I said. "Even I know what those are. He's sure to know."

Mr. Pettibone suddenly smiled. "I've got one for you," he said. "Every investment adviser knows what it means or should know. If your man doesn't recognize it, I'd have serious doubts about how legit he is. It's called the Magic of Seventy-two."

"Never heard of it," I said. "But it sounds interesting. What is it?"

"It's a method of estimating how long it will take to double your money. It's not accurate to the penny but it's close enough. The whole thing is based on the number seventy-two. Suppose you invest a million dollars in some gilt-edged security earning ten percent a year. You divide seventy-two by ten and learn that in seven-point-two years you'll have two million dollars. It works the other way too. Say you have a million dollars to invest and want to double it in five years. You divide seventy-two by five and learn you'll have to get a yield of fourteen-point-four percent to do it."

"Crazy," I said. "And this little trick works for any amount you want to invest, from ten bucks on up?"

"That's right."

"Explain it," I urged. "Why the number is seventy-two and not, say, sixty-four or ninety-three."

Mr. Pettibone shrugged. "Beats me," he said. "I've never been able to figure it out. All I know is it works only with the number seventy-two."

"And all investment advisers know about this?"

"They *should* know," he said. "If they don't they better get in another line of business. It's a very basic and useful rule of thumb. Every investor wants to know how long it will take to double his stake."

"Mr. Pettibone, I thank you. I think the Magic of Seventy-two will serve as an excellent ploy to test this fellow's financial expertise."

"Let me know how you make out," he said. "There are a lot of sharks in South Florida and they're not all in the ocean."

Much buoyed by the arrow he had added to my quiver, I carried what remained of my drink into the dining area, where I lunched alone. I had one of Leroy's special Canadian bacon cheeseburgers with a side order of thick garlic-flavored potato chips. I figured if the investment adviser wasn't rattled by mention of the Magic of 72, my breath might do the trick.

It was a leisurely lunch; I had time to devise

a scenario I hoped Clemens would find believable. I decided to avoid any reference to Mrs. Edythe Westmore unless I was asked directly if I knew the lady. And I had no desire to reveal my interest in the Fabergé egg. I wanted to continue playing the role of an amateur investor concerned only with seeking higher yields.

I had little fear that even if the object of my Discreet Inquiry was a consummate confidence man he would be suspicious of my story and my motives. It has been my experience that professional swindlers are remarkably easy to swindle. It is because their egos are so monumental—even more Brobdingnagian than my own! Accustomed to regarding everyone as potential marks, it never seems to occur to them they might also be the target of a scam. Who in a world of dorks would dare attempt to defraud them?

I would.

CHAPTER 12

BINKY'S PERCEPTION OF the physical layout of Clemens Investments had been accurate. If anything, my loopy helot was restrained in describing the condo-cum-office as posh and spacious. I found it vast, impressive, decorated with chilly elegance, and generally presenting a no-expense-spared appearance. It was difficult to believe it might in reality be an upper-class bucket shop.

The apartment occupied an entire floor of a rather austere ten-story edifice which apparently offered only one residence per floor, plus a penthouse. When I emerged from the small elevator on the fourth floor, after having been buzzed into the building via the lobby intercom, the door of Frederick Clemens's abode was wide open, offering entrance to a reception area larger than the McNally dining room.

Standing behind a glass-topped desk was an individual who had to be Felix, the assistant Binky had claimed was *really* tall and *really* skinny. How right he was—but wrong in reporting Felix never smiled, for he greeted me with an expression I interpreted as a smile although it was more teeth than warmth and came close to being a grimace.

"Mr. McNally?" he said, pronouncing my name MackNally instead of MickNally.

"Yes," I said. "I have an appointment with Mr. Clemens."

"My name is Felix," he said, teeth still glistening, "Mr. Clemens's secretary. He is on the phone at the moment but won't be long. Meanwhile, please be seated and make yourself comfortable. May I bring you a coffee or anything else?"

I don't think he would have been flummoxed if I had said, "A glass of Dom Perignon, please." But I said, "Nothing, thank you," and remained standing. I looked about at the lean decor, noting Felix's desk was bare of everything but a combination telephone-fax-answering machine.

94

A red light glowed on the telephone panel. The square chamber itself resembled an efficient machine, furnishings precisely placed, the off-white walls bearing groupings of abstract graphics I could not identify.

Felix seemed amused by my interest in the artwork. "Fractals," he said. "Created by computers. Do you like them?"

"Different," I said.

"A bore," he said. "I try to disregard them. The decorator insisted the room needed a touch of the infinite. Her words: 'A touch of the infinite.' I would have preferred hunting prints or even travel posters."

As Binky had said, the man did have an unblinking stare. But I did not think it cold. Direct and searching perhaps but not hostile. He had a coffin-shaped face, eyes deep-set and glowing. His features bore a saturnine cast, not sullen you understand, but I doubted if he was a man much given to mirth. No white suit today; he was wearing a gray linen jacket and black trousers with an almost metallic sheen. This time the shirt was white and the knitted silk four-in-hand black. His costume fitted the sterile room perfectly.

He glanced at the gadget on his desk. The red light had gone off. "Mr. Clemens is free now," he said. "This way, please."

He ushered me through a door I hadn't noticed before since it was also painted off-white and set flush into the wall. And it had no knob or lock. Felix opened it by pressing lightly on the edge. The door swung silently inward and I wondered if it could be locked electronically by remote control. Curious.

We marched down a tiled hallway to a closed portal also set smoothly into the wall and sans knob and lock. Felix knocked once and pressed in without waiting for a response. He stepped back, motioned me forward, and then disappeared. The door closed silently behind me and I had the oddest notion of being imprisoned in the lair of a beast.

But there was nothing beastly about the smiling man who came toward me, hand outstretched. He was as tall as I but burlier, and if some of his bulk was fat it was effectively concealed by the bespoke three-piece suit he wore—worsted wool gabardine in a cool shade of French blue. I wished I could afford his tailor, for that suit was a masterpiece, with gently rolled lapels, beautifully fitted neck, and wrinkle-free sleeves with four-button cuffs. They worked of course.

The color was right for him, for his complexion was burnished, his smoothly brushed hair halfway between blond and silver. He had the look and manner of a CEO or perhaps a brigadier in mufti. His handclasp was firm and dry, his voice as resonant as it had been on the phone, full but not boomy. I saw no indication of the oiliness disturbing Natalie Westmore. I thought him a handsome man with enough crag in his face to save it from vapidity. The only unsettling detail of his dress and manner was his wristwatch: a gold Rolex studded with diamonds. I thought it a bit much.

He got me seated in a comfortable leather armchair alongside his desk—and what a desk it was! A polished slab of veined black marble was supported on a frame and twisted legs of verdigrised wrought iron. Atop the marble were the red, white, and blue telephones Binky had mentioned and a desk set (blotter, portfolio, letter file, calendar, and engagement book) trimmed in mellow calfskin. No framed photographs, knickknacks, or stained coffee cup.

The computing equipment occupied a separate table and was placed so Clemens could scoot in front of the monitor and keyboard without rising from his castered swivel chair. To my untrained eye the equipment seemed enormous and complex; I couldn't guess the function of those power cords, metal boxes and their attached screens, and really had no desire to know. I still haven't mastered the percentage key on my pocket calculator (two AA batteries).

"There are a number of questions I'd like to ask, Archy," Clemens started. "If you feel any are too personal or you don't wish to answer for whatever reason, have no hesitation in telling me so. I won't be insulted, I assure you." It was hard to resist his grin—an invitation to share a private joke.

"Ask away," I said airily.

"How old are you?"

"Thirty-seven."

"A resident of West Palm?"

"No. The Town of Palm Beach."

"Married?"

"Single."

"You live alone?"

"No, with my parents."

"How long have you lived in Palm Beach?"

"All my life."

"You're a native Floridian?" he asked, apparently astounded.

"I am indeed."

He shook his head. "Amazing. The first of the breed I've met. Education?"

"B.A. degree."

"You are employed?"

"Yes. As a paralegal. The salary is not munificent."

"You have other sources of income?"

"A trust fund," I lied cheerfully. "Left to me by my paternal grandfather. And my investments of course."

"Are you heavily in debt?"

"Heavily? Oh no. I do owe but nothing onerous."

"Where are most of your investments now?"

"The bulk is in two jumbo CD's, both of which mature next month. A total of slightly more than two hundred thousand. I have no desire to roll them over. The yield offered is miserable."

"What yield would make you happy? Ten percent? Fifteen? Twenty?"

"I don't think I can realistically expect more than fifteen, do you? Let's see—with a fifteen percent return, how long would it take to double my money using the Magic of Seventy-two?"

I said it casually but I was watching him closely. He gave me what I can only describe as a glassy smile. Then he suddenly snapped his fingers and glanced at his watch.

"Good lord!" he said in a fretful tone. "I'm waiting for an important FedEx package and it hasn't arrived yet. Please excuse me a moment while I check with Felix. Perhaps it's been delivered and he neglected to inform me. Be right back."

Then he was gone and I was left alone in that silent room. I was tempted to light a gasper but there was no ashtray in sight and so I refrained. Clemens couldn't have been absent more than two minutes, then came striding back.

"Hasn't arrived yet," he reported. "I asked Felix to call FedEx. Now then—what were we talking about?"

"I mentioned I had two hundred thousand to invest and wondered how long it would take to double under the Magic of Seventy-two if I was able to get a fifteen percent yield."

"About four-point-eight years," he said immediately. "But your desire for a fifteen percent return is modest. I think we can do better than that with only slightly more risk. How do you feel about risk, Archy? Would you say you have a high tolerance or low?"

"About average," I said. "Well, perhaps that is not absolutely correct. Risk doesn't spook me if the potential benefit is large enough. In other words, under the right conditions I'm willing to take a flier."

"Good for you," Frederick Clemens said approvingly. "Well, I think I have a clear picture of your investment objectives. Thank you for your patience and cooperation. Now it's your turn to ask questions and I'm sure you have many. I'll answer them to the best of my ability."

"All right," I said. "Here we go.... How long has Clemens Investments been in business?"

"Slightly more than ten years. Formerly in La Jolla, California. I made the move to West Palm less than a year ago."

"Are you a registered investment adviser?"

"Not yet in the state of Florida but my application has been filed."

"Do you have an M.B.A.?"

"No, I do not," he said. "But prior to starting my own firm I worked at two of the largest stock brokerages on Wall Street. I also spent two years in the A and M department of a five-star investment banker."

"A and M?"

"Acquisitions and mergers."

"Would you call yourself essentially a trader or an investor, Fred?"

"A very cogent question, Archy. I'd say I'm both but favor investing more than I do speculation. I am a buy-and-hold type and usually try to avoid quick in-and-out tactics but I'll do it if the potential return is too tempting to resist."

"Do you charge a fixed fee as your compensation or a percentage based on the size of a client's original investment or investment income?"

"I work in a variety of ways—whichever the client is most comfortable with. Occasionally the client pays me nothing at all; my compensation comes in the form of commissions on the sale of securities to the client."

"Have you ever been the subject of an investigation by the SEC or any other law enforcement agency?"

"Not to my knowledge. I had several minor complaints made by clients who lost money. This was when I was employed as a stockbroker. The few cases that went to arbitration were decided in my favor. Some people go ballistic when they lose money, you know. My reply to the poor losers is that I never held a gun to their head and demanded they invest. It was their choice."

This last was uttered in a serious, almost a solemn voice as Clemens leaned toward me. He had the ability to communicate sincerity. Looking into those steady blue eyes, it was almost impossible for me to doubt the man's probity.

I could denigrate his appeal by saying he was a skilled actor giving an effective performance. But I could not detect the slightest hint of dramaturgy in his speech or manner. He seemed open, without pretense, a nonfiction man who was what he appeared to be. It required a conscious and deliberate effort on my part to refrain from surrendering completely.

"Well, Fred," I said, "I am impressed by your

responses and I appreciate your speaking so frankly. Suppose we do this: I shall invest with you half the funds becoming available when my two jumbo CD's mature. If the initial investment proves successful, I will be willing to let you manage the remaining half and perhaps other moneys from the sale of securities I now own and from my trust fund. In other words I propose dipping my toes in the water to test the temperature before plunging in."

"A wise decision," he said. "I like the way you think, Archy. Then I presume you will contact me when you have the first hundred thousand in hand?"

"Correct."

"Excellent. Meanwhile I'll do some digging and see if I can come up with three or four opportunities offering the yield you hope to receive or more. The final choice will be yours of course."

"Do you want me to fill out an application, Fred? Or sign an agreement with your company?"

"Not at the moment. We can complete the paperwork when your funds are available and you have selected the investment you prefer."

There didn't seem to be anything more to say. We both rose and shook hands. Clemens opened the door and escorted me down the hallway to the reception area. Felix was seated at his desk, hands folded atop the glass, and I noticed the stub of the missing finger. But I saw no papers, magazines, or books and wondered if he spent his working hours sitting stonily with folded hands. Not bloody likely.

I stepped through the opened door of Clemens Investments and rang for the elevator. I glanced back and saw both men were looking at me, smiling and nodding. The elevator arrived. I lifted a hand in farewell and departed.

Why did I have an irritating fancy that after I left, the two men exchanged a conspiratorial wink?

I CHAPTER 13

EXITED FROM the building in a rankled mood. I had confidently expected Frederick Clemens to reveal himself as a flimflammer peddling penny stocks and fake Fabergé eggs to gullible clients. But I was chagrined to find myself favorably impressed by the man. And the thought he might actually be honest and respectable made me cranky. If he was indeed a legitimate investment adviser it meant my Discreet Inquiry was a silly waste of time and effort and both my father and I were over-suspicious churls condemning a man on insufficient evidence.

I was about to board the Miata when I noted a maroon Bentley parked nearby. It had to be the car that had wafted Binky Watrous to his meal of brains and eggs. I wandered over to take a closer look. It really was a stately vehicle, lacking the panache of a Rolls—which was the reason many people prefer it. But it surprised me Clemens would select this particular marque. It had absolutely no kinship to a gold Rolex studded with diamonds.

I drove home still peeved by the ambiguity of my encounter with Clemens. I reviewed it slowly and carefully: what was said and what we all did—gestures, expressions, body language. I was seeking a false note: a slipup, no matter how minor, that might indicate the man was a sleazy conniver despite how convincing his words and manner had been.

I continued to reexamine our meeting during the family cocktail hour and a dinner of coq au vin, which is one of my several hundred favorite dishes. But so engrossed was I in finding a blunder in Clemens's presentation, a loose button on his custom-made duds so to speak, I was able to manage only two helpings of the winy chicken and lacked my usual volubility. In fact, I was so silent and withdrawn that mother inquired anxiously if I was coming down with something.

"Only a slight case of frustration," I told her.

"A lot of that going around these days," father remarked. Sometimes his attempts at humor approach the ponderous. But what can you expect of a man who believes Calvin Coolidge had a rapier-sharp wit?

I went upstairs after dinner and shucked my clothing to don a new silk robe. It was printed with images of the golden goddesses of moviedom. A portrait of Carole Lombard lay over my heart—where she belonged.

I opened my journal and began to scratch an account of my conversation with Frederick

Clemens. It was less than half completed when I suddenly stopped and reread what I had just scribbled. I did not shout "Ah-ha!" or "Eureka!" or even "Gotcha!" But I did feel I had uncovered something mighty peculiar, apparently trifling but significant enough to rejuvenate my doubts of Clemens's genuineness.

Consider this sequence of events:

1. When Binky Watrous first phoned Clemens Investments, he was answered by Felix, who then switched the call to Frederick Clemens.

2. When I entered I was told by Felix that Clemens was on the phone. A few moments later he glanced at the dingus on his desk, saw the red light was gone, and told me his boss was now off the phone.

Ergo: There was direct telephonic communication between the desks of Felix and Frederick.

3. Seated in Clemens's office, I made reference to the Magic of 72 to test the investment adviser's expertise, as suggested by Simon Pettibone.

4. Clemens almost immediately snapped his fingers, said he was expecting a FedEx package, and left the room ostensibly to ask Felix if it had arrived.

5. Clemens returned a few minutes later and gave a rapid answer to my inquiry concerning the Magic of 72.

Question: Why hadn't Clemens merely picked up one of his three telephones, buzzed Felix, and asked if the package had arrived?

My answer: Clemens was totally bewildered by my reference to the Magic of 72, and rather than betray his ignorance had left the room on a pretext to consult with Felix, who obviously supplied the correct response to my query.

Now you may think my interpretation of what occurred is flapdoodle and there are several completely innocent explanations of Frederick's behavior. You may also feel that even if my reasoning was accurate, it didn't necessarily prove the financial guru was a phony.

If you do believe that, you can't play on my team. Credulity will get you nowhere if you expect to make a career of Discreet Inquiries.

And if my construct of the incident was correct—and I was convinced it was—it implied more than Clemens's villainy; it also suggested Felix was not just a secretary. If he knew more of the obscure vocabulary of investing than his alleged employer—and apparently he did—it was quite possible he was actually an equal partner in or perhaps even the honcho of Clemens Investments. It was an intriguing conjecture.

I was still musing on the role Felix might be playing in this affair when my phone rang. I picked it up hoping Connie Garcia was calling. I needed a spell of Palm Beach tittle-tattle to provide diversion from ruminating on how financial dupery so often succeeds because of the greed of the duped.

'Twasn't Connie, 'twas Natalie Westmore.

"What a pleasant surprise!" I caroled, and feared I might be speaking with forked tongue.

"Am I disturbing you?" she inquired stiffly.

"Not at all. How are you, Nettie?"

But she scorned politesse. She abruptly said, "Walter is coming home tomorrow morning."

"Is he? I'm sure you'll be happy to see him."

"Yes. I want you to meet him, Archy."

"Of course."

"You said we might have like a picnic in my studio. I want to do it at twelve-thirty tomorrow. I'll have my brother there and you can meet him then."

"Nettie, won't he be busy? After all, he's been gone a year and will want to spend some time with his wife and mother. Shouldn't we wait a few days?"

"No," she said flatly. "I want it to be tomorrow. Please don't fight me on this."

"Fight you?" I said, mildly outraged. "I'm merely making what I feel is a perfectly reasonable suggestion: Let your brother unpack and recover from jet lag before you ask him to meet a stranger."

"He'll do it for me," she said doggedly. "Now will you do it or won't you?"

It wasn't, I decided, worth a tussle; she had obviously made up her mind; I added obstinacy to her résumé. "Naturally, I'll do it, Nettie. Twelve-thirty tomorrow in your studio. Let me bring the lunch. How does pizza sound? With a cold six-pack of beer."

"All right for Walter and you. I'll bring my own food. I didn't tell you—I'm a vegan."

And she hung up. I sat there a moment staring stupidly at the dead phone, wondering why it was so necessary I meet her brother on the morrow. And she was a rabid vegetarian? It explained why she hadn't joined her mother and me at our luncheon and made her even more quirky than I had surmised. I recalled Connie's epithet: kooky. It was beginning to seem appropriate.

I finished working on my journal, sipped a marc and smoked a final cig while I listened to a tape of Tony Bennett singing "The Boulevard of Broken Dreams." Then I went to bed. But my dream wasn't broken. It involved the Rockettes, me, and thirty-six hula hoops.

The following morning was peculiar. I seemed to be functioning in a daze, even more disoriented than usual. It couldn't have been the weather, which was crisp and bracing. But I was unable to focus on anything; every time I tried, my concentration just fuzzed away. I finally decided my condition was due to the confusing telephone conversation with Natalie Westmore. I had been a Laplander trying to converse with a Bantu.

My anomie began to fade during my drive to the McNally Building. A container of black coffee and two glazed doughnuts from the company cafeteria helped. I had breakfasted at home but my stomach still seemed as vacant as my brain. The caffeine and a jolt of nicotine removed most of the cobwebs remaining and I convinced myself I would live to play the kazoo again.

Having nothing better to do before my lunch with Nettie and Walter Westmore, I found a pad of scratch paper and began to compile my Christmas list. The holiday loomed and I hadn't even begun shopping or mailed out a single card.

I started with my parents, of course, followed by Ursi and Jamie Olson. That took care of the McNally household except for Hobo. I decided he deserved a new rawhide bone at least. Then came Connie Garcia, Binky Watrous and his Bridget, the four Pettibones at the Pelican Club, Mrs. Trelawney (my father's secretary), Sgt. Al Rogoff, gossip columnist Lolly Spindrift, Herman Pincus (my barber), Wang Lo (stockbroker), Dr. Gussie Pearlberg, and a long roster of friends and coworkers.

Finished, I gazed in horrified amazement at the number of gifts I'd be required to purchase. I knew the wizened state of my checking account and wondered if I could possibly obtain a home equity loan on Hobo's doghouse. I remembered my nonchalant prevarications to Frederick Clemens concerning jumbo CD's and $200,000 to invest. It was a moment for hollow laughter but I was saved from that hackneyed response when my phone rang.

The caller was Sydney Smythe and I knew immediately what he was going to ask. The challenge to my talent for improv was enough to dissipate the remnants of my morning's attack of mindlessness.

"I was wondering, dear boy," he said, "if you've had an opportunity to examine the 'surprise' in the Fabergé Imperial Easter egg you mentioned."

"I have indeed," I said, slipping on my Ananias cap. "The most remarkable thing I've ever seen. It's a teeny-tiny model of the 1907 Rolls-Royce Silver Ghost. No more than an inch and a half long and fashioned of sterling silver. Crystal windshield and head-lights. Real leather upholstery. It really is an amazing work of artistic craftsmanship. The wheels actually turn."

I heard his sharp intake of breath and then there was silence for a beat or two. Finally he exclaimed, "What a marvelous find! But understandable. I'm sure such distinguished cars were owned by royalty in 1917 St. Petersburg. I must look it up in my library. If I find any references to the Rolls-Royce model I'll certainly let you know. It might help establish the provenance and market value of your deceased client's egg."

"I would appreciate that," I told him. "Thank you so much for all your trouble, Mr. Smythe."

"No trouble at all, dear boy," he sang out gaily. "I shall enjoy the search."

After we disconnected I wondered again about his continuing interest in my imaginary Fabergé Imperial egg. But then a greater wonder—awe at my own inventiveness—took over and I questioned how I had come up with the creation of a model car "surprise."

I finally decided it had its origin in my inspection of Frederick Clemens's Bentley, my puzzlement at his choice and why he hadn't selected a Rolls-Royce with more pizzazz.

But I put all my musings into a mental deep six, doubting if I would ever hear more on the subject from Sydney Smythe. It was true I had sent him off on wild-goose research of an object that didn't exist, but he had assured me he would enjoy the pursuit, so I was able to endure a feeling of guilt. I'm good at that.

As a further assuagement I added his name to my Christmas gift list. Then, realizing it was time to go shopping for luncheon pizza and beer, I also added Natalie Westmore's name. The list was beginning to resemble a telephone directory and I dreamed of sending each of my donees a chaste card saying a contribution in their name had been made to some worthwhile charity—such as the Society for the Prevention of Drinking Brandy Stingers. Would that scam work? I didn't think so. Christmas is a time for giving till it hurts—right? How true, how true.

CHAPTER 14

MOTHER HAD DESCRIBED Walter Westmore as being nerdish, a science wonk whose most fervid dreams probably involved algorithms known only to him and the ghost of Pascal. I found a totally different man and I could only conclude a year in Africa searching for old bones had wrought the transformation.

He was stalwartly built and on the afternoon we met he was wearing a neatly pressed khaki safari suit and looked physically capable of wrestling a black rhinoceros to a draw. The short-sleeved jacket revealed muscular arms with a pelt of fine golden hair noticeable because he was suntanned to almost a mahogany shade.

His handclasp was strong without being crushing and his voice had a nice timbre. He said he was happy to meet me. "Nettie has told me a lot about you, Archy."

"Don't believe a word of it," I advised him, and we all laughed.

I was glad to see Natalie had acquired a new steel cot, much sturdier than the one we had demolished. Walter and I sat on that while we worked on the pepperoni pizza and cold six-pack of Heinekens I had brought. Nettie perched on the high stool at the drawing table. She was wearing short shorts which looked as if they had been hacked from a pair of denim jeans with a dull razor. And she nibbled a paste she told me was minced mushrooms and eggplant moistened with extra-virgin olive oil. This mire was spread on cracked wheat wafers and looked loathsome. Never did pepperoni pizza taste more delectable.

"In what part of Africa did you work?" I asked Walter.

"Mostly in Kenya near Lake Turkana, although I spent a month in Tanzania. But Kenya offered the best possibilities."

"What were you looking for?"

He answered carefully. "Bones, teeth, or any other evidence of early hominids. My specialty is bipedalism. I assume you know what that is."

"Oh sure," I said. "Being able to jump into the air on two feet and click your heels together."

He smiled. His teeth were white tile against his sunburned face. "Something like that. There is a continuing controversy about when it began. And where. Millions of years' difference in the estimates. Guesses actually."

He spoke elliptically, as if he thought I had little interest in bipedalism. How right he was. But I was curious about when Homo sapiens learned to stomp on grapes with both feet, which eventually resulted in 1982 Lafite-Rothschild.

"Fascinating," I said. "And old bones help determine the date we stopped walking on our knuckles?"

"Sometimes," he said. "If sufficient fragments are found to reconstruct a skeleton, even partially."

"Walter can't go back," Natalie said bluntly. "He had a one-year grant and it's over."

He shrugged. "Grant money is tight right now. The universities are cutting back and so are the foundations."

"Mother could finance you," she said angrily. "But no, she's just interested in buying a Fabergé egg."

He shrugged again. "It's her money. She can do with it what she pleases."

113

He tried to express insouciance and failed miserably. There was no mistaking the bitterness in his voice.

"It's not fair!" Nettie burst out.

They both looked at me as if expecting an instant solution of the problem of getting Walter back to Africa to continue his search for ancient bones or perhaps a rack of stained bicuspids.

"It's important to you, is it?" was the best I could do.

He nodded and gave me a sheepish grin. "It starts out as a scientific investigation. Then it becomes an obsession. For all of us. Something like prospecting for gold I suppose. The lure never dies. It's all accident and chance, of course. But sometimes it does happen."

"Talk to mother again," his sister commanded. "She won't listen to me."

He shook his head. "I asked her once and she turned me down. I won't beg. I think I better start looking for a teaching job somewhere—or maybe I can get into a research lab."

"Oh God!" Nettie cried out. "There goes your life."

He stood up to kiss her cheek and give her a sweet smile. Then he resumed his seat on the cot. "It's not that bad, dear," he said evenly. "We all have to make compromises. Don't you agree, Archy?"

"Absolutely," I said. "And occasionally the compromise turns out more happily than we anticipated."

I don't think either of them believed me. Why should they? I didn't believe it myself.

"Let's talk about something more cheerful," Walter said. "Mother is having a cocktail party on Friday. Around five o'clock. Of course you're invited, Archy. Can you make it?"

"Delighted."

"Good," he said. "Bring anyone you like. Most of the guests will be mother's friends."

"And Helen's," Natalie said darkly.

He made no response to that but rose and rubbed his fingers through his sun-streaked brown hair cut *en brosse*. "How do you like the crew cut?" he asked me. "I usually wear it long but barbers were few and far between in the Kenyan outback so I settled for a brush cut. Helen says it makes me look like a fugitive from a chain gang."

"She would," Nettie said scornfully. "Well, I like it."

"I've got to go," he said. "I have to finish unpacking and make a start on my report. It's been a pleasure meeting you, Archy, and I'll see you again on Friday."

I stood briefly to shake his proffered hand. He gave sis another cheek kiss and then he left. I looked at the two unopened cans of Heineken.

"I don't suppose you drink beer," I said to Natalie.

"No, I do not."

"It's made of grain, you know. No animal fat."

"I still won't drink it. Take it home."

"I should have given them to Walter to aid his labors."

"Do you like him?" she challenged.

"Very much. But he does seem unhappy."

"Worse," she said. "It's despair. Because he can't get back to Africa and do what he loves most."

"He's a big boy," I told her. "I'm sure he knows how to endure disappointment."

She slid off the stool and began pacing back and forth, hugging her elbows. "It makes me so furious!" she cried. "Just furious. Mother could easily finance one or two years in Africa. It doesn't cost that much. But all she can think about is that stupid egg. I could kill her!"

If I had thought her last declaration was a brief and temporary explosion of anger I would have made cooing noises and attempted to soothe her. But there was such vitriol in her tone she was obviously expressing a deep, long-standing passion. I didn't know how to respond to her rage.

"You don't mean that," I said feebly.

She paused in her pacing to face me and glare. "I do mean it. Every word of it. Walter lets mother and Helen walk all over him. Not because he's weak but because he thinks it's unimportant compared to his work."

"His obsession," I suggested.

"Yes, his obsession," she agreed. "And meanwhile they're destroying him. Well, I won't let it happen. If he won't do anything about it, I will."

"Do what?" I asked, fearful of what she might answer.

But "Something" was all she said.

I realized I was uncomfortable in her presence as if she might be suffering a petit mal and I was ignorant of how to aid her. So I was somewhat relieved when she said, "I don't want to make love this afternoon, Archy."

"All right," I said equably.

"I'm too upset," she explained. "You can see how things are, can't you?"

I couldn't, of course. I had only the haziest notion of how things were in the Westmore ménage. But I nodded and she accepted that. She plopped down alongside me on the cot and put a bare and slender arm around my neck. I kissed her wrist.

"You're a yum-yum devil," she said.

For some reason I recalled the classic line from *The Ten Commandments,* spoken by Anne Baxter to Charlton Heston: "Oh Moses, you adorable fool!"

"Tell me a story," Nettie enjoined. "Take my mind off my problems."

"Okay," I said. "What kind of story?"

"A true one but a funny one."

I thought a moment. Then: "Well, here's one you may find mildly amusing. I work for my father's legal firm and not too long ago..."

I told her about the Franklin kidnapping and how the Boston bubbleheads had been nabbed simply because their intended victim had a phone equipped with Caller ID. Natalie didn't laugh uproariously but she smiled and tightened the arm about my neck.

"The boy wasn't hurt?" she asked.

"Nope. He was fine."

"And what happened to the kidnappers?"

"Durance Vile, I hope."

"What do you do at your father's firm, Archy?"

"This and that," I said casually. "I'm a sort of paralegal. I don't have a law degree."

She accepted it with no further questions about my occupation, for which I was thankful. She withdrew her arm and took up her perch on the high stool again. My recital of the attempted Franklin kidnapping had enlivened her for a few moments but now she seemed to have slipped back into her broody mode, planning, no doubt, how to slaughter her mother, discombobulate her sister-in-law, and finance her brother's African explorations. Then, her self-imposed tasks successfully completed, she would take me to cot in celebration.

I thought it time to depart and she made no effort to persuade me to linger. She did insist I take the two remaining cans of Heineken with me and I finally acquiesced, hoping they were still cool enough to be drinkable. I also received a light kiss before I left.

"See you on Friday?" she asked. "At the cocktail party."

"I'll be there," I promised.

She gave me a lidded glance but said nothing more.

I drove home reflecting I had learned a great deal about the Westmores that afternoon but nothing directly concerning my Discreet Inquiry into Mr. F. Clemens. But isn't there a folk saying to the effect that the longest way round is the shortest way home? There is no such bromide? Strange; I could have sworn there was.

Even stranger was the character of Natalie Westmore. What a contradiction she was! At our first meeting I had been initially aware of her apparent apathy and indifference. Then came the Paroxysm of the Collapsing Cot during which she displayed a physical passion I had not suspected. And more recently she had revealed an emotional intensity scary to such an easygoing, laid-back chap as your 'umble 'ero.

A windless calm outside and raging squalls within—that was the only conclusion I could arrive at, and wondered if my gamble on an intimate relationship might be a losing proposition. Women and men who present a serene persona to the world but who carry repressed storms within can prove extremely dangerous when finally thunder rumbles and lightning flashes. And I abhor violence. Except for the Three Stooges, of course.

CHAPTER 15

WHEN I PULLED into the graveled turn-around at the rear of the McNally manse I saw Jamie Olson sitting on the step leading to the back door. Hobo was lying beside him. The pooch was on his spine, all four paws in the air, and Jamie was slowly scratching his belly. Lucky dog. No one ever did that for me.

Hobo was alerted by my arrival. He raised his head, saw me, scrambled upright and came dashing. I gave him the customary ear tweak and assured him he was the handsomest hound in dogdom. I retrieved the two beers and went over to join Jamie on the step. I gave him one of the cans.

"Not cold," I warned. "But I think it's still cool enough to drink."

"Thankee," he said.

We popped the tabs, sipped, sat placidly in the waning sunlight and watched Hobo chase a fluttering moth. Jamie filled his old briar from an oilskin pouch and I lighted a cigarette to protect myself. I think Jamie smokes shredded tar paper.

When he had the pipe alight he said, "Al Canfield," and lapsed into silence. I waited for what seemed like minutes. No one has ever accused Jamie of being mouthy. "Had a brew with him and some others," he finally added, pausing midspeech to quaff his beer and puff his pipe.

I reckoned the "others" he referred to were all staff employees of Palm Beach richniks, which meant the gathering was probably a gossipfest.

"Hear anything?" I asked. "From Al. About the Westmores."

"Got a boyfriend. Canfield says."

"Who's got a boyfriend?"

"Mrs. Westmore."

"Jamie," I protested, "she's as old as my mother. I can't see her fooling around."

"Not her. T'other one."

"Mrs. Helen Westmore, the daughter-in-law?"

"Yep."

"Did the houseman say who he was—the boyfriend?"

"Nope. Don't know."

"Well, I suppose it's possible. She's a flashy woman and her husband was away for a year. But he's back now."

"Uh-huh."

I heard amusement in that interjection, a cynical recognition of the ways of the world.

"You mean that even with hubby at home she's continuing her affair?"

"Al says."

I did not pursue the subject further. Natalie had hinted at her sister-in-law's misbehavior and now a servant had confirmed her suspicion. I believed it. I had met Helen Westmore only once, briefly, but she had impressed me as a woman likely to consider chastity an absurdity.

That's the way I saw her. It takes one to know one.

After a while I wandered into the house and went up to my den much bemused by what I had learned from Jamie about Helen Westmore's concupiscence. Poor Walter, I would have wagered, suffered from uxoriousness. (Look it up, fevvin's sake.)

I entered all this in my journal along with an account of my luncheon at Natalie's studio. Then I reread everything I had recorded since my current Discreet Inquiry began. I found no startling revelations but there were some tantalizing snippets meriting further investigation.

It would be a help, I knew, if I dared ask Sgt. Al Rogoff to search for possible police dossiers on Frederick Clemens and his alleged secretary, Felix. But Rogoff would demand to know why I wanted the information and I was silenced by my father's insistence on discretion. I could earn the sergeant's cooperation only if it involved criminal activity, and I had no evidence of that. As yet.

During the family cocktail hour I announced I had been invited to attend a cocktail party at the home of Mrs. Edythe Westmore on Friday. Mother said she and father had also been asked and would probably make a short *pro forma* appearance. She didn't have to explain the reason for their brief attendance. The pater has a thing about socializing with clients, preferring to keep the relationship on a professional level. He feels familiarity breeds contempt—and a casual delay in the payment of retainers.

Dinner that evening was a proletarian meal but not to be scorned. Ursi Olson had prepared a huge platter of spaghetti with marinara sauce. Accompanying this dish were two bowls of roasted Italian sausage, one of hot for father and me and the other of the sweet variety for mother, who because of her high blood pressure tries to avoid spicy foods.

We also had a small salad of romaine and radicchio and a basket of garlic bread to sop up excess spaghetti sauce. And to help digest this savory feast we drank red wine from a jug with a handle and screw-top, vintage of last Tuesday. Nothing subtle about that vino, but its biting harshness was exactly what was needed to cut the richness of sauce and sausage. Dessert was amaretti with espresso and I staggered upstairs singing *"O Sole Mio."*

My appetite may have been satisfied but my curiosity remained unfulfilled. I began leafing through my up-to-the-minute journal again, hoping to find a startling factoid which might help unlock the mystery of Frederick Clemens. Instead I found myself dawdling over the entries concerning Natalie Westmore.

That young lady fascinated and, I must admit, spooked me. She was so volatile, y'see, and I feared her capriciousness. It was highly unlikely to happen but I could imagine her blurting out a merry account of our fervid tussle on the collapsing cot to her brother, mother, or—heaven forfend!—to the astonished but delighted guests at the cocktail party. Impossible she might be so lacking in prudence? I didn't think so; the woman was totally unpredictable.

The more I read and mused on her actions and utterances, the more firmly convinced I became that I would be wise not to encourage our intimacy. I knew from the beginning it was a gamble. Now I regretfully admitted it was a no-win situation and I had better cool the relationship before I became a hapless victim of her caprices.

I could make a start at withdrawing from our incipient liaison during the cocktail party Friday evening, and I thought I knew how to do it. Hadn't Walter Westmore said I could bring anyone I chose? I phoned Connie Garcia.

"Hi, hon," I said. "How's by you?"

"Okay, I guess," she said, sighing. "It's been a heavy week and I'll be glad when it's over. I'm frazzled."

"Got just the thing to unfrazzle you," I said breezily. "Remember we spoke about Mrs. Edythe Westmore? As I told you, she's a client of ours and she's throwing this great cocktail party on Friday evening. Lots of food, drinks, and maybe even funny hats and confetti. My parents are invited and so am I. The balloon goes up at five o'clock. Can you make it?"

"Oh Archy," she wailed. "No can do. Friday is the night of Lady Cynthia's sit-down dinner for the pols—the shindig I've been working on so hard for so long. I'll have to be there to make sure everything goes like silk. There's no way I can see you on Friday night."

"Drat!" I said. "Also hell and damnation. I was hoping you'd come along to provide aid and comfort and make certain I don't put a lampshade on my head."

"I can provide aid and comfort on Saturday night," she consoled me. "And I'll be even more in need of unfrazzling. How about it?"

"You betcha," I said bravely. "Saturday

night it is. I'll give you a buzz to decide where and when. But I'm sorry you can't make the cocktail bash. It reduces the gaiety potential by ninety percent."

"We'll make up for it on Saturday," she promised. "And behave yourself at the Westmores."

"I'll have to," I said sadly. "My parents will be present."

"Good. They'll keep you on a short leash. See you Saturday, sweet. I hope the party is a hoot."

"And I hope you have a grand time at the Lady's dinner."

"Fat chance," she said, and rang off.

I sat there practically grinding the McNally molars in frustration. I'm sure you ken my attempted ploy. I had wanted Connie to accompany me as protection against any untoward advances by Natalie. I wanted Ms. Westmore to see and recognize there was a woman in my life I had known longer than I had known her, an attractive woman whom, I intended to make evident, I cherished and possibly loved.

But the stratagem had come to naught and I was faced with the problem of finding another way to lessen the intensity of Nettie's emotional attachment to me while retaining her friendship. Students of ego giantism will note that never once did I consider she might be utterly indifferent to my charms and just as eager as I to be casual pals rather than impassioned lovers.

In defense of my machismo I can only point to the evidence of the collapsed cot. And if you wish to remind me I was as much seductee as seducer, I suggest we terminate this conversation at once. It is a spiteful thing to rob a man of his illusions.

Nothing of any great consequence occurred during the following forty-eight hours. The weather was, as the French put it, *lousay,* and I could think of nothing better to do than Christmas shopping. I bought everything on plastic and refused to brood about the bills arriving in January.

I shall not distract you by detailing the items selected for everyone on my list. I only wish to mention I was stumped in finding a proper gift for Natalie Westmore. I think you'll agree I had to give her some token of my esteem no matter how impersonal. But a card saying "Best wishes for a jolly holiday season" seemed insufficient for a woman with whom I had played adult patty-cake. I finally decided to postpone the purchase of her present until I could find a trinket she might appreciate but which wouldn't signify undying passion on my part.

At noontime on Friday I decided to take a break from my shopping orgy and escape the relentless rain for a few moments by ducking into the Pelican Club for a wee bit of the old nasty. And there, standing at the bar, was my number one (and only) aider and abettor, the bedlamite Binky Watrous himself. He greeted me effusively.

"Hey, old sport!" he shouted. "Merry Xmas and all that sort of thing. Let me buy you a snifter to chase the winter chill."

I looked at him in amazement. "I appreciate your kind offer," I told him. "A generous impulse on your part. But do you have the wherewithal?"

"Floating," he assured me. "Awash in cash. Mr. Pettibone, did I or did I not show you a plump bundle of spondulicks?"

"You did indeed, Mr. Watrous," the bartender said gravely.

"In that case," I said, "I'll have a double vodka rocks with the merest tincture of aqua. Binky, tell me at once; what is the source of your unusual liquidity? Have you tunneled into Fort Knox?"

"Frederick Clemens," he said with a smirky grin. "I told you he promised me a hundred-buck finder's fee for every person I suggest who becomes a client. Two of the people I touted signed up, and Fred forked over the moola with heartfelt thanks. Archy, he's a true gentleman. A paragon one might even say and I do say it."

"Uh-huh," I said, and waited until Mr. Pettibone was out of earshot. "Binky, I don't wish to push the panic button but I feel it my duty to remind you the purpose of our Discreet Inquiry is to determine if Frederick Clemens is or is not a swindler. Should it be proved he is and has been acting with criminal intent it may put you in an awkward or even indefensible position, since you are serving as his paid assistant, profiting when he profits, and so might be held equally culpable."

"Say what?" Binky said.

"I'm beginning to talk like my father," I admitted. "To put it bluntly, old boy, if Clemens is a crook you may find yourself in the clink as an accessory before the fact."

He considered that, staring into his tumbler of Irish whiskey. I really didn't believe he was in any danger of suffering the fate I had described, but I would have preferred he wasn't playing kneesies with the formidable Mr. Clemens.

"You really think I might be popped in the cooler?" he asked.

"Well," I said judiciously, "you could always plead insanity."

He ignored that. "I'd hate to give up the commish Clemens pays me," he said wistfully. "It's nice having walking-around money in my pocket. Especially since I'm losing hope of ever getting any monetary reward from you for the valuable services I render. And whatever happened to those fringe benefits you're always dangling in your sly way?"

I didn't shout "Shazam!" but his chiding resulted in an inspiration that pleased me mightily. "Why, Binky," I said, "how odd you should mention it. I was going to phone to ask if you'd care to attend a lavish cocktail party tonight at the home of the Westmore family on Ocean Boulevard. Much to eat and drink. Laughs aplenty and possibly scantily clad dancing girls."

"What time?" Binky said eagerly.

And so, denied the company of Connie Garcia, I had found a substitute chaperon in the person of my squirrelly henchman. Binky and I would be inseparable at the Westmore party, I decided, and there would be little opportunity for private conversation with Natalie during which she might seek to further an intimacy I had solemnly vowed to resist. I thought I had planned wisely.

How could I have been such a pompous ass?

CHAPTER 16

HOW DOES THIS rig-out grab you? Ivory cashmere blazer, butterscotch suede vest, band-collar shirt with burgundy awning stripes, fawny linen slacks, black crocodile slip-ons. No socks. And to avoid excess the only jewelry I wore was my Mickey Mouse wristwatch—an original, not a replica.

Nifty, eh? I thought so, and thus caparisoned, I set out for the Westmores' shindy. The rain had ceased but the air was still dampish and winterly. Of course it's a South Florida winter I speak of—which means a temperature of perhaps 60°F, give or take, but definitely chill.

I was fashionably late (twenty minutes) but the Westmore driveway was already crowded with cars. I espied my father's black Lexus and the battered 1970 MB cabriolet belonging to Binky Watrous. Trust that dingbat to be on time for free belts and noshes. I also spotted Frederick Clemens's maroon Bentley and thought I discerned someone within. I strolled over and found Felix sitting behind the wheel, not smoking or reading, just sitting placidly and not even bothering to yawn. I admired his composedness. The man was a cat.

"Good evening, Felix," I said through his open window.

He turned his head slowly to look at me. "Good evening, Mr. McNally," he said, and I ignored his mispronunciation of my name.

"You're not coming inside?" I asked.

"Think not," he said. "I try to avoid mob scenes."

I thought it an odd thing to say. I mean it was merely a cocktail party, not Times Square on New Year's Eve.

"You may be missing a rollicking jamboree," I told him.

"Later," he said, and once again I couldn't decide if the expression he put on was a smile or a grimace.

I nodded, left him alone, and went into the Westmore home through the open door. So began what turned out to be a kaleidoscopic evening, and I must warn you I am not certain I accurately recall the correct sequence of incidents, conversations, and events. No matter. They all did occur I assure you, discontinuous though they may seem.

It had been my fear after enduring the so-so luncheon with Mrs. Westmore that the viands offered at her party would be more of

130

the same—a whimpering board rather than groaning, so to speak. But she or someone in her household had had the great good sense to hire a caterer, and I was happy to see the dining room table laden with a tempting selection of hot meats, cold seafood, pasta salads, and an iced salver of chocolate profiteroles. I saw nothing to object to.

A bar had been set up in the sitting room, and it was there I found Binky Watrous working on what I hoped was his first drink.

"Satisfied?" I asked him.

"Not bad," he admitted. "After I finish this torpedo I'm going to stage a raid on the buffet before all the stone crabs are gone."

"Good thinking," I said, and ordered a vodka gimlet from the bartender, who appeared to be 382 years old. "See anyone interesting of the female ilk?"

"I did indeed," he said. "But she was accompanied by a mastodon. Even his muscles had muscles and so I passed. But I did meet the hostess, told her I was your closest friend and role model. She said you should be sure to look her up; she has something to tell you. I also met Mrs. Helen Westmore. She patted my cheek and said I was cute. You think there's anything doing there, Archy?"

"Not for you. Meet the son or daughter?"

"Nope. What's the daughter like?"

"Different," I said.

The room was filling up and we were being elbowed away from the bar. Binky finished his drink and headed for the dining room. I followed closely, carrying my gimlet. There was already a crush at the buffet. I stood back while my hungry helot went to fill a plate. Suddenly Frederick Clemens was planted before me, hand outstretched.

"Good to see you again, Archy," he said, smiling. "I didn't realize you knew Edythe Westmore."

"She's really my mother's friend," I explained. "But I can't resist a party."

"Don't blame you," he said, still smiling. "And it's a good one." He paused and looked around. "There's something I'd like to talk to you about but there's such a crowd in here. Could we step out in the hall a minute? It's a bit quieter there."

I saw no way to refuse even though it meant I'd have to leave Binky—temporarily I hoped. I followed Clemens out to the hallway, which held only a few guests to-ing and fro-ing.

"You say Mrs. Westmore is a friend of your mother," he said. "Then you probably know Edythe is a client of mine. I've been working on a special deal for her. It was supposed to be confidential but apparently the dear woman has informed several of her friends about it. It concerns the purchase of a Fabergé egg. Do you happen to know if Mrs. Westmore told your mother?"

He wasn't smiling now. I thought his tone was almost grim.

"A Fabergé egg?" I repeated. "Why, yes, I believe mother did mention something about it. I wasn't really listening but I remember thinking what an unusual investment it was."

He nodded. "A few people have asked me about it, so it's obvious Mrs. Westmore has been talking. I thought she had agreed to keep the matter private but I guess I was expecting too much. You know what women are like."

I thought it was a rhetorical observation, but he seemed to await a response. I said, "Mmm."

"In any event," he continued, "it is potentially a once-in-a-lifetime opportunity with a possible three or four hundred percent return. But of course the purchase is contingent on what the appraiser says of the object's authenticity, condition, and probable market value."

"Understandable," I said. "I hope you have an expert appraiser."

"The best," he said with emphasis.

He said nothing more, I said nothing, and our silence was becoming awkward when Helen Westmore came prancing up to take Clemens's arm in a firm grasp. Her gown was phenomenal and she was flaunting a small black *mouche* on her left cheek.

"You deserted me, Fred," she said reprovingly to Clemens. "Mama no like. Now get me some nibbles; I'm famished."

"Of course," he said. "What would you like?"

"Everything," she said, and gave me a dismissive "Hi, Archy" before tugging him into the dining room. I waited a mo and then followed, looking about for Binky. But he wasn't at the buffet and I went back to the bar, figuring I'd surely find him there. No Binky, so I asked for a gimlet refill before continuing my search.

I didn't find him in the throng but I found *her*—Natalie Westmore. She was standing near the front entrance, deep in an animated conversation with her brother. I stared at her from afar and what a revelation it was!

She was wearing a creamy sleeveless sheath of some glittery stuff. It wasn't skintight but it clung to her pliant body here and there and here and there. The dress was quite short and I was reminded of the elegance of her tanned legs. She wasn't wearing makeup and her hair was as raggedy as before, but she seemed to me absolutely luscious.

Well, you get the picture. I had spent hours brooding on how I might temper our relationship and in one brief moment the hyperkinetic McNally glands took command and my knees turned to lime Jell-O. I staggered away before I lost control and rushed to her babbling, "Take me, take me, take me!" Yes, I fled, although my corpuscles continued to dance a Highland fling.

I wandered through the house, ignoring the chattering merrymakers, giving no thought to the whereabouts of Binky Watrous. I was conscious of wearing a sappy grin and I tried, I really *tried* to censure my weak character. How quickly I had surrendered lofty resolves to baser instincts. But all my attempted *mea culpas* were to no avail. I could think of nothing but

Natalie, a quicksilver woman. And a new steel cot. I thought of that as well.

I found myself with a drained glass and headed for the bar again, needing Dutch courage for what I knew I would inevitably endeavor. There was a row of guests clamoring for their drinks to be mixed and I stood aside until the press of the thirsty slackened.

I saw a tall woman also standing at a distance, gripping an empty glass and apparently waiting a chance to be served. I guessed her age at about eighty but she was erect and seemed untroubled by the noise and confusion about her. It was noteworthy because she was wearing opaque black eyeglasses and there was a white cane hooked over one arm.

I went up to her and her face turned in my direction. It was a strong, handsome face. There were many wrinkles, many, but the cheekbones were high, the jaw firm. She had a pleasantly amused expression and I reckoned she had laughed a great deal in her lifetime. She wore a tweed suit with a mannish shirt and tie. Her shoes were clunky brogues.

"Ma'am," I said, "may I have the pleasure of fetching you a drink?" Her head turned a little more at the sound of my voice so those black specs were facing me directly.

"You're very kind," she said in a deep, rumbling voice, and held out her glass. I took it from her fingers. "Bourbon, please," she said, "Straight. And quite small; I'll be leaving soon."

It took almost five minutes to get our drinks but when I returned with her half-shot of Jim Beam she was still standing exactly where I had left her.

"Here you are," I said. "A small bourbon straight." She held out her hand and I placed the glass within her encircling fingers.

"Thank you so much," she said, and took a sip. "I'm usually able to cope but mobs are daunting. What is your name?"

"Archy McNally. And yours?"

"Barney Newfield," she said.

"Any relation to Barney Oldfield?" I asked.

She laughed. "How old are you, Archy?"

"Thirty-seven, ma'am."

"Then how do you know about Barney Oldfield?"

"I'm a nostalgia buff. And a trivia maven. Barney Oldfield set the one-mile speed record in 1910."

"And won many other races as well," she said. "My father was a car-racing nut and insisted I be named Barney."

"Unusual for a woman. It's a variation of Barnaby, which means 'son of consolation.' "

"Does it? I needed consolation when I was a kid and the song 'Barney Google' was popular. Have you heard it?"

"Of course," I said, happy I could display my knowledge of antique tunes. I sang, "Barney Google, with the goo-goo googly eyes."

"That's the one," she said, smiling. "My school chums made my life miserable by singing it when I appeared. And now my eyes

136

really are googly. God has a divine sense of humor."

"Are you totally blind?" I asked boldly, but she wasn't offended.

"Almost," she said quite cheerfully. "A degenerative condition due to diabetes. Fortunately I had a full career before the curtain came down."

"Please forgive my insatiable curiosity," I said, "but what *was* your career?"

"Why, I was a paleontologist. I'm sure a clever young man like you knows what that is."

"Similar to a paleoanthropologist?"

"Very similar. If there's any difference it's in the degree of specialization. The ontologist may be interested in the total life-forms of ancient periods while the anthropologist concentrates on fossil hominids. But the fields certainly overlap. All of which explains what I'm doing here drinking bourbon. I was Walter Westmore's teacher and mentor for many years and the dear man has never forgotten me."

"How could he?" I said. "Tell me, is Walter good at what he does?"

"Good?" she said. "I don't use the term genius lightly but I consider Walter a genius. Not only does he now far surpass me in technical knowledge but he has a natural talent for demodulation. I do believe he can extrapolate a complete skeleton from a chip of shinbone. The only thing he lacks is field experience."

"I know he's eager to get back to Africa."

"And he deserves to go. It's a bloody shame he can't get the funds to continue his work.

137

He has a new theory of bipedalism that will cause a sensation if he can prove it out. But it will require more physical evidence than he has now. And the only place to find the evidence is in Africa." She suddenly turned her head and said, "Walter? We were just talking about you."

I also turned and there he was, quite close to us although I hadn't been aware of his presence.

"How on earth did you know he was here?" I asked Barney Newfield.

Westmore laughed. "My aftershave," he explained. "I've been using the same brand for years and Barney can spot it a mile away."

"At least," she said, smiling.

"I'm glad you two met," he said. "Barney, I hope you can stay a while longer."

"Afraid not," she said. "I better get home before my companion panics and phones nine-one-one."

"Whenever you're ready," Walter said. Then to me: "Barney lives in Manalapan and her companion, Ruby, is a tyrant."

"She is that," Barney agreed. "But I don't know what I'd do without the darling."

"Ma'am," I said, "do you require transportation? My car is right outside if you don't mind riding in an open convertible."

"Thanks, Archy," Westmore said, "but I'll make sure Barney gets home."

"It's been a joy meeting you, ma'am," I said, "and I hope we may have another chat sometime soon."

"Would you mind if I touched your face?" she asked.

"Not at all," I said, and thrust my phiz forward. Her hand found it and she began to trace forehead, eye sockets, nose, cheekbones, lips, chin, and jaw. Her fingertips were light, almost caressing. It was a very pleasurable sensation. Dare I say erotic?

"Oh my," she said. "What a handsome man you are!"

"Thank you," I said, "but it's really a plastic mask. Underneath I am The Phantom of the Opera."

They laughed and I started away. Walter called after me, "Oh, Archy, Natalie is looking for you."

Did I begin to pant? No. Hyperventilate? Yes.

CHAPTER 17

I PASSED THE dining room, glanced in, and there was Binky Watrous grazing at what remained of the buffet. I wondered if he might be stuffing a doggie bag. I didn't stop to inquire; I no longer had need of a chaperon—not even a quasi chaperon. I continued an increasingly frantic search for Natalie. The crowd was thinning but I was unable to find her.

Finally, finally, while I was pacing fretfully near the front entrance, she came slowly down the stairway from the second floor. She had donned a ratty coat sweater that concealed her enchanting bare shoulders and arms. (The Earl of Cardigan has a lot to answer for.) I hustled forward to greet her.

"Good evening, Natalie," I said beamishly.

"Good evening, Archy," she said with what I thought was a tight smile. "Having a good time?"

"Oh yes. Excellent party. I saw you earlier but you were talking to your brother and I didn't want to interrupt. What a great outfit you're wearing. You look smashing!"

She glanced down at herself. "Mother insisted I wear a dress. Helen picked it out. I hate it."

"Oh no," I dissented. "It really does look super."

"It isn't me," she said defiantly.

I couldn't think of an intelligent response so all I said was, "May I get you a drink or a snack?"

"No, thank you," she said coldly. "I don't drink alcohol and all the food they have is garbage as far as I'm concerned."

This wasn't going well at all. She seemed in a particularly tense mood and my hopes were rapidly evaporating when she came to the rescue. "Archy," she said, "could we go over to my studio for a while? I have something for you."

"Of course," I said heartily, my pulse going pit-a-pat. "Be happy to."

We started out but paused when Barney Newfield and Walter Westmore came along. She was holding his arm and he was carrying her cane. We all exchanged adieus and they left us. Nettie and I waited outside until they drove away in the lavender Riviera. They waved and we waved back.

I looked about at the remaining cars. My father's Lexus was gone but Binky's heap was still parked and so was Clemens's Bentley. Then Natalie took my hand and we strolled toward the studio hut.

"Barney is a wonderful woman," I offered.

"A saint," Nettie said. "She's done so much for Walter. She's devoted to him. He should have married her."

"There's a slight age difference," I pointed out.

She shook her head. "Doesn't make any difference," she said, and I didn't argue, not wanting a silly disagreement to endanger what I anticipated would be a paradisiacal interlude.

"Archy," she said in a low voice, "there's no electricity in the studio but I have a battery-powered lantern. It should be enough for us."

"It will do nicely," I assured her with what sounded to me like a nervous giggle. I mean I felt a certain trepidation about the approaching encounter despite my lickerishness. Doesn't every man?

The lantern had been placed on the floor and after unlocking the door Nettie reached in to switch on the light. The small room was flooded with a white glare and I hoped it wouldn't attract curious guests from the party.

"Here it is," she said, motioning toward a watercolor lying on her drawing table. "I worked on it for two days and had it framed yesterday. Do you like it?"

I looked. "Very nice," I said. "It resembles a petunia."

"Well, I started copying a print of a petunia but then I added things. Do you really like it?"

"I do indeed," I lied bravely. "The colors are striking, especially the red leaves."

"I'm glad you like it, Archy, because I painted it for you. I want you to have it."

I swallowed. "Oh, I couldn't accept," I protested. "After the work you did on it. And the frame and all."

"No, no," she said firmly. "I want you to have it. It's my Christmas gift to you."

"You're very kind. I'll certainly treasure it."

"I have a plastic shopping bag from Publix you can carry it in."

"Wonderful," I said.

"I think we better go back now," she said.

"Must we go?" I said weakly.

"Yes," she said.

A few moments later the light was off, the door locked, and we were walking silently toward the main house. I was carrying my petunia in a shopping bag and feeling a new empathy for Napoleon trudging home from Moscow.

We were nearing the lighted portico when Natalie stopped me. She was staring at the open front door. I looked and saw Helen Westmore

142

and Frederick Clemens pausing to light cigarettes. Helen was wearing a short mink jacket as a cape. Clemens put his arm about her
waist, said something, and they both laughed.
Nettie and I heard their continued laughter
as they went down to the maroon Bentley
and slid in. We waited in the semidarkness until
the car pulled away.

"Bitch!" Natalie said, and I was shocked by
the venom in her voice.

She said nothing more until we were inside.
Then she gave me a quick peck on the cheek,
muttered good-bye, and darted up the stairs.
"Thank you for the painting," I called after
her, but I don't think she heard me. I wanted desperately to kick something—anything.

Gruntled I was not. The evening had lost
its savor and I determined to make my departure as soon as I found the hostess and thanked
her for such a *fun* occasion. It was easy to locate
Mrs. Edythe Westmore. All I had to do was
trace a braying voice to its source.

She was wearing a brocaded gown that
looked stiff enough to stand up by itself. And
she was festooned with jewelry: pearls and gold
and precious stones. Every time she moved she
clanked, clinked, chimed, or pealed. I waited
for a break in her monologue to two stunned
guests before I could catch her eye and smile.
She deserted her relieved listeners and bustled
to my side. I received a warm, moist kiss.

"Edythe," I said, "I must be going but I wanted to thank you for an evening I shall never
forget."

"It was a wonderful party, wasn't it?" she crowed. "I'm sure everyone had a marvy time."

"Oh, we did," I agreed, and then topped her dated cliché. "We all had a fab time. Edythe, what was it you wished to say to me?"

She was puzzled.

"My friend Binky Watrous said you wanted to tell me something."

"Oh yes," she said, "now I remember. Well, when you and I had that nice lunch together we talked about the Fabergé egg I'm going to buy and you said I should ask Fred Clemens if it contained a 'surprise' like all the other Imperial eggs. Fred says it does, and you know what it is?"

"Can't guess."

"Well, I haven't seen it of course because the egg is still in Paris, but Fred says you open it up and inside is this tiny, beautiful model of a 1907 Rolls-Royce Silver Ghost made of sterling. Fred says it's the most remarkable thing he's ever seen. It has a crystal windshield and real leather upholstery. And Fred says the wheels actually turn! Isn't it the most incredible thing you've ever heard?" She looked at me expectantly.

In previous tales of my adventures I have mentioned how certain unexpected happenings gasted my flabber. But none of those reactions matched the intensity of the astonishment I felt at that precise moment. And when the initial shock subsided I was left in a condition I can only describe as utter bafflement.

"Amazing," I said hoarsely. "Yes. Truly astounding."

"I knew you'd be impressed," she said brightly, pleased with the effect her words had caused.

I was finally able to flee when other guests came up to make their farewells. I left Binky to continue his depredations at the bar and buffet and staggered outside to the Miata, still lugging my petunia. The evening, I decided, had been a crazy quilt of frustrations and perplexities. And to heighten my distraction I realized I had eaten nothing since lunch and was suddenly stricken by a hunger so extreme I feared I might faint if I didn't soon quiet my stomach's growl. I sped homeward.

Ursi Olson had not prepared dinner for the family, believing we would eat our fill at the party. It was an accurate assessment of my parents; they had dined at the Westmore buffet. But I was famished and headed for the kitchen immediately, not even pausing to give Hobo a pat.

I discovered the Olsons' dinner had been mutton, which they loved but never served to us. Many people loathe mutton and my mother and father are two of them. I admit eating the flesh of a geriatric sheep is an acquired taste but I fancy the strong, gamy flavor of the meat. So you can imagine my delight when upon jerking open the refrigerator door I discovered an enormous mutton chop still retaining a bit of warmth from the broiler. I glommed on to it, grabbed a cold bottle of Rolling Rock, and scuttled upstairs to enjoy a delayed feast.

I was glad no one was present to see me tear into the chop at my desk. I was ravenous, devoured every shred of meat and was sorry my teeth weren't strong enough to grind the bone to meal. Naturally by the time I finished, my hands and mug were a greasy mess and I needed a washup before I could relax with the beer and muse on the bewilderments of the evening.

I found I had no desire to reflect on the unusual relationship between Barney Newfield and Walter Westmore or the apparent intimacy shared by Helen Westmore and Frederick Clemens. Nor—and you may find this difficult to believe—did I wish to ponder the reason for Natalie dooming my hope to test the resilience of her new steel cot. Later, I knew, I would brood on the cause of my failure and the resulting wound to my *amour propre*.

No, what concerned me most, to the exclusion of everything else, was Edythe Westmore's account (via Frederick Clemens) of the surprise contained within the Fabergé egg she intended to buy. It was an exact duplication of the invented surprise I had told Sydney Smythe was inside the imaginary egg of an equally imaginary deceased client.

Coincidence? Impossible! If Clemens had said the Imperial egg supposedly in Paris contained a tiny reproduction of a classic motorcar, marque and model year not specified, I might have accepted it as an extraordinary

146

similarity. But not only was the description detailed but many of the words and phrases used were mine! I had created an illusion only to be informed it actually existed.

Did I believe that? Of course. And I also have an abiding faith in the tooth fairy.

The only possible conclusion was that somehow, at some time, for some reason Sydney Smythe had communicated what I had told him of the fictitious surprise to Frederick Clemens. Their exchange might have been quite innocent, of course. Perhaps Clemens stopped at Windsor Antiques by chance and began to chat with the proprietor about Fabergé eggs, a subject of interest to both of them. And during the conversation Smythe had repeated my scam, including my paean to the 1907 Rolls-Royce Silver Ghost.

But if Sydney Smythe's role in this incident was blameless, what was I to make of the behavior of Clemens? When questioned by Edythe Westmore, he had told her the Paris egg he was recommending she purchase as an investment contained a surprise he obviously knew didn't exist. Was it because he didn't know what it contained and didn't wish to reveal his ignorance? Or was it because the egg itself was a chimera?

I decided my first step would be a meeting with Mr. Smythe. During small talk I should be able to ascertain if he was acquainted with Fred Clemens and had repeated to him my feigned report on the dead client and the Fabergé egg included in his estate.

Now all I needed was an innocuous excuse for visiting Windsor Antiques. The answer was easy. I still hadn't purchased a Christmas present for Natalie Westmore—and she had already given me a gift beyond compare. Shopping for some unusual curio would provide a perfect pretext for pawing through the shop's hodgepodge while I casually elicited from the decrepit dandy what I needed to know.

Thinking about Nettie moved my thoughts sluggishly to the evening's romantic fiasco. I had yearned for a perennial wildflower and had ended up with a painted petunia—now hidden hurriedly behind my dresser. It called for gnashing of the McNally choppers.

But I suddenly found myself succumbing to torpidity. I could no longer concentrate except on the lure of sleep, blessed sleep. So I postponed any attempt to analyze the reasons for Natalie's cruel rejection. Those vodka gimlets and the beer were doing their soporific best, and I disrobed and fell into bed.

Scarlett O'Hara's last line had it right.

CHAPTER 18

REGARDLESS OF THE season, weather, or impending nuclear catastrophe, my father plays golf every Saturday—and the next morning was no exception. He was clad in his usual plus fours, argyle hose, and spectator wing tips in brown and beige. He had added the hand-knitted sweater—mother's birthday gift to him. I noted the pater wore it with cuff rolled up to his elbows to conceal those mismatched sleeves.

A lesser man might have looked ridiculous in such a costume but the guv, with his erect posture and guardsman's mustache, carried it off with great dignity. He was an impressive figure on the links for he approached the game of golf with the same thoughtful solemnity he brought to every challenge. For instance, was it de rigueur or gauche to pop a whole hard-boiled egg into one's mouth rather than nibble at it with a resulting cascade of yolk crumbs? It was a decision requiring intense mulling.

He paused before leaving for his club to draw me aside in the hallway. His mien revealed nothing of what he might be thinking or feeling.

"At the party last evening," he began abruptly, "I was approached by Natalie and Walter Westmore. In concert they asked if they might confer with me with no mention of the consultation relayed to their mother. Archy, do you have any idea why they appeared so eager for a confidential meeting?"

"Not definitely, no, sir," I answered. "But if I had to guess I'd say it concerns their mother's willingness to pay half a million dollars for a Fabergé egg. Both Natalie and Walter are unalterably opposed."

He nodded. "I thought it was likely although they gave no reason and I didn't ask. Have you made any progress in determining the legitimacy of the investment and the probity of Mrs. Westmore's financial adviser?"

"Some progress, father, but not enough to state positively the bauble in question does or does not exist. Nor have I yet come to any final judgment on the trustworthiness of Frederick Clemens."

(Have you ever noticed that when my father and I converse our speech resembles oral arguments presented by prolix advocates to the Supreme Court?)

He accepted my temporary failure with no rebuke. "In any event I have agreed to meet with the Westmore siblings at eleven o'clock Tuesday morning. If, during our conversation, they suggest McNally and Son engage in any actions I deem possibly injurious to our client I shall refuse to advise them or act on their behalf. It is a very delicate situation and I think it wise to have a witness present. Will you be able to attend?"

"Of course," I said. "But will they accept my presence, sir? It may have the effect of silencing them or at least dampening the confidence they'd have in speaking to you alone."

"I shall make it plain to them your attendance or that of another witness is necessary. If they continue to object, I shall then suggest they consult another attorney."

Having handed down his decision, there was no appeal to a higher court. He went off to his golf game and, the weather being inclement, I retired to my digs and set to work recording details of the Westmore cocktail party. It was not the way I would have preferred to spend a Saturday but so much had happened I wanted to have a written reminder.

I interrupted my labors for a half-hour frolic with Hobo during which we roughhoused and then searched the grounds for any marauding raccoons that might have invaded the McNally acres. Finally I gave his coat a good brushing, which he endured although I think he'd have much preferred watching a rerun of *Lassie Come Home.*

I demolished a sardine salad for lunch and then resumed scribbling in my professional diary. I was jotting an honest (and heartrending) account of my misadventure in Natalie's studio when the recollection of how my lascivious hopes were thwarted drove me to phone Consuela Garcia. I wanted to make certain I had not suddenly become persona non grata to the entire female world.

"I just got up twenty minutes ago, hon," she confessed. "I'm glad you didn't call earlier. I must have slept ten hours. Managing that dinner wiped me out."

"How did it go?"

"Fine. None of the pols got too drunk or too loud."

"Did they bring wives or mistresses?"

"Are you kidding? It was strictly stag: eleven men and Lady C. Those are the odds she likes."

I laughed. "She just doesn't want competition, Connie. The queen surrounded by her courtiers. Did she ask anyone to stay?"

"One."

"Which one?"

"I'm not saying."

"I'll bet he was the youngest."

"You win your bet. Am I seeing you tonight, sweetie?"

"Of course. Where and when?"

"Oh, I don't know. I don't feel like doing the fancy bit, Archy. I've had enough dress-up and rich food to hold me for a while."

"How about this...? I'll pick up a tub of barbecued chicken and maybe some potato salad and coleslaw. And a cold six-pack naturally. Nothing fancy about that, is there? You pull on a T-shirt and jeans and unfrazzle—the way we planned."

"Just right," she approved. "By the way, how was the Westmores' cocktail party?"

"Dull, duller, dullest. I cut out early. I need a little excitement in my life."

"Come over around seven," she said, and giggled.

Understanding, sympathetic, *cooperative* Connie!

I skipped the family cocktail hour and went shopping for provisions. I bought the barbecued chicken at a West Palm deli and asked for half with lemon-pepper sauce and half Cajun. I didn't forget the potato salad and coleslaw, and added two kosher dills to serve as a green vegetable. And two squares of baklava, dripping with honey, for dessert.

It turned out to be a splendid evening—everything a growing boy could want. Connie was at her foxiest, a winning combination of sly humor and artless charm. The picnic-type food was just right, although the Cajun chicken could have used a little more cayenne. Afterward we drank beer and listened to the original cast recording of *My Fair Lady*. Great songs—but I don't want a woman to be more like a man. What if she turned out to be the spitting image of Binky Watrous?

There was, glory be, no danger of Connie flipping her gender. She proved that later in the evening and her eagerness was doubly welcome, for not only was I physically pleasured but my masculine ego regained the bloom it needed after being cruelly shriveled by Natalie's cold dismissal.

Even more important to me than Connie's flashy aptitudes is her normalcy. No gym bloomers and middy blouses for her. And no confusing alternations of mood between apathy and scary malevolence. Ms. Consuela Garcia is not a complex woman but her honest simplicity is admirable—and lovable. What you see is what you get—and I see a blessing.

And so a pleasant time was had by all and I drove home shortly after midnight feeling at peace with the world and singing "With a Little Bit of Luck." Knowing the sardonicism of fate, I should have been wary of my optimistic humor and crossed my fingers or taken some other action to ward off the evil eye. But I didn't and within three days destiny had kneed me in the groin and my chirpy tune had become a dismal lament.

Sunday was sodden and I didn't stir from the house, not even to accompany my parents to church. (I felt a wee pang of guilt about that—but not for long.) Instead, I read for a few hours, listened to some early recordings of Blind Lemon Jefferson and Big Bill Broonzy, tried (and failed) to balance my checkbook, and generally futzed the day away.

Dinner was Swiss steak, which no one, including restaurants, seems to prepare these days—a sadness because it's an excellent dish, especially with smothered onions. The meal was enhanced by father's decision to uncork one of his bottles of vintage pinot noir, kept in a locked, temperature-controlled cabinet in his study. I know where he hides the key but have never dared filch since he maintains a meticulous inventory.

I would like to alert you to one other happening on that lazy Sabbath. It was, I thought at the time, of minor import but it had momentous consequences as you shall shortly learn.

I was at my desk after dinner, enjoying the bite of a small marc, when my thoughts turned to possible scenarios for the visit to Windsor Antiques I planned for Monday morning. I tried several gambits but none of them pleased me. I wanted to believe Sydney Smythe was innocent but I hoped to discover how and why he had informed Fred Clemens about my imaginary 1907 Silver Ghost "surprise."

A direct, brusque question was never seriously considered. It would sound accusatory and might offend Mr. Smythe. In which case his further cooperation would be snuffed.

Besides, direct questions are not my style; I much prefer dissembling.

I finally devised a plan that made me smile because it was almost diabolical in its cunning. At the same time it offered a simple and elegant solution to my problems. It would help determine the closeness of the Smythe-Clemens relationship. And it could conceivably push the investment adviser to rash actions which might reveal his true colors.

I was so impressed by my wiliness I treated myself to a second brandy. I thought my scheme was designed for complete success. The oft misquoted proverb declares pride goeth before a fall. I never did quite understand it; shouldn't pride goeth *after* a fall? However you slice it, I took a fall, as you shall see, and my pride wenteth.

Monday made its appearance, and I was happy to greet a clear, sunshiny day, taking it as a good omen. I saw no reason to make an early appearance at work and so I dawdled at home, collecting my laundry and dry cleaning for the weekly pickup. I drove to the McNally Building around ten-thirty, parked in our underground garage, and walked over to Worth Avenue. I recall I was wearing a new fedora in a jazzy taupe shade. It was wide-brimmed and I fancied it made me look like Ronald Colman in *Lost Horizon*. Connie's vote was for Ray Milland in *The Lost Weekend*.

Once again I was startled at how grungy Windsor Antiques looked on that street of sparkling jewelry stores and trendy boutiques. I was amazed Sydney Smythe hadn't been evicted for maintaining a public eyesore—if such an act is proscribed by law. I doubt if it is or half the falafel joints in the country would be shuttered.

I entered, called "Hallo!" to the empty shop. The proprietor came mincing from the back room he uses as an office and, I suspect, to take an occasional nap, since it includes a black leather couch so ancient and crackled it could have been original equipment in Sigmund's study.

Mr. Smythe greeted me genially with two outstretched hands and we exchanged the usual salutations. He was wearing his habitual seedy apparel and I was sad he apparently could not afford a new silk ascot. Perhaps, I thought suddenly, I'll give him a handsome foulard for Christmas.

"Mr. Smythe," I said, "I'm looking for an unusual gift for a young lady of rather eccentric tastes. Can you suggest something different she might like?"

"A bracelet?" he offered. "Earrings? A necklace?"

"I think not," I said. "She's the denim jeans type and I've never seen her wear jewelry."

He thought a moment, eyes glittering behind his pince-nez. Then he snapped his fingers. "Ah-ha!" he cried. "I think I have a treasure that will delight you, dear boy. And your young lady as well. Be right back."

He darted into the back office and emerged a moment later bearing a small object swathed in tissue paper. He unwrapped it carefully to reveal a little porcelain box with a hinged lid. It was hand-painted and scarcely large enough to contain a dozen Tums. Atop the cover was a bouquet of flowers, none of which I could identify.

"Isn't it exquisite?" Smythe said. "Limoges, you know. A fine collectible."

"Just the thing," I agreed. "She worships flowers."

"Two hundred," he said. "And for you, dear boy, I'll put a penny inside for good luck."

"I'd prefer a twenty-dollar gold piece," I said. "I need more than a penny's worth of good luck."

We both laughed and he accepted the credit card I offered. "Unfortunately I cannot gift-wrap it," he said. "I lack the paper and ribbons."

"No matter," I said. "I'll do the honors. Just swaddle it in tissue again and pop it into a bag."

Our transaction was concluded and I prepared to launch my planned spiel but he forestalled me.

"Incidentally," he said, "about the 'surprise' in the Fabergé egg you mentioned, the 1907 Rolls-Royce Silver Ghost—I was unable to find any reference to it in the books and catalogues I consulted."

"Disappointing," I said.

"Not completely unexpected. As I told you

during our first discussion, there are several Imperial eggs that have never been discovered so to speak. I mean they are not in museums and have never been exhibited in public by private collectors. They include the final two eggs made for Czar Nicholas in 1917. While some or even all of the missing eggs may have been lost or destroyed, the chances are just as good that several are being held by persons who, for whatever reason, do not want it known they possess a Fabergé egg."

"So it's possible our deceased client's egg and its surprise are authentic?"

"Oh my yes," he said. "Other Fabergé surprises included a model coach, yacht, and a train, so it's likely a tiny motorcar was fashioned. If it's as remarkable as you described, it is quite valuable."

My time had come. "I'm glad to hear you say that," I told him. "The heirs and beneficiaries have agreed to send the egg and its surprise to Sotheby's in New York for auction."

The pince-nez fell from his nose to the floor. He stooped to retrieve it. When he slowly straightened up I saw no change of expression in his face. No change at all. I thought it significant.

"An auction at Sotheby's," he repeated. "In New York?"

"Correct," I said cheerily. "I expect you'll be seeing a lot of publicity in newspapers, magazines, and on TV. I'm sure Sotheby's will make a media event of its auction. Why, they might even persuade Rolls-Royce to feature a color photo of Fabergé's miniature model in their ads."

"Yes," he said. "Shouldn't wonder."

Obviously he didn't wish to comment further on the matter. Nor did I. So we wished each other a happy holiday and I departed carrying Natalie's Christmas gift in a brown paper bag.

CHAPTER 19

I LUNCHED AT Ta-boo (grilled salmon with sweet pepper salsa) but it was not until my second cup of oolong that I allowed myself to review the conversation with the decadent proprietor of Windsor Antiques.

I was satisfied with the way things had gone. My fabricated story would, I reckoned, have one of two possible results. If the relationship between Smythe and Clemens was merely a casual onetime thing, occurring by chance, the investment adviser would probably never learn of the Sotheby's auction fantasy.

But if the two men were closer than I imagined, Clemens would hear of the auction soon enough. And if he did, I could envision his fury and despair. He had described the "surprise" in the Fabergé egg Mrs. Westmore planned to buy, and now it was to be hawked in New York with a blizzard of publicity. Edythe would be sure to ask some very pointed questions. Panic time, folks.

Unless of course the silver-tongued financial counselor could convince his client
Fabergé had created identical surprises for *two*
Imperial eggs—but I thought it highly unlikely. No, Mr. Clemens would be confronted with
a crisis—and the fact it had been wholly
invented by your scribe did not affect the
peril he faced.

I returned to Royal Palm Way in a chipper
mood. I am never happier than when I have
launched a devilish scheme, especially when
it may result in the discomfiture of miscreants.
Why should villains have all the fun?

Back in the McNally Building I did something I should have done days ago: I visited
the office of Mrs. Lenore Crittenden, who heads
the department of McNally & Son dealing
with estate planning and investment advising.

Lennie is a frisky middle-aged lady, cheerfully
overweight, with a fondness for loose dresses
in flowered Pulitzer prints. She is one of the
two women I've known who use a monocle,
which she wields with great éclat. Her knowledge
of high finance is awesome and her judgment
so sensible that father is content to let her
handle the firm's capital. She manages it very
well indeed.

I found the money whiz at her desk lunching on a toasted BLT and what appeared to
be a chocolate milk shake.

"On a diet, Lennie?" I asked pleasantly.

"Go to hell, Archy," she said just as pleasantly. "And if you're looking for a stock tip,
here it is: Buy low and sell high."

I sighed. "I know a bartender who repeats the same mantra. Actually, I was hoping you could spare me some time."

"If you have a candlelit dinner for two in mind I'm afraid I can't make it tonight. My husband's in town."

"Doggone it," I said. "And I was chilling the bubbly. Well, maybe some other time. Lennie, I'm investigating a bloke who claims to be an investment adviser, financial planner, money manager—whatever. He says he's worked for a few brokerage houses and a banker. He also says he had no bad marks except for a few arbitration hearings settled in his favor. He apparently moved to West Palm from California about a year ago. Question: Are there government agencies and professional associations which might provide the inside poop on this guy and say whether he's soiled or as pure as the d.s.?"

"Of course. At least a dozen organizations you can check, from the Securities and Exchange Commission in Washington to the Division of Securities in Tallahassee."

"Glad to hear it. But not that *I* can check but *you* can check. Will you handle it for me, Lennie darling? Send them faxes or E-mail or however you do it."

She slurped her milk shake. "What's in it for me?" she demanded.

"A candlelit dinner for two when your husband's out of town."

"With bubbly?"

"Naturally."

She laughed. "You sly conniver! All right,

give me the man's name and address, and I'll see if he's got a rap sheet."

I dictated Clemens's full name, street address, and telephone number. Mrs. Crittenden scrawled the info on a pad of Post-it Notes bearing the legend "The Buck Stops Here."

"When do you need this stuff?" she asked. "Yesterday?"

"Nah," I said. "Tomorrow will do excellently."

"It figures. Don't forget to tell your papa how helpful I am."

"Is that why you're doing it—to score brownie points? And I thought it was my animal magnetism."

"You got the animal part right," she said. "Begone!"

I returned to my office happy I had put the pot on to boil, especially since it entailed no labor on my part. But there was something I could do personally, and I called Clemens Investments intending to set up a meeting with the pooh-bah himself for later in the week. I would offer some fraudulent reason for wanting to see him but actually I hoped to discover if Sydney Smythe had repeated to him my fictional opus about the Sotheby auction.

I phoned but was greeted by an answering machine and hung up. I detest talking to machines; they never reply to one's queries or engage in lighthearted banter. Does that make me a traditionalist? So be it.

I sat there momentarily paralyzed by a mild

state of confusion. Then the phone shrilled and I was told the caller was Natalie Westmore.

"How delightful to hear from you," I said—not a lie but a slight exaggeration.

She wasted no time. "I'd like to see you this afternoon," she said, and her tone was almost peremptory. "Can you come to my studio? I have something for you, Archy."

I instantly thought of a bitter response; to wit, "What are you peddling today—peonies?" But I didn't voice it of course. I merely wondered what this elusive woman was up to. She was as confusing as Schrödinger's cat.

"Now?" I bleated. "This afternoon? Your studio?" All of which added up to "Duh."

"Yes," she said crisply. "As soon as possible."

I surrendered, craven that I am. Ten minutes later I was in the Miata heading for Ocean Boulevard. I didn't forget to bring along Natalie's Christmas present in the brown bag. The lack of festive paper and a gay bow didn't bother me. She didn't gift-wrap my petunia, did she?

I parked at one end of the Westmore driveway. It would do little harm if Edythe spotted and identified my distinctive quadriga. She'd probably think her plan of my becoming her son-in-law was beginning to show promise.

Natalie was standing at the studio entrance as I approached; she had obviously been awaiting my arrival. After I was inside she closed and bolted the door. Hmm. She greeted me with a wide smile and then a kiss. Not a swift cheek buss but a lingering smackeroo on the lips. Enjoyable, but like a student of method acting I wondered, What's her motivation?

She was barefoot, wearing her cutoff minishorts with a man's blue denim work shirt, sleeves rolled up to her biceps, the top two buttons undone. What came as something of a shock was her makeup—the first time I had seen her with mascara, lipstick, and a faint rouging of the cheekbones. The cosmetics had been inexpertly applied; the effect was more clownish than seductive. I found myself regretting the makeover. I preferred the unadorned original.

"You've already given me my Christmas gift, Nettie," I said. "Now here is yours."

She literally tore open the paper bag and ripped off the tissue. The sight of the little porcelain box with the bouquet on the lid brought forth a squeal of delight and my reward was another smooch. I hoped her lip gloss was kiss-proof.

"Oh it's divine!" she cried. "The nicest, sweetest, cunningest present in the whole world!"

I wasn't certain there is such a word as "cunningest" but there was no mistaking her enthusiasm, which, quite honestly, I found suspect. I mean my gift might have been Limoges but it wasn't Cartier. I couldn't believe such effusiveness from a woman I originally thought apathetic.

"Now you sit there," she said, motioning toward the new cot, "while I put this lovely, lovely present in a safe place."

I sat gingerly on the cot but it seemed stable enough. Nettie had turned away to place the porcelain box atop the cupboard. When she faced me again I saw the top *three* buttons of her shirt were now open. Listen, I'm an experienced investigator and trained to notice such details.

"Here's what I wanted to show you," she said, picked up a single sheet of stiff paper from the drawing table, and handed it to me.

It was a color photo of a Fabergé Imperial egg. A ruler placed at the bottom of the reproduction provided a handy guide to the dimensions. I estimated the egg to be almost four inches high, the top quarter being a hinged lid, closed in the photo. The outer coating appeared to be a gleaming yellow enamel in a repeated starburst design. The entire exterior was bound within a trellis of gold bands of leaves. At each intersection of the lattice was a tiny black enameled royal eagle set with what was apparently a diamond.

All in all, it was breathtaking objet d'art, rich and lustrous. The proportions were perfect, the craftsmanship precise and elegant. It may have been designed to be a czarina's toy but it was much more than a bibelot. I thought it beautiful and could understand wanting to own it, to see it every day and feel the lift of spirit a flawless creation can produce.

"It's magnificent!" I burst out, and discovered immediately I had said the wrong thing.

"Magnificent?" Natalie repeated in a tone

of great disgust. "How can you say such a thing? It's just a trinket, a novelty for the wealthy to show off and boast about. But can't you see it has no real value? It's garish and vulgar."

I didn't want to argue with her. *Chacun à son goût.* I said only, "I presume this is the Fabergé egg your mother wants to buy?"

She nodded. "Half a million dollars," she said acidly. "And she refuses to give my brother one red cent to help him get back to Africa. She says his work is a waste of money and time. Walter is furious, I know, even though he tries to hide it. Archy, it's just not fair! You don't think it's fair, do you?"

"I can comprehend how Walter feels," I said carefully. "Nettie, where did you get this photo?"

"I took it from mother's desk drawer."

I looked at her, remembering what Connie had told me of her kleptomania at the aerobic sessions. "I suggest you put it back as soon as possible," I said.

"What difference does it make?" she said offhandedly.

Suddenly she sat down close to me on the cot and slid a warm arm about my neck.

"Archy, you're sympathetic with what Walter wants to do, aren't you?"

"Of course."

"It means so much to him. It's his whole life, his happiness, which certainly should be more important to mother than buying a silly ornament."

"Your concern is understandable," I said, trying hard to be noncommittal.

"I knew I could depend on you, sweet-heart!" she said joyously, embraced me with both arms, pressed me back onto the cot.

If I had an ounce of pride—or even a gram—I would have risen from my recumbent position, uttered a cutting remark (e.g.: "What do you take me for—passion's plaything?"), and stalked out in a state of high dudgeon—or even low dudgeon. That is what I *should* have done.

But in situations such as this my backbone becomes wet twine. I am bereft of any sense whatsoever. So it happened and in a trice we were thrashing about on the sturdy cot like finalists in a world championship match of Greco-Roman wrestlers.

I shall not describe our encounter in more explicit detail since this chronicle may be read by devout celibates and I don't wish to excite them unnecessarily.

Much later, after we had relaxed, rested, and were reclaiming and donning the garments so frantically flung aside, Natalie vowed I had introduced her to a whole new world of sensory pleasure for which she would be eternally grateful. And in the future, she hinted, her favors would be mine for the asking. She was, she implied, looking forward to a long, intimate relationship during which I was to lead the way to nirvana.

Was I delighted my gamble had paid off? I was not. On the trip homeward I attempted to suss out the reason for Natalie's unexpected largesse. I regretfully admitted she was not swept away by my charm, or even the aroma of my aftershave. Nettie's motives were more byzantine. I did not resent what she was attempting to do but I was somewhat peeved she apparently believed I could be so primitively manipulated.

I verified my theory that evening at the family cocktail hour. I asked my father, "Did you inform Natalie and Walter Westmore I will be present at their conference with you tomorrow?"

"I did," he said. "I phoned them this morning."

"Uh-huh," I said. "And did they object?"

"Initially. Until I explained they really had no choice. Then they accepted your presence as a witness and perhaps as a participant in the consultation."

"Thank you, sir," I said, thinking, Ah-ha!

CHAPTER 20

I DRESSED IN sober threads on Tuesday morning, knowing my father would be outraged if I appeared in his office attired like Ronald McDonald. The only spark I allowed myself was a four-in-hand of silk jacquard with a pattern of brightly colored carousels. Incidentally, I tied it in a Windsor knot, which brought to mind Windsor Antiques and my Machiavellian ploy involving Sydney

Smythe and Frederick Clemens. And so I went to work with a smile on my lips and a song in my heart.

I lollygagged in my office for almost an hour, smoked an English Oval, doodled on a scratch pad, and wondered why I hadn't heard from Binky Watrous. Possibly, I thought, because Bridget Houlihan, his inamorata, had returned from Ireland. If so, the turtledoves would probably be busy with their musical recitals, during which Binky does birdcalls accompanied by Bridget on the tambourine. They perform gratis at local nursing homes for the entertainment of aged residents many of whom, I am reliably informed, refer to them as The Crackpots.

My summons arrived a few minutes after eleven o'clock via a phone call from Mrs. Trelawney.

"Boss wants you," she reported laconically.

"Be there forthwith," I replied. "If not sooner."

I climbed the back stairs one flight to m'lord's sanctum on the uppermost floor. Although the McNally Building is a modern cube of stainless steel and tinted glass daddy-o had insisted his private office be wood-paneled, equipped with leather-upholstered furniture, and designed to accommodate his enormous antique rolltop desk. Steel engravings of judicial luminaries decorated the walls. Roger B. Taney would feel right at home in that chamber. The only thing it lacked was a brass gaboon on a rubber mat.

The Westmores were sunk into club chairs when I entered but Walter struggled to his feet to shake my hand: a gentlemanly act. He was clad in a three-piece suit of rusty tweed with a white dress shirt the collar of which was obviously too tight. Natalie, lost in a nondescript shirtwaist dress of beigy cotton, gave me a smile I thought strained.

I sat down in one corner of the bottle-green chesterfield and looked at my father. He was planted in his tall swivel chair, swung around so he faced us, his back to the rolltop desk.

"Now then," he said almost genially, addressing the Westmores, "we are all assembled. How may McNally and Son be of service?"

Apparently it had been decided Walter was to make the pitch. He began to speak in unemotional tones: complete sentences in an orderly sequence as if he had composed the speech on paper, then memorized and possibly rehearsed it. Fluent, you understand, but neither rambling nor glib.

Hizzoner and I listened in polite silence, both trying to evince interest and not reveal we were already privy to everything he was telling us.

Their mother, Walter said, had surrendered the management of her financial affairs to a man named Frederick Clemens who claimed to be an investment counselor but about whose expertise and antecedents little was known. On the advice of Clemens, Edythe Westmore had made several investments her daughter and son considered imprudent, to say the least.

And now she planned to spend a half-million dollars to buy a Fabergé Imperial egg she had never seen from a man in France she had never met. She was being urged to make this purchase by Clemens, who vouched for the authenticity of the curio and had assured Edythe she could easily resell the egg or have it auctioned for triple the cost.

He paused briefly and Natalie could keep quiet no longer. "It's just a trinket!" she cried.

Walter ignored his sister's interruption. Was there any way, he asked, addressing my father, any legal way the Westmore siblings could prevent their mother from putting a half-million into a speculative investment they were certain would end in disaster, a total loss? They stared at my father expectantly, awaiting his response.

In the silence that followed, during which, I knew, McNally Sr. was mulling over a proper reply, I had time to reflect that Walter had not mentioned his own desperate need of funds to continue his African research. He had not alluded to it, I guessed, because he didn't want father to know of his selfish interest in how Edythe spent her money. He wished to imply their motive was pure; they sought only to protect their mother from the larcenous machinations of an unscrupulous con man.

Finally my father spoke.

"I am aware," he said in measured tones, "as I am certain you are, that your mother is sole trustee of the two funds your father established prior to his passing. Those funds are to be of benefit to each of you in the form of periodic disbursements while your mother is alive and capable of serving as trustee. You will inherit the funds *in toto* and assume full control of the funds' assets upon the demise of your mother. But while she is animate, the powers conferred upon a trustee are hers, and they are quite extensive I assure you. There is very little a trustee cannot do—excepting illegal behavior of course—if in his or her judgment the action is warranted and will benefit the trust funds. Should the judgment of the trustee prove faulty and a loss is incurred, the beneficiaries have little recourse in law unless they can claim criminal intent on the part of the trustee—something extremely difficult to prove in court."

"Wait a minute, sir," Walter said hastily. "Mother isn't using dollars from our trust funds to buy the Fabergé egg. It is her own capital she intends to invest."

I was positive father already knew this or had assumed it, but he hoisted one brambly eyebrow aloft as if surprised by the news.

"Her own money?" he repeated. "Then there is nothing, nil, you can do to prevent it. Unless you wish to assert she is of unsound mind and incapable of managing her own affairs. I must warn you, however, that I, as her attorney, would dispute such a claim with all the resources at my command."

It was such a ringing declaration I do believe it shocked and perhaps even frightened the

Westmores. In any event it left Walter abashed.

"Oh no, no, no," he said brokenly. "I didn't mean to say— We wouldn't— Of course not. No, no!"

Natalie remained quiet, head bowed.

Walter drew a deep breath. "In other words, sir," he said, "you're telling us it's impossible to keep mother from throwing her money away on what we consider a swindle?"

The sire looked at me directly. "Archy," he said, "what is your reaction to all this?"

Then Natalie raised her head to stare at me hopefully. I knew what my father wanted me to say and I said it.

"From what I have heard," I began, "it is evident Mrs. Westmore has been persuaded to purchase the Fabergé egg by Frederick Clemens, her financial adviser, who promises her an enormous return on the investment. It seems to me that even before considering the authenticity and intrinsic value of the egg itself it would be wise to make a Discreet Inquiry into what Walter termed the antecedents and expertise of Clemens to firmly establish he is the person he purports to be—an experienced investment counselor whose word can be trusted. If the inquiry reveals he is who he claims, with a clean record of successful financial planning, then I doubt if Mrs. Westmore can be dissuaded from the purchase. But if, on the other hand, the inquiry uncovers a shadowy past including several instances of proven chicanery, then I think Mrs. Westmore can be convinced the Fabergé egg investment is much too risky to be attempted."

I paused, waiting for my father to ask the logical question, to cue my reply as I was certain he would—Abbott and Costello McNally—but Walter did the prompting.

"Who do you suggest might make an investigation?" he asked. "I can't. I wouldn't know where to begin."

"I would be happy to conduct such an inquiry," I volunteered. "With the proviso my participation be known only to you and Natalie. I have handled similar tasks in the past and have learned the value and advantage of the utmost discretion. If my probing into the history and character of Frederick Clemens is bruited about and becomes generally known, a successful inquiry will become more difficult if not impossible. I cannot stress the importance of discretion too strongly. It means, Walter, your mother and your wife are not to be informed of my activities. I must insist on it."

He made no objection but said, "How do you propose going about investigating Clemens?"

"There are many things to be done," I answered. "For instance, at least a dozen government agencies and professional associations exist which are capable of supplying information on individuals claiming to be financial advisers, investment counselors, or estate planners. There are computerized records of the legitimate and of those suspected, accused, or convicted of unethical, immoral, or illegal behavior. These sources range from the Securities and Exchange Commission in Washington to the Division of Securities in Tallahassee."

I thought the old man looked at me with some amazement, surprised no doubt by my apparent proficiency. But then he must have realized I was cribbing from someone (we know from whom, don't we?), for he gave me a wintry smile and began to smooth his mustache with a knuckle.

"I think it's a wonderful idea!" Nettie said excitedly. "How clever of you to think of an investigation, Archy. It's exactly what should be done. How long do you think it will take?"

"I'll start at once," I promised. "I certainly hope to have an answer one way or another before your mother hands over the half-million."

"I should hope so," she said. "I'm sure you're going to find out Clemens is just an oily crook."

"Please," I said, "let me urge you again to mention nothing of my inquiry to anyone else. If Clemens is, as you suspect, not to be trusted and he learns of my investigation, he will surely attempt to make my job more arduous."

Both the Westmores vowed they would be most circumspect, farewells were exchanged, and they filed out. Father and I looked at each other.

"I believe it went as well as might be expected," he commented. "Now, if Mrs. Edythe

Westmore learns of your actions and is affront-
ed thereby, we can honestly assert the inquiry
was conducted with her children's knowledge and approval."

"Yes, sir," I said. "But there is another
factor involved here of which you should be
cognizant."

I told him of Walter's eagerness to return
to Africa to continue his research on the ori-
gins of bipedalism and his inability to obtain
university or foundation grants.

"Father, both he and his sister were hoping
their mother would finance his work but
apparently she refuses. They are rankled by
her attitude and so their determination to
forestall the Fabergé egg investment is based
not solely on filial devotion, a desire to protect their mother from a possibly rapacious
swindler. I believe they also harbor a hope that
if they prevent a foolish and disastrous loss of
half a million dollars she may be grateful
enough to contribute to her son's continued
African explorations. It is, I admit, conjecture
on my part."

He sighed. "Archy, these intrafamily conflicts are one of the most disturbing and difficult problems the legal profession is sometimes
called upon to solve. Rarely is there a resolution
which satisfies everyone. It is, in effect, a
zero-sum game."

"Yes, sir," I said. "Except in the McNally
family."

His smile was wry-crisp. "Precisely," he said.

I returned to my office reflecting we now had

a semiofficial go-ahead for a Discreet Inquiry from at least part of the Westmore clan. My main concern, after reviewing the conversation in father's office, was whether Walter would keep his promise not to tell his wife of the investigation. If Helen learned I was prying into the rectitude of Frederick Clemens I reckoned the subject himself would hear of it within minutes.

The palaver with the Westmore siblings had given me a thirst and an appetite I judged could only be slaked by a lunch at the Pelican Club chock-full of calories both liquid and solid. I was about to set out when the phone's ring stopped me and I wondered if it might be Natalie offering a physical bonanza in gratitude for my efforts on her behalf. But the caller was Sydney Smythe.

"I'm glad I caught you in, dear boy," he said.

"Is something amiss, Mr. Smythe?" I said. "You sound subdued."

"I do have a slight problem," he admitted. "But I'm sure a clever lad like you will be able to suggest an answer. Might I see you as soon as possible?"

"Surely," I said. "Suppose I drop in this afternoon around three o'clock."

Short pause. "Ah," he said faintly. "No chance of your popping over now?"

"It's important?" I asked.

"Oh yes," he said. "Quite, dear boy. I think you and I—"

Suddenly he stopped speaking and there was silence.

"Mr. Smythe?" I said. "Are you on the line?"

No response. Then I heard a series of bumps. It sounded to me as if his phone had fallen to the floor.

"Mr. Smythe!" I shouted. "Are you all right?"

Again no reply. But I heard a heavier thump, not a crash but the thud of a body falling and a brief scrabbling noise.

"Hello? Hello?!" I yelled. "What is it? What's going on?"

No one spoke. But there were muffled sounds I could not identify. Then nothing more.

I replaced my own phone, thought a moment of calling 911, and realized I could not accurately describe the emergency although I feared the old codger had suffered cardiac arrest. I hurried out thinking I'd make better time walking quickly rather than driving and bucking midday traffic.

CHAPTER 21

THE FRONT DOOR of Windsor Antiques was slightly ajar, and I paused a moment, not really wanting to enter. I glanced up and down the avenue for no particular reason. I saw cars, pedestrians, the usual bustling activities of noontime. Nothing strange. Nothing suspicious.

I took a deep breath, pushed the door open, stepped inside. No one in the front room. No sounds.

"Hello!" I called. "Anyone home?" I added stupidly.

I threaded my way slowly through the jumble of dusty antiques and rusted curios. I halted at the doorway to the back room, peered in cautiously. The phone was on the floor all right. So was Sydney Smythe.

I stepped around him carefully to open another door leading to a small loo. No one lurking in there. I returned to the body crumpled on a piece of threadbare carpeting and did a deep knee bend for a closer look.

I didn't know how to locate the carotid artery and I had no mirror to hold up to his lips, but I had no doubt the poor man was dead, dead, dead. The pince-nez had fallen off and had been stepped on; the glass was slivered. Blank, unseeing eyes stared at the stained ceiling. I saw no signs of respiration. I did see a steel blade driven into his chest just below the breastbone. The wooden grip of the weapon had a steel pommel and a guard fitted with a ring. I knew what it was.

There was very little blood: a small puddle and a thin trickle from one corner of his mouth. I stood shakily, glad I had not yet eaten lunch or I might have lost it. He looked so shrunken, you see, so old and sad in his foppish shroud.

"Good-bye, sir," I said aloud. I don't know why.

I didn't touch a thing. I left Windsor Antiques, closed the door, walked down the avenue to a bookstore I sometimes patronize.

"Hi, Mr. McNally," the clerk said cheerfully. "Haven't seen you in a while. Happy Holiday!"

"Same to you, John," I said. "Have a good one. May I use your phone for a short local call?"

"Sure thing," he said. "Help yourself."

He wandered away from the counter to give me privacy. I phoned the PBPD, praying Sgt. Al Rogoff would be in. He was.

"Archy McNally," I said.

"Goodness gracious," he said. "I haven't heard from you in ages. Why, I was afraid you were mad at me. Listen, sonny boy, call me back in an hour or so. My lunch was just brought in."

"An hour?" I said. "Sure. The homicide victim isn't going anywhere."

"What the hell are you talking about?"

"Sydney Smythe, proprietor of Windsor Antiques on Worth Avenue. He's lying kaput in his back room. Someone shoved a blade in his gizzard."

Rogoff groaned. "For real?"

"For real," I assured him. "He's gone to the great antique shop in the sky."

"What's *with* you?" Al demanded indignantly. "This has got to be the third or fourth body you've found."

"Only the second," I said. "I think."

"Well, don't touch anything. Wait for me outside on the sidewalk. I'm on my way."

I thanked the bookshop clerk, returned to Windsor Antiques, and took up my station outside. It was a super day: warm sun, azure sky

180

with a few shreds of clouds. The cool breeze had a nice salty tang. I felt sick.

The police car pulled up about ten minutes later, driven by a young officer I didn't recognize. No siren. They didn't want to offend the natives or scare the tourists. Both cops got out to join me on the sidewalk. Sgt. Rogoff was finishing the remnants of a folded slice of pizza.

"My lunch," he said to me. "Thanks a lot. Where is he?"

I led the way to the back room. We stood looking down at the remains.

"Mr. Sydney Smythe," I said, introducing the corpse.

"Is he dead?" the young officer asked.

"Nah," Al said. "Just taking a nap with six inches of steel in his brisket. Now you go back to the car and call in an apparent homicide. Alert the crime scene crew, the ME's office, traffic control, the brass, and so forth. Think you can handle all that?"

"Sure, sarge. Just like we were taught in training school."

"Just like it," Rogoff agreed. "Except in this school the guy doesn't get up and go out for a beer."

The officer left to alert headquarters.

"They say you're getting old when cops start looking young," I commented.

"How do you think I feel?" Al said. "The kid could be my son." He squatted alongside the body.

The sergeant is limber enough. And fast? You

181

wouldn't believe. But he's a heavy hulk with a squarish body and a big head. He has a truculent walk and some of his gestures look as if he's pounding a tough steak. Despite the good ol' boy persona he projects, he's a closet balletomane—a secret shared by only a few friends but none of his colleagues.

"Crazy-looking shiv," he said. "You got any idea what it is?"

"I know exactly what it is," I told him. "It was part of Smythe's stock-in-trade. He picked it up somewhere a few years ago and showed it to me then. I guess he was never able to sell it. It's a Turkish Mauser bayonet, circa 1915. Ten-inch blade. The ring on the top of the guard encircled the muzzle of the rifle. That bayonet may have been used at Gallipoli."

"Thank you, professor. It was kept with the other garbage in the front room?"

"Correct. When Smythe first showed it to me it was in a steel scabbard."

"You buy a lot of stuff here?"

"No. One or two purchases a year. Occasionally I dropped by just to chat awhile. He was interesting. Knew a great deal about antiques."

"Is that why you were here today—just stepped in to gab?"

I hesitated a beat. Then: "No, he phoned me around noon at the office. He said he wanted to see me as soon as possible."

"Did he say why?"

"No. He started to explain but suddenly

stopped speaking. I heard what sounded like his phone dropping to the floor. Then there was a louder thud. I presumed it was him falling. I hurried over fearing he might have had a heart attack."

"How did he sound to you on the phone?"

This time I didn't hesitate. "He sounded all right. Normal. I thought he might have acquired a rare bibelot he wanted me to see."

"Bibelot," Rogoff repeated. "Love the way you talk." He stood up and dusted his palms although he hadn't touched anything. "You think it's possible someone was in the store while he was talking to you on the phone?"

"Yes, it's possible."

"How about this scenario: Someone was in the front room who spooked him. He was afraid of being robbed so he came back here and called you for help?"

"Why wouldn't he call you or nine-one-one?"

"Maybe he wasn't certain he was in danger and didn't want to phone in a false alarm."

"Yes, Al, that too is possible."

The sergeant stared at me. "You wouldn't be scamming a guardian of law and order, would you, kiddo?"

"Not me. I've told you what happened."

"Uh-huh. Do you know where he kept his cash?"

"I remember once he made change from a tin box in the upper left drawer of the desk."

Rogoff used one fingertip to pull the drawer open. The black tin box was in there. He lifted the lid with the point of a pencil. The box was empty.

"How much cash did he keep in there—do you know?"

"No."

"Doesn't make much difference," he said. "These days you can be snuffed for fifty-nine cents."

"You think that's what it was, Al—a robbery?"

"Could be. A crime of opportunity. A wrongo wanders in. Nothing on his mind. No weapon. No plan. He hasn't even cased the joint. Then he sees the bayonet, picks it up, slides the blade out of the scabbard. Nice. He realizes he's alone in the place with the owner. Maybe he figures he'll just threaten the old man. But then he hears Smythe phoning and he panics, figuring he's calling the cops. So he sticks him with the bayonet, makes a quick search, finds cash in the tin box, grabs it and runs."

"Is that what you think happened?" I asked him.

"No," he said. "A panicky killer and crook wouldn't waste time closing the lid of the tin box and sliding the drawer shut."

We heard the sounds of several sirens and the blasting of horns and whistles.

"The troops are arriving," Sgt. Rogoff said. "You'll be in the way. Take off and I'll contact you later. I'll need a signed statement from you."

"Sorry I spoiled your lunch, Al."

"Anchovy pizza," he reported. "I got to

184

eat half of it. By the way, do you know Smythe's next of kin?"

"No."

"Do you know where he lived?"

"No."

"There's a lot you don't know, isn't there, buster?"

"Too much," I admitted.

I walked back to the McNally Building, reclaimed the Miata, and drove to the Pelican Club. I found it packed with the luncheon crowd but I finally found space at the bar and asked Simon Pettibone for a Rémy Martin.

"Before lunch?" he said. "Since when has cognac been an aperitif?"

"Since right now," I said. "Due to serious trauma of the nervous system."

"Have one of Leroy's double cheeseburgers with bacon," he advised. "It deadens all pain."

"Splendid idea," I said.

But the burger didn't work; the pain persisted. Not pain exactly but sorrow. I could not stop brooding on the death of Sydney Smythe, trying to find meaning in what Al Rogoff had called a crime of opportunity, the result of chance and accident.

It had to be a stranger, maybe a druggie, who had wandered into Windsor Antiques, found himself alone with the aged proprietor, and decided to rip him off. Murder had followed when he thought he heard Smythe phone for assistance. I discounted what Rogoff had said about a panicky assailant not pausing to close the tin box or shut the desk drawer. How long would it take—a second or two? And the man might not have been panicky at all, but a cool villain moving steadily and deliberately.

I am a great believer in Occam's razor, a principle which, roughly stated, holds that when more than one solution to a problem exists, the simplest and most obvious answer is likely to be the most valid. Ergo, Sydney Smythe was slain by a stranger, an intruder who acted from conscienceless greed.

I held to that belief throughout lunch and the remainder of the day. It was after dinner when I had retired to my aerie in the McNally manse that I attempted to phone Sgt. Rogoff, hoping the confused initial stages of the investigation had been concluded. I found him still at headquarters and inquired if any progress had been made.

"Some," he said cautiously. Al doesn't like to tell me all he knows and, as you are undoubtedly aware, I treat him in a similar fashion. "We found where he lived: a fleabag motel out in the West Palm boonies. The owner says Smythe had been a tenant for almost five years. The place looked to me like the last stop before skid row. We sealed his rooms until we can toss them."

"Have you located his next of kin?"

"So far it looks like a cousin in England. Get this: the coz lives in a village called Thornton-le-Beans. How do you like that?"

"Intriguing," I said.

"Yeah. Your favorite word."

"Discover anything about his private life?"

"We discovered he didn't have any—if you can believe the motel owner, which I don't. Anyway he claims Smythe never went out at night, never had visitors, had no friends, made no phone calls, and never talked about his past. Nada, zip, zilch, and zero."

"Al, I still think he was killed by a stranger, maybe an addict, who just happened to wander in, found himself alone with a fragile old man, and decided to score—even a few bucks."

"You believe that, do you?"

"It certainly looks like a spur-of-the-moment thing."

"Not to me it doesn't," the sergeant said. "We found the steel scabbard you mentioned. It was on the floor in the front room. Looked like it had just been dropped amongst all the other junk. We dusted the scabbard and the wooden grip of the bayonet for prints."

"Find anything?"

"Sure did. But not fingerprints. Gloves. Our wonk thinks the last person to handle the scabbard and bayonet was wearing pigskin gloves. Who in South Florida wears gloves unless he wants to cover his hands during the commission of a crime? Am I right? And if our desperado was wearing gloves it's a clear indication of premeditation and planning. Isn't that intriguing?"

"I guess so..." I said faintly.

He laughed. "There goes your random killing theory. Listen, I've got to cut this short and get back to work. Talk to you tomorrow or whenever." He hung up.

Was I shocked by Rogoff's suggestion of a premeditated and planned murder? I was not. Ever since I had discovered the crumpled body a tiny pilot light of suspicion had been burning. But I had willfully ignored it, deluding myself with the fantasy of a drugged stranger stabbing Sydney Smythe during a stupid theft.

But in view of what Rogoff had just told me, my re-creation of what had happened became a base exercise in self-deception. My scenario and my dependence on Occam's razor had all been part of an almost irrational attempt to disavow the tiny pilot light. But now it was a large, consuming flame and I could no longer deny it.

Why had I striven so mightily to evade the truth? Because if Sydney Smythe had not been murdered by a thieving interloper, then it was possible, perhaps even probable he was killed by someone he knew—a category conceivably including Frederick Clemens and his inscrutable secretary, Felix.

If either or both of those men were involved in Smythe's quietus the fault was partly mine. If not the fault, then certainly the guilt. For I had launched a ploy which, with an excess of hubris, I thought fiendishly clever enough to precipitate a crisis between Smythe and Clemens if the two were partners in a plan to swindle Mrs. Edythe Westmore.

My scheme had precipitated a crisis all

right—resulting in one of the conspirators lying defunct on a scrap of carpeting with a Turkish bayonet thrust into him.

What evidence did I have of a conspiracy? Very little. I had Clemens's description of the "surprise" in the Fabergé Imperial egg he was selling which mimicked the imaginary surprise I had portrayed to Smythe. And I had the latter's final phone call to me during which he spoke of a vexing problem and a need to see me as soon as possible. Could not his call concern the fairy tale I had spun about my invented egg being auctioned in New York?

Not a great deal to go on I agree. But I surrendered to a conviction Clemens and Smythe had been acting in concert and my sly ruse had had a totally unexpected and tragic denouement. I could not escape my guilt in the death of Sydney Smythe. If he had served as a henchman of an immoral knave he had acted reprehensibly, true. But had he been so culpable as to deserve the ignoble end he earned? I didn't think so.

I feared I might live the remainder of my life with the acknowledgment of my guilt in the slaying of an aged fop. But there was one way to make partial amends: conclusively identify the killer and bring him to justice.

If I could do that perhaps my self-reproach would fade with time and my egotism would regain its healthy vigor and thrive.

CHAPTER 22

THE MURDER OF Sydney Smythe did not make blaring headlines in our local newspaper the following morning but it did earn a one-column story titled "Antique Dealer Slain"—leaving it to the reader to decide if the victim dealt in antiques or was an ancient merchant. In this case, both.

I read the article carefully. It stated: "Law enforcement authorities are investigating several leads"—journalese for, "The police are stumped and don't know which way to turn." But the account did give the name and address of Smythe's motel. It also mentioned, "Windsor Antiques has been a fixture on Worth Avenue for almost twenty years." I scissored the story from the newspaper, folded it carefully, and placed it in my wallet. Then I went to work.

The Real Estate Department of McNally & Son advises clients on the purchase or lease of residences, commercial properties, and raw land. For many years this section has been under the direction of Mrs. Evelyn Sharif, a jovial lady married to a Lebanese who sells Oriental rugs to the nouveau riche with nary a qualm about the prices he charges. But Evelyn was currently on maternity leave, having dropped twins, and real estate matters were temporarily being handled by her assistant, Timothy Hogan.

Hogan's office was my first stop on Wednesday. I found him working on a large black coffee and two of the loathsome bran muffins available in our company cafeteria.

"Tim," I said, "did you hear about the murder yesterday on Worth Avenue?"

"Yeah, I saw it on TV last night. A helluva thing. My guess is a dopehead did it."

"Probably. You know, I've been in that antique store a few times. It looked like a rat's nest, worse than a thrift shop. Never saw any customers in there. Never found anything expensive worth buying. Yet the newspaper report says the store's been there for almost twenty years. How on earth did the owner manage to stay in business while paying Worth Avenue rents?"

Hogan took a gulp of coffee and then a bite of a bran muffin. "It's an interesting story. The dealer had a twenty-year lease on the space with no option to renew. The lease is up at midnight on New Year's Eve this year. I'm betting the rent will triple or quadruple or—what's larger than quadruple?"

"Fivefold?" I suggested. "Sextuple? Sevenfold?"

"Whatever, the rent is going up one hell of a lot on January first. An antique shop will never be able to make it. The space will be taken over by a trendy boutique or an upscale jewelry store. They can carry the overhead."

"You're probably right, Tim. Enjoy your fiber."

I returned to my office satisfied but saddened by what I had learned. I reckoned Smythe had really been on his uppers. He had been eking out a barren existence from his antique shop but he was to lose it on the last day of the year; he'd never be able to afford tripled or quadrupled rent.

I could understand his desperation. Retaining the shop had become secondary to bare living: food, shelter, perhaps necessary medicines. His fears must have been horrendous; it was hard to blame him for grasping at any source of income no matter how sordid. The impoverished can afford nothing—not even morality.

His motives and actions might have been justified—can you condemn a starving man for stealing a loaf of bread?—but those of Frederick Clemens were more problematic. I was forced to admit that so far the financial adviser had committed no provable crime or even a minor misdeed. He was simply acting as a broker in the purchase of a valuable object and I had no evidence he would profit unconscionably from the transaction.

But still, as I told my father at the start of this Discreet Inquiry, the whole affair had a distinct aroma of flimflam. The murder of Sydney Smythe only intensified my desire to expose the sins of a man I thought morally corrupt. I had only the vaguest idea how that might be accomplished, but decided I would be guided by Danton: "Audacity, more audacity, always audacity!" And so I phoned Clemens Investments.

Somewhat to my surprise my call was answered by the man himself with no preliminary queries from Felix. We exchanged holiday greetings, and I asked if it might be possible to meet at two o'clock in the afternoon.

He seemed in an expansive mood. "Of course!" he said. "I'll be delighted to see you. I think you and I will discover we have a great deal in common."

What a salesman! He made me feel I was important to him. And perhaps I was—if Sydney Smythe had named me as the source of the Fabergé "surprise."

I had no sooner hung up than my phone rang and I plucked it up again thinking Clemens might be calling back. But it was a woman's voice, dulcet and wooing.

"Archy McNally?" she inquired.

"Speaking. And with whom do I have the pleasure... ?"

"Helen Westmore," she said with a throaty laugh. "And I'm insulted you didn't recognize my voice."

"It will never happen again," I promised. "How are you, Helen?"

"In the pink," she said, her giggle calling to mind dented pillows and mussed sheets. "But I do have a personal problem I'd like to discuss with you, Archy. In private."

"Of course. Would you like me to come to your home or would you prefer my office?"

"Neither," she said definitely. And she named a restaurant on South Ocean Boulevard.

I shall not repeat it here since it is a dreadful place where drinks are served with little paper parasols and the boiled shrimp are consistently limp.

"I have a luncheon date there at noon," she continued, "but I can arrive half an hour early. I thought we might sit in my car at one end of the parking lot and have our talk. It won't take more than twenty or thirty minutes and we'll certainly have privacy. Just don't park too close; everyone recognizes your little fire engine."

I thought it an odd arrangement but assured her I would be happy to follow her instructions.

"I knew I could depend on you, Archy," she said, now using an intimate purr. "You're *such* a darling."

She disconnected, leaving me much bemused by my two recent conversations. First the salesman, then the actress. But it was the latter I found more curious. Her plan to ensure privacy seemed strange enough but just as queerish was her selection of that touristy restaurant for luncheon. Had her taste buds become atrophied—or was the joint her date's choice?

I departed at once, happy I was nattily dressed in a navy blazer and gray flannel slacks. Conventional you say? Of course. But the cerise polo shirt gave my garb the distinctive McNally imprimatur—and the puce beret was an added attraction.

I arrived at the designated rendezvous a few minutes early but the enormous parking lot was already filling and camera-laden tourists were hastening toward the restaurant, eager for their mai tais and the specialty of the house: grilled mahimahi on a cinnamon bagel.

The lavender Riviera was at one end and, following orders, I parked some distance away and walked over. Mrs. Helen Westmore was seated behind the wheel wearing something too tight, too short, and too sheer. She saw me approaching and leaned to open the passenger door. I slid in, closed the door, and was immediately greeted with a fervent embrace and kiss that knocked my beret awry. I took it off, becoming aware the interior of the car was fuggy with Helen's scent, a ripe perfume suitable for a Persian odalisque.

"You sweetheart!" she yelped. "A friend in need is a friend indeed."

"And your wish is my command," I said with a goofy grin.

Suddenly she sobered, became solemn and intent. "Archy, I've decided to divorce Walter."

She paused and stared, waiting expectantly for my reaction. All I could manage was a weak, "Ah."

And just as abruptly she became desperate. Her moods seemed to flip with every speech. She needed a new scriptwriter or a clever director.

"It's hopeless!" she cried. "I've tried. God knows I've tried."

"Surely—" I started.

"We're just two different people," she said

as if uttering a profound truth. "Two completely different people."

"Can't you—"

"It was wrong from the beginning," she mourned, and I guessed she wished for a little square of cambric to dab nonexistent tears. "Oh Archy, I should have known. But I had stars in my eyes."

And diamonds on your fingers, I thought, glancing at the rocks she was sporting.

"But I can no longer live a lie," she declaimed dramatically, and I was tempted to applaud and shout, "Brava!" "Archy, please help me."

"What can—"

"I need a lawyer," she rattled on. "Someone sympathetic and smart."

"But I'm not—"

"Someone who will understand me. Someone I feel *here*"—she pressed a palm to her imposing bosom—"is on my side. Someone nice and not too expensive."

It was all so stagy I couldn't stand it and spoke rapidly before she could interrupt again. "Helen, I am not an attorney and our firm does not handle divorce actions. But I can ask my father to recommend a lawyer I'm sure you'll find suitable."

She turned widened eyes on me, leaned close to put a warm hand on my knee. I should have felt stirrings of musth but her heavy perfume made me sneeze.

"Bless you," she said, back to a throaty voice again. "When will you be able to give me a name?"

"As soon as possible."

"Good. I don't want to waste any time. I want it settled quickly in case Walter goes back to his old bones in Africa. Darling, I can't tell you how much better I feel now. You're the first person I've told."

I was startled. "Walter doesn't know?"

"Not yet," she said breezily. "And not Edythe. And definitely not Natalie. Boy, are they going to be surprised."

"I can imagine."

"Listen, toots," she said, "I've got to get to my lunch. Don't bother walking me to the door. It's best if we're not seen together."

I nodded, having absolutely no idea what she implied. I received a hasty cheek kiss in farewell. We both alighted from the Riviera, she gave me a toothy smile, and I watched her dance away to the restaurant. I wasn't the only male admiring her undulations. All she needed was the head of John the Baptist on a platter.

I strolled back to the Miata, tugging on my beret, and found a lanky individual slouched against the right front fender. He straightened as I came up but even then he was droopy. I mean his nose and jowls drooped, his shoulders drooped, and his soiled seersucker suit drooped.

"You Archy McNally?" he demanded.

I saw no reason to identify myself. "Who are you?" I asked.

"Police Department," he said. His voice had a smoker's rasp.

"Oh? Which one?"

"Local."

"Town of Palm Beach?"

"Yeah."

"Then you must know Roscoe Arbuckle," I said. "The one they call Fatty."

"Sure, I know Fatty."

"Remarkable," I said. "Since he died in 1933. If you are, as you claim, a member of the gendarmerie, you'll have no objection to showing me your ID."

Droopy glanced about to see if any arriving lunchers were observing us. None were. He fished a short-barreled revolver from the sagging pocket of his jacket and held it, muzzle down, close to his leg. "How's this for ID?" he rasped.

"Is it loaded?" I inquired, proud of my coolth. You say there is no such word? There is now.

"Of course it's loaded," he said indignantly. "Now you and me are going to take a little ride in your wagon. You drive."

" 'You and I' is the correct grammatical construction," I instructed him. "And I have no desire whatsoever to take a ride with you anywhere at any time."

"But I've got a gun," he protested plaintively.

"So you do," I acknowledged. "And if I persist in my refusal to accompany you, which I fully intend to do, you may decide to shoot me. However, please let me call to your attention the number of passersby certain to be alerted by the discharge of a firearm. Surely some of them will be capable of serving as witnesses, giving a detailed and accurate description of your appearance as you flee the scene. And, I might add, able to pick you out of a lineup after you have been apprehended. Assuming you possess a brain, I strongly urge you to use it now and recognize your dilemma."

He looked about wildly, flummoxed. "It's my first job," he confessed. "I ain't never done anything like this before."

"We all must start at the bottom," I consoled him, "and ascend the ladder of success rung by rung. Who hired you?"

"I won't tell you," Droopy said. "But they're going to be plenty sore."

"That you made a botch of a kidnapping possibly planned to end with an assassination? How much were you paid?"

"Half," was all he'd say.

"In advance—the remainder to be paid on the delivery of my corpus?"

"Yeah."

"My advice to you is take the money and run. Don't return to your employer and try to explain your failure. Use your advance to get as far out of town as possible."

"I already spent it—the advance," he said sadly.

I sighed. "I can let you have fifty," I told him. "It's not much but it will get you on your way. You have a car?"

"A clunker."

"As long as you have wheels."

He pocketed the revolver and plucked my fifty-dollar bill eagerly.

"You're okay," he said.

"Of course I am," I agreed. "And I suggest you get in another line of business. You simply do not have the resolve and gumption required for strong-arm work."

He was offended and addressed four words to me. They were not "Have a nice day." Then he turned and slouched away, droopier than ever.

Unless I had just been bilked by an imaginative panhandling scam, which I doubted, I had been the intended victim of a setup designed with the connivance of Helen Westmore to facilitate my premature extinction: a shivery realization. Along with exultancy at my escaping such a fate came contempt for the stupidity of my would-be executioners in employing such an inept hit man as Droopy. But then we all know, do we not, how hard it is to get good help these days.

As for the identity of the rotters who launched the ridiculously ineffectual plot, I certainly had my suspicions as I'm sure you have yours. But my truncated legal education had taught me the nullity of suspicion in a court of law. Evidence and proof are rightly demanded, and at the moment those requisites were in short supply.

I started the Miata and made a slow tour through the parking area, up one lane and down the next. I was looking for a maroon Bentley, y'see, but didn't spot it. I was disappointed; I could have sworn that vehicle had conveyed Helen Westmore's date.

I headed northward on Ocean Boulevard and decided to stop at home for a spot of lunch. I found Ursi Olson in the kitchen preparing a meat loaf for dinner. She paused long enough to make me a three-egg omelette with shallots. I also had a hefty portion of warm German potato salad and two slices of Ursi's homemade sour rye, toasted and slathered with a cream cheese spread alleged to contain smoked salmon although I could not detect it. And a cold bottle of lager.

Thus fortified, I set out for my meeting with Frederick Clemens. I had a lunatic idea of how I might rattle his cage. One never knows, does one?

CHAPTER 23

I found the door of Clemens Investments closed and locked. Taped to the jamb was a neat typewritten note: "Please ring the buzzer for entrance." I thought it incorrect. One doesn't ring a buzzer; one rings a bell and buzzes or presses a buzzer. Do you think I suffer from a terminal case of pedantry?

Anyway I pushed the buzzer button and a moment later the door was opened by a smiling Fred Clemens who shook my hand most heartily, drawing me into the reception area and closing the door behind us. I heard the snap of a lock.

"Felix is off today," he said casually, "and your appointment is the only one I have scheduled, so we have all the time in the world."

Pushing open the knobless doors, he led the way down the corridor to his private office. He motioned toward an easeful armchair and waited until I was seated before he went behind his desk to the swivel chair on casters.

"I'd love to have a cigar," he said. "You, Archy?"

"Thank you, no," I said. "But you go ahead."

"Sure it won't bother you?"

"Not at all. It'll give me an excuse to smoke a cigarette."

He opened a lower drawer, brought out a large crystal ashtray and placed it on the desk between us.

"I keep it hidden," he admitted. "Many of my clients object to smoking."

He slipped a narrow pigskin case from his inside jacket pocket and extracted a plump, dark cigar. No band. He used a small gold cutter to snip off the tip and lighted the cigar with a paper book match. He took a deep puff and half closed his eyes with pleasure.

"Havana," he said. "But please don't tell the authorities. What are you smoking?"

I had already lighted an English Oval and showed him the packet.

"Oval, eh?" he said. "That's interesting. I once received a prospectus touting an investment in a machine which mass-produced square cigarettes."

"Square?" I said, laughing.

"Oh, they were still tubes of paper holding tobacco but the tubes were four-sided."

"What was the purpose?"

"The inventor claimed they eliminated wasted space, making the pack firmer."

"Did you invest in it?"

"I did not. I thought it was unusual but would never become universally popular. People enjoy having a round tube between their lips. And most consumers are conventional and stick with traditional ways of doing things until it's proved they can benefit from new methods. The square cigarette conferred no benefits to the smoker. It was just a novelty."

"Do you have that problem in your business, Fred—trying to convince clients there are unconventional ways to invest which might benefit them?"

"Oh lord, yes! Most people think investing begins and ends with stocks and bonds, when they're not putting their cash in CD's and money market funds. The most difficult part of my job is advising clients about the enormous variety of financial opportunities available."

He smoked his cigar slowly and rather grandly, as if handling a scepter. He seemed perfectly at ease, comfortable with himself and his surroundings. He was wearing a beautifully tailored suit of raw black silk with a blindingly white shirt. The gold Rolex studded with diamonds had been replaced by a severely elegant wristwatch I judged to be platinum. I wondered if Felix had persuaded him to wear something less dazzling. If so, it was wise counsel. Clemens was now a complete authoritative personage, immaculate and serious.

"Fred," I said, trying to match his gravitas, "I'm glad you brought up the subject of alternative investments. I have a proposition to present to you but first I need your pledge of complete confidentiality."

"You have it," he said promptly. "Success in my business demands the nth degree of discretion."

Mine too, I was tempted to add. But instead I said, "It concerns the purchase of a Fabergé Imperial egg by Mrs. Edythe Westmore. Has she given final approval?"

"It is not yet a done deal," he admitted.

"I didn't think so," I said.

His expression was amused but I caught the agitation in his voice when he asked, "Why do you say that, Archy?"

"I've been made aware of the strong objections of her son Walter and daughter Natalie to their mother investing half a million in a curio."

I had hoped to yank his chain and I succeeded. He tried to control himself, moving slowly to place the half-smoked cigar in the ashtray. But I saw the tight jaw and slight tremor of his hands. And when he leaned

toward me his smile was a rictus and his mellifluous voice had coarsened with an under-
tone of venom.

"Kooks!" he almost spat. "Both of them are
morons! They are totally ignorant of financial
matters, spiteful, and greedy. They would
never admit it but they resent their mother
spending their inheritance."

I didn't think it a propitious time to tell him
Natalie had already admitted it to me. "Their
objections may be selfishly motivated," I
agreed. "But they have close daily contact
with their mother. I think it quite possible she
may eventually be swayed by their negative opinions."

He sat back forcibly, clenched his fingers,
stared down at his whitened knuckles. "Yes,"
he said in a low voice, "it's possible the gruesome twosome might convince their mother
to reject the project. I don't mind telling you
I have seen recent indications she may be
wavering. The owner of the egg, a former
Parisian banker, is becoming more anxious to
close the deal. If not, he intends to find another buyer—which would not be difficult. But
Edythe keeps postponing the actual transfer
of funds."

"How would it be accomplished?" I asked,
not really expecting he would reveal details.
But he surprised me.

"The seller demands cash," he said.
"Obviously I don't wish to carry that amount
of money overseas. Edythe will execute a
bank check made out to me. I will take it to

Paris, where I have banking contacts enabling me to convert it to French francs and pay the seller."

"Edythe won't go to France herself?"

"No," he said. "She's afraid of flying."

I looked at him with some amazement. If he had a con game going he had found the perfect pigeon—one who wouldn't fly. And apparently Edythe was so ditzy she would approve of such a risky plan.

"Archy," Clemens said, sounding distracted, "you started this talk about the Fabergé egg by saying you have a proposition to make. Let's have it."

"If Mrs. Westmore should renege on the deal," I said determinedly, "I'd like you to consider me as an interested and potential buyer under the same terms offered to her."

He stared at me a moment, then took his cold cigar from the ashtray and relighted it. He puffed with obvious satisfaction, his composure once more intact.

"You would be able to provide the funds?"

"No problem," I assured him. "But I wish to make an additional proposal. Was your income from Mrs. Westmore's deal to be in excess of the regular fee you charge for acting as her financial adviser?"

"Oh no," he said quickly. "There was to be no extra billing on my part other than travel expenses. It was to be included in the services provided by Clemens Investments."

He said this so earnestly it was difficult to doubt him. But I managed.

"Fred, I would be happy to pay you personally an additional fifty thousand dollars if you'd be willing to remove Mrs. Westmore from the deal and negotiate the purchase of the egg on my behalf."

It was a test of his scrupulosity you understand. If he became indignant at my offer and immediately rejected it as being unethical or just too tricky to be accepted, I would have been forced to blot out all my conceptions of the man and start over. But he was not indignant. He wasn't even startled by my suggestion.

"May I ask the reason for your interest in this particular investment, Archy?" His cold smile indicated he had already decided what my motive was.

"Greed," I admitted at once. "Since first hearing about the Fabergé egg I've done some research on the subject. I'm convinced I could double or perhaps even triple my stake. An additional fifty thousand to you, in cash, would hardly dent the potential profit."

"You're quite right," he said. He understood me very well; I was speaking his language. "I presume, Archy, you'd want to fly to Paris and examine the egg before purchase."

"Naturally. And have it appraised by an expert of my choosing before handing over my half-million clams."

He nodded. "I see no problems there. Getting the egg back to the U.S. without paying an enormous duty might prove difficult but I daresay it can be worked out. Those are details of course and have little bearing on whether or not I accept your generous offer."

I could detect no irony in his final phrase. "Well?" I said. "Which is it to be: yes or no?"

He laughed gently. "Surely you don't expect an immediate answer. This is an important matter, Archy, and deserves serious consideration. For instance, my acceptance of your proposal would undoubtedly mark the end of my business relationship with Mrs. Westmore— and probably with her friends who are presently clients but would leave me to prove their sympathy with Edythe. I must do some heavy thinking on what agreeing to your request would do to my reputation as a trustworthy adviser—a reputation I value highly, I might add, and one I'd hate to see besmirched."

"Perfectly understandable," I told him. "It's your decision to make and I know you'll do what you think best."

We smiled at each other a long moment. I think we were both conscious of being foes in a contest which had no rules and hence no referee or umpire.

"Please let me know as soon as possible what you decide," I said, suspecting he was delaying his answer to give himself time to discuss the matter with Felix. I rose to leave but he put out a hand to detain me.

"You can do me a favor, Archy," he said. "I wish you'd tell me if Walter and Natalie Westmore make any defaming remarks about me in your presence. Others have told me those children from hell have referred to me in terms which may be the basis for a lawsuit against them for slander."

I nodded. "I'll tell you if I hear them say anything which might make them liable. Thank you for your time, Fred."

"And thank *you*, Archy, for a very intriguing visit."

He was using *my* word!

When I exited from his condo I looked about for the maroon Bentley as I had when I arrived at two o'clock. Again, it was nowhere to be seen. I drove back to the McNally Building, ruminating on my talk with Clemens and wondering if he'd accept my deal or refuse it. I thought I knew the answer to that.

I took the automatic elevator up from our underground garage. It stopped on the second floor and Mrs. Lenore Crittenden entered, carrying a stack of files.

"Hi, Archy," she said. "Love your beret. Cinnabar?"

"Puce."

"Oh no," she said. "Perhaps plum."

"Puce," I insisted.

The third-floor door slid open and she got off but held the door back with her foot.

"I was going to give you a call later, Archy. You know that guy you asked me to trace?"

"Frederick Clemens? Find out anything about him?"

"So far I've only heard from about half the agencies I queried but all the replies are the same: nothing."

"Nothing?" I repeated, stunned.

"You've got it," she said. "Or rather you don't have it. No one has heard of him. No one has his name or address in their files."

"The man does exist, Lennie," I said angrily. "And claims to be an investment adviser."

"Probably a fake name," she said blithely. "Happens all the time. A no-good gets caught, fined, and barred from the securities business. So he just takes on a new identity—it's ridiculously easy to do these days—moves to another state, and continues his dirty work. Caveat emptor, kiddo."

"You can say that again," I gloomed.

"Caveat emptor, kiddo," she said again, winked at me behind her monocle, and let the door close.

The moment I was back in my office I phoned Binky Watrous and was told by the houseman Master Binky was not presently at home. I shuffled through a heap of scraps in my desk drawer and finally found the number of Bridget Houlihan. I called, hoping she had returned from Ireland. She had.

"Faith and begorra and all that sort of thing, Bridget," I said. "Welcome back. Have a good time?"

"Loverly," she said. "It rained every day. Archy, did you ever drink a Shillelagh?"

"No, and I've never drunk a knobkerrie either. What's in a Shillelagh?"

"Irish whiskey, sloe gin, rum, sugar, lemon juice, and three fresh raspberries. It's very powerful."

"Probably the raspberries that give it a kick. Listen, ducky, is Binky there by any chance? I'm trying to locate him."

"He's here. While I was gone he learned the call of a whooping crane and we've been rehearsing."

"Well, Binky's very good at whooping. I remember he once ate— But you don't want to hear that story."

"No, I don't," she said firmly. "Wait a minute; I'll put him on."

My scatty amigo came on the line by giving me a mercifully brief imitation of a whooping crane.

"Incredible," I said. "Take two aspirin and don't call me in the morning. Binky, are you still providing Frederick Clemens with the names of potential clients?"

"Oh sure. He's good for a yard or two a week."

"Stick with me, kid, and you'll be wearing zircons. Now I've got another job for you. I want you to find out the last name of Felix, the secretary."

"I already know it."

"You do?" I said, hearing Bridget's tambourine in the background. "How did you discover it?"

"I asked him."

I laughed. "Good thinking on your part. What is it?"

"Katz. K-a-t-z."

"He's Felix Katz? And I am The Man in the Iron Mask. Binky, Felix the Cat was a movie

211

cartoon, even older than Mickey Mouse."

Silence. Then: "You think he's using a phony name?"

"A distinct possibility," I said. "Thanks for the info. Now go back to your whooping."

I hung up knowing what I must do next.

I CHAPTER 24

I LOVE MY father but it doesn't blind me to the home truth he can be intimidating and occasionally dictatorial. Until recently I had generally deferred to his judgments and obeyed his diktats, recognizing his superior learning and experience. Of course there were times I simply didn't request his advice, foreseeing it would not be in accord with what I considered a clever and sometimes sneaky method of conducting a Discreet Inquiry. Oh, he could be stodgy! Like his private library he was hidebound.

But during a previous case I had made an important decision without consulting him. It had aroused his ire especially since it concerned the outlay of a considerable sum of money by McNally & Son. He had become so outraged I offered to resign. He ignored my declaration of independence and allowed my decision to stand. It had proved efficacious and nothing more was said of the matter.

The incident had subtly changed our relationship. It had given me an increased desire for freedom to do my job the way I wanted to do it, without first obtaining his approval. It was not bald defiance you understand, merely a more deliberate and more frequent refrainment from informing him of my *modus operandi*. In many cases I was certain he would have withheld permission, not because I proposed a particularly outlandish course of action but because he had a lawyerly tendency to defer any action at all which might have unexpected consequences.

All this is a preamble to explaining why I did not inform him I intended to seek the assistance of the Palm Beach Police Department in my investigation of Frederick Clemens. The pater had stated vehemently my inquiry was to be conducted with the utmost discretion, an injunction which surely excluded bringing in the cops. But I felt events now required their aid and cooperation. And so, without telling the senior McNally what I planned, I phoned Sgt. Al Rogoff.

I found him at headquarters and he sounded cranky. I guessed his investigation of the Sydney Smythe homicide wasn't going well and resolved not to refer to it.

"Any chance of seeing you tonight?" I asked him.

"No," he said bluntly. "I'm stuck here for another couple of hours and then I'm going to grab a burger somewhere, go home, and fall into bed. I'm beat."

"I'd really like to talk to you, Al."

"Can't it wait?"

"Everything can wait I suppose but this is important."

"I'll bet. What happened—someone steal your Bugs Bunny lunch box? Give me a break."

His surliness annoyed me and I changed my mind. "It concerns the murder of Sydney Smythe," I said flatly. "Now do you want to talk about it or don't you?"

Brief pause. Then: "Are you shucking me?"

"No, I am not shucking you. Forget about the burger, Al. Go directly home and I'll show up with provisions about eight o'clock." I hung up without waiting for his yea or nay.

I had phoned from my desk at home. I smoked half a gasper, reflecting it would take hours to record in my journal all the events of a tumultuous day. But a more pressing problem was how much to reveal to Sgt. Rogoff and what I would be wise not to disclose. I was still unsure when I went downstairs to join the family cocktail hour.

While we inhaled our martinis I informed my parents I would not be present at dinner.

"An old friend in town," I explained. "A dreadful bore. He wants a tour of the flesh-pots of Palm Beach. He'd do better in Dubuque."

"Oh Archy," mother said. "And Ursi baked such a nice meat loaf."

"What a shame I have to miss it," I said, another falsehood since I consider meat loaf a plebeian dish with all the lip-smacking allure of chocolate-covered dottle.

During my brief visit home I had cast off my

beret and dressy apparel to don casual duds: khaki jeans, scuffed mocs, a blue denim work shirt, and a tweed jacket so old it was a bit hairy about the elbows and cuffs. Thus attired, I gave Hobo a farewell pat, vaulted into the Miata, and sped to my favorite West Palm deli.

I purchased two Reubens, each so humongous it must have contained a pound of corned beef. I also bought a big bag of matchstick French fries and a cold six-pack of pale ale from a local microbrewery I had never tried. And for dessert, two mammoth Uglis, which I dearly love. I then drove back across the lake and arrived at Rogoff's mobile home only a few minutes late.

Al's place is rather grotty and always reminds me of a dilapidated fraternity house. But the scarred wood armchairs are comfortable enough, and the lingering odor of cigars and garlic is not strong enough to be offensive. It is an unpretentious bachelor's pad, and you'd expect a poker or pinochle game to be played at the round oak table every Saturday night— and you'd be right!

I found the sergeant in a tetchy mood but he thawed when he opened the bags of food I had brought.

"I haven't had a Reuben in years," he said. "A welcome change from cheeseburgers and anchovy pizza."

"Listen, Al," I said, "I have a lot to tell you so let's talk while we eat."

"Suits me. You want hot ketchup for your fries?"

"Why not?" I said. "And don't bother with glasses for the ale. Just pop the caps."

"Great grub," he said, looking at our food. "You must want something bad."

"I do," I admitted. "But it's back-scratching time. First of all, how are you doing on the Sydney Smythe homicide?"

"Getting nowhere fast."

"I thought so. Well, I have a confession to make: I didn't tell you everything Smythe said in his final phone call to me."

I related how the antique dealer had spoken of a problem he had and asked for my assistance to help solve it.

"He was worried?" Rogoff asked.

"No doubt about it. He was trying to be casual but it was obvious he was in a bind."

"Why didn't you tell me about this before?"

"Because I didn't think it important. Now I do. And here's why..."

I started from the beginning and told him how a client, Mrs. Edythe Westmore, intended to buy a Fabergé Imperial egg through her financial adviser, Frederick Clemens. I explained why I had consulted Sydney Smythe in the first place and how our meeting had led to my fanciful creation of a "surprise" in an invented egg, and how Clemens had adopted my description and repeated it to Mrs. Westmore.

I even told Rogoff of the scam about my imaginary egg being auctioned by Sotheby's in New York.

"Why did you pull that one?" he asked.

"I wanted to determine just how close Smythe was to Clemens. And if the former repeated my story to the latter, the whole freaky deal might just die."

"Yeah," the sergeant said, "but it was Smythe who died."

"Don't think I don't feel guilty about that."

"All right, so you feel guilty. What else?"

I spoke of the opposition of Walter and Natalie Westmore to their mother spending half a million for the egg and the enmity Clemens had expressed because of their attitude. (Naturally I said nothing of my personal relationship with Natalie.)

"What kind of a guy is this Clemens?" Rogoff asked.

I told him what I knew and what I guessed. I described his office, how he operated, and the puzzling role of his secretary, Felix Katz. I detailed my failed efforts to learn anything about Clemens's background. I admitted he had committed no crimes of which I was aware.

"But I now believe the man is a pirate," I said. "If our client agrees to the deal he has planned, he's going to grab her bank check, cash it somewhere or sell it at a discount to some other shark, and promptly vamoose, whistling a merry tune. Al, I've seen a color photo of the alleged egg involved but I don't think Clemens has any intention of buying it. The whole thing is an ingenious con game from the git-go."

"Could be," he said, starting on the second

half of his sandwich. "You got any proof?"

"No," I said miserably. "None."

"And your office hasn't been able to find his name on the records of any financial agency?"

"Not a mention."

He nodded. "It's probably phony. Archy, producing and peddling fake ID is the most lucrative cottage industry in America."

"That's why I need your help. There are computer files on criminals cross-indexed with their known aliases, aren't there?"

"Yep."

"Will you do a computer trace on Frederick Clemens and Felix Katz?"

"Nope."

I was angered. "Why the hell not?"

"You may be right. Those two ginks may have a world-class con in the works. But you have no proof and so far they've done nothing illegal. There are no indictments, no warrants, no probable cause. How in God's name can I justify a nationwide computer trace on the basis of your suspicions?"

"It's more than just a swindle," I said hotly. "I think they're guilty of the murder of Sydney Smythe."

"Why should they kill the old man or have him iced?"

"Because he gave them the information about the nonexistent surprise I described to him. And then he had to tell them it and the egg containing it would be auctioned in New York, garnering a lot of publicity that would demolish their plot to fleece Mrs. Westmore.

They figured he had made too many mistakes, represented too much of a danger, especially if he decided to talk—to me or to you—and so he had to be terminated."

"Proof?" Rogoff asked again. "Hard evidence?"

"None," I admitted again.

"Old buddy," he said, finishing his sandwich and beginning to peel his Ugli, "I just can't spend the time on the trace you want. It would mean a lot of work and cost a lot of bucks. And there's no guarantee a computer check of aliases would succeed. Maybe they're using new names not on record. Sorry, sonny boy, but no can do. Now if you could supply their fingerprints a search might be a lot easier."

"Their fingerprints?" I exclaimed. "How on earth am I supposed to obtain them?"

He shrugged. "Pinch some papers they've handled. Almost anything."

"Besides," I said, half laughing, "they wouldn't be complete. The one who calls himself Felix Katz is missing a finger."

The sergeant stared at me strangely, then rose and began rummaging through a kitchen cabinet, his back turned to me. "I think we can use some paper napkins. Should have put them out before." He returned to the table with a stack, sat down again, and resumed eating his Ugli. "So Katz has lost a finger?"

"Correct. Index finger on his right hand."

"Uh-huh. I'll tell you what I'll do for you, pal. You bring in their fingerprints, of one or both, and I'll put them through the wringer for you."

"Is that the best you can do?"

"It's the *only* thing I can do."

I sighed. "All right, I'll try to get their prints. But don't ask me how. I have no ideas."

"If those two are the villains you think they are, which one do you figure is the honcho? Or are they equal?"

"I honestly don't know, Al, but I'd guess Katz is the heavy. He gives me an impression of barely suppressed violence. Clemens is the front man, a smooth salesman with more charm than one man can legitimately use."

We had finished the food but there was plenty of pale ale remaining and we settled down with that. It was potable enough but not as tartish as I had hoped.

I must have been quiet a long time, for Rogoff finally said, "Well? You got more you haven't told me?"

I had been silent because I was uncertain whether or not to tell him of my encounter in the restaurant parking lot. I finally decided.

"There is something," I admitted. "But I'm not sure it has anything to do with Clemens and Katz."

"Tell me!" the sergeant said. "I want to hear it."

I was startled by his eagerness. A few moments previously he had seemed indifferent to my recital, showing no enthusiasm for tracing Clemens and Katz. But now he was keen to hear more. I couldn't understand the abrupt change.

I told him about my rendezvous with Mrs.

Helen Westmore and the attempted abduction by Droopy. Al listened intently.

"The woman was the bait to get you to the parking lot?"

"It's the way I see it."

"What did you talk about?"

"She claims she wants a divorce from Walter and—"

"A lot of that going around these days."

"—she asked me to find her a lawyer. Now I think she was blowing smoke. Her sister-in-law, Natalie, hinted Helen has been catting around. I think she might have a thing going with Clemens; they seemed awfully cozy when I saw them together at a party. So I figured she was probably lunching with him. But I didn't spot his car and he was in his office, cool as the proverbial cuke, when I met him at two o'clock. I really don't know who she was meeting at that vile restaurant."

"You think she knew you were an intended victim?"

"I doubt it. She's such an airhead I think she set me up only as a favor to someone. Besides, it gave her a chance to act and she used to be on the stage. But I don't think she knew there was going to be rough stuff involved."

"This dorky gunman you call Droopy—he knew your name?"

"He did."

"So it had to be a setup."

"Definitely."

"By Clemens and Katz?"

"Possibly."

"Why would they want to put you down, Archy?"

"For the same reasons they bayoneted Sydney Smythe. I represent a danger to their campaign. I'm the guy who fed them the description of the Fabergé 'surprise.' Maybe they don't know Mrs. Westmore told me Clemens's identical description of the surprise in the egg he's peddling. Maybe they're afraid she will tell me and then their con game is blitzed. Maybe they just don't like the way I part my hair."

I had feared my story of the attempted kidnapping would amuse Rogoff and he would respond with laughter and a ribald comment. But no, he accepted my account with nary a smirk. In fact, he seemed to give it more import than I.

"You want us to look for this Droopy gink?"

"Don't waste your time, Al," I said. "If he took my advice—and I expect he did—he's out of town by now."

"Archy, I think you better start watching your back."

I was touched by his concern. "I intend to. The first attempt was a farce. I don't want the second to be a tragedy."

"You don't own a gun, do you?"

"Good lord, no! Wouldn't know which end to point. But I am armed with faith, righteousness, and a pure heart."

"Yeah," he said. "Lots of luck. Finished your ale? How about taking off and letting me get some sleep."

"Sure. Thanks for listening to my tale of woe."

"Thanks for the grub. The Reuben was super. Listen, don't neglect those fingerprints. Try to get them to me as soon as possible."

Once more I was perplexed. What had begun as an offhand suggestion now seemed an urgent request. I wondered what had impressed him enough to justify his remarkable conversion.

It was almost eleven o'clock when I started home. I was reasonably content with the way our klatch had gone. Sometimes Al and I are competitors but our rivalry is usually in methods, not in aims. We both want the same happy ending.

I customarily sing when I drive alone at night but I didn't feel like warbling on that occasion. I was too intent in mulling over what impels men like Clemens and Katz. Inordinate greed I suppose, and surely covetousness is the most sordid of the Seven Deadly Sins, even more than sloth or gluttony.

I remember Lady Cynthia Horowitz once told me, "When it comes to money, enough is never enough." It implies a kind of addiction in those like Fred and Felix: a compulsive need requiring larger and larger injections to produce a satisfaction always temporary. Avarice is a passion doomed to be unconsummated.

The Good Book has it right. Money is not the root of all evil. It is the love of money.

CHAPTER 25

I DIDN'T EVEN consider going to the office on Thursday. After breakfast with my parents I changed to sweats and planted myself at my desk, determined to bring my journal up to date even if it required eight hours of labor. It almost did because I was interrupted by several phone calls and discovered I preferred yakking to scribbling.

The first was from Sgt. Al Rogoff.

"I had one of your leftover ales for breakfast," he announced. "Hit the spot."

"And that's what you called to tell me?"

"Nah. I thought you'd like to know Sydney Smythe's English cousin is in town."

"Oh? What kind of a guy is he?"

"She. A very straight, solid lady. We explained we can't release the body for a few days and it didn't upset her. Says it's her first visit to the Land of the Brave and she plans to look around a little. Want to meet her?"

"No."

"Still got the guilts, huh? The cousin—her name's Penelope Blakely-Jones—found out Smythe owed two months' rent at his motel. I guess the guy was scraping bottom."

"I think he was."

"Anyway she's going to take a few personal things and give the rest of Smythe's belongings to the motel owner to sell for the back rent."

"Makes sense," I said. "Have you unsealed his apartment?"

"Yep. We went through all his stuff. A lot of junk. Nothing was any help. You get the fingerprints of Clemens and Katz?"

"Al," I protested, "it was only last night you told me you wanted them. Give me some time."

"The sooner the better," he said, and hung up.

I went back to scrawling in my professional journal. Memories of the previous day's events came crowding and I dutifully jotted them down without attempting to judge their importance or significance. It was purely mechanical labor requiring little thought and so enabled my fancy to soar.

Lest you think me totally gormless (actually I have as much gorm as the next chap), my dreams were firmly rooted in reality. The facts were these:

Lady Cynthia Horowitz, doyenne of Palm Beach society, was temporarily deserting our shores on Friday morning to spend the holiday season at her St. Tropez villa. During her absence her social secretary, my very own Consuela Garcia, was driving south to spend Christmas and New Year's with her multitudinous family in Miami.

And so that Thursday night would be my last opportunity to enjoy Connie's company until the new year. We had agreed on a farewell dinner at the Ritz-Carlton in Manalapan and decided it should be a black-tie occasion. I had already made our reservation and had my Christmas gift to her, diamond stud earrings, gift-wrapped and ready to be handed over with many wishes for a fabulous Christmastide.

And then after dinner? As stated, I allowed my fancy to soar and my anticipatory visions had me snorting like a randy sophomore.

My daydreams were demolished by a second phone call, this one from Walter Westmore.

"I know it's too soon to expect results, Archy," he said anxiously, "but Natalie and I wondered how your investigation is coming along."

"Excellently," I said, lying briskly. "I have already queried the professional agencies I mentioned in my father's office. No replies received as yet. Also—and this is *entre nous* you understand—I have persuaded law enforcement officers to conduct a computer trace on Clemens and his secretary to determine if any criminal record exists. In addition, I have managed to place my assistant, an extremely clever and experienced operative, as an employee of the subjects to observe and report on their activities. He will serve as an undercover agent, one might say."

"It sounds like you're really making progress," Walter said relievedly. "When do you think you'll have something definite to tell us?"

"As soon as possible," I said, wearying of the repetition.

"Wait a sec," he said. "Natalie wants to speak to you."

"Archy," she said in a snarky voice, "you've really got to *do* something. Clemens talks to mother every day, and I'm afraid he'll get her to hand over the money before you can prove he's an oily crook."

"Natalie," I said as equably as I could, "you must be patient. I've been overseeing this investigation for only two days, you know, and Walter will tell you how much I have already accomplished."

"You must do more," she said, still snappish. "And if you take too long, Walter and I will have to do something ourselves. I don't think you realize how important this is to us."

I did not relish being dressed down by a client—and a nonpaying client to boot. (At the moment I would have liked to.)

"I fully realize its importance," I said coldly, "and am doing my best to bring the matter to a successful conclusion. You're quite at liberty to seek assistance elsewhere, you know, if that is your wish."

"Oh God!" she wailed. "You can be *such* a prig!"

She slammed down the receiver and I yelled, "I detest your petunia!" at the dead phone.

It took a cigarette to soothe my shredded nerves. I finally calmed sufficiently to resume my chores as a diarist. I recalled Fred Clemens had referred to the Westmore siblings as kooks, as children from hell, and as a gruesome twosome. I was beginning to think he was a perspicacious analyst of human behavior.

I prepared my own lunch, only a small salad of ersatz crabmeat because I had already decided what Connie and I would have at dinner: a luscious chateaubriand. Or perhaps, if it was available, beef Wellington. I returned to my desk debating a proper wine for the tender slab of meat I envisioned. Merlot? Pinot noir? A fine old cabernet? Burgundy? It was, I decided happily, a no-lose decision.

I finished my journal entries about three o'clock with the feeling I had achieved a great deal. The illusion faded when I reread my jottings. All the details were there but the pattern, the big picture, eluded me.

Connie phoned in an exuberant mood compounded of her freedom from her employer's whims for two weeks (she was sometimes referred to by enemies as Lady Horrorwitz); the planned visit to her family in Miami; and our dinner date that evening. I hoped it was the last which made the biggest contribution to her high spirits.

I promised to pick her up at six o'clock and the moment we disconnected I flopped into bed for a short nap, knowing it was going to be a long evening. I awoke in time to shower, shave, and don my black tropical worsted dinner jacket and all its accoutrements. Then I made certain I had keys, handkerchief, wallet, credit cards, cigarettes, lighter, and Connie's gift.

I bounced downstairs ready to slay dragons or rescue a damsel in distress—and received a five-star surprise. My father had just returned from the office and we met in the hallway. He observed my finery and hoisted an inquiring eyebrow. I explained I was escorting Connie Garcia to a farewell dinner at the Ritz-Carlton before her departure on a Christmas vacation.

"I do not believe your convertible is suitable for such a festive event," he said, po-faced. "I suggest you borrow the Lexus for the evening."

I was shocked, *shocked*! I could count on the thumb of one hand the number of times he had made that offer.

"Thank you, sir," I said. "I promise to return it with no scratches or dings."

"See that you do," he said gruffly, and handed over the keys.

Driving the big Lexus was like piloting a safe on wheels after breezing about in my sprightly Miata. But I must admit I enjoyed the solidity and comfort. I opened the sunroof and fiddled with the radio until I found an acceptable station. I shunned my father's tapes and CD's, knowing they'd be Guy Lombardo or Mantovani.

I couldn't have ordered a more enchanting evening. The faintly luminescent sky was cloudless and salted with stars. A pale moon was half a key lime pie and a tangy breeze billowed, too cool for a T-shirt, too warm for a sweater, just right for a dinner jacket. Even inland I thought I could hear the susurrus of the sea. What a night! I prayed it might end as felicitously as it had begun.

I pulled up in front of Connie's building and saw her waiting inside the glassed lobby. She glimpsed the black Lexus but made no move to exit, obviously expecting my fiery roadster.

She was garbed in a drop-dead gown of shimmery satin in periwinkle blue. Her long black hair was up, braided and held in place with a glittering ornamental comb—something a flamenco dancer might wear. And she carried a small tapestried minaudière.

Connie could never be called elegant—at least by me. I think elegance demands cool serenity, physical slenderness if not emaciation, and sometimes a bloodless hauteur. Connie had something better: a fleshy vitality, open passions, a bursting energy I found bewitching if occasionally daunting.

I gave the horn a brief tottle, and when she glanced at the Lexus again, I waved a beckoning arm through the open window. She came from the lobby and I alighted to greet her. She paused a mo to inspect our transportation delightedly.

"Oh Archy," she said, "how grand!"

"Only for tonight," I told her. "A royal coach for a royal princess." I moved to kiss her cheek but she fended me off.

"Wait! Wait!" she cried, opened her little bag, fumbled within and brought out a sprig of mistletoe, complete with white berries. She held it over her head. "Now!" she commanded.

Laughing, I kissed her lightly once, twice, thrice. "Good planning on your part, luv. Keep the shrub handy; I'm sure we'll put it to use."

"I intend to," she said firmly.

We drove south on Ocean Boulevard, the radio turned low until "Because You Loved Me," a pop ballad of the day, came on, and then Connie turned up the volume. She lay back on the leather and gazed at the sequined sky through the open sunroof.

We chatted of this and that as we sped southward on the almost deserted corniche. Connie told me of the holiday parties her family had scheduled. When we passed the first sign announcing the distance from our destination I mentioned I had met a blind woman at the Westmores' fete who lived in Manalapan.

"Her name is Barney Newfield," I told Connie. "Isn't that choice? What a wonderful old lady! She was Walter's professor and mentor, and apparently they're still quite close. She's remarkably sharp and spry considering her age and blindness."

"You shouldn't say she's blind," Connie chided. "You should say 'visually-impaired.'"

"Correct. And you shouldn't say I smoke too much. You should say I'm nicotinically challenged."

"And I should say you're mentally deprived instead of calling you a nut."

We both giggled, she held the mistletoe over her head, and I took my eyes off the road long enough to kiss her chin.

We were ushered to a primo table in the dining room of the Ritz. And while I will not claim we were the cynosure of all, we did attract attention. I'm sure some of the curious/envious reaction was due to our formal attire but I think it was Connie's game with the mistletoe that drew most eyes in our direction. No one seemed to object to our osculation. I certainly didn't.

I shall not describe our dinner in detail other than to mention the wine I selected was a '92 Haut-Brion. (I hope you approve.) The reason for my reticence is because I have found when writing about succulent, mouthwatering foods I am invariably driven to dash wildly to the refrigerator to see what's available. So to prevent my waistline from exceeding my IQ I shall merely report it was a most enjoyable occasion made more memorable by a poignant tenderness I am certain we both felt. It was, after all, a farewell and if our separation was to be of only two weeks' duration it was sufficient to give our pleasure an elegiac tinge.

We exchanged Christmas presents before our postprandial liqueurs were served. I gave Connie the stud earrings. She gave me gold cuff links in the shape of love knots. I was delighted with my gift, and her joy at receiving the diamonds was obvious. I helped her insert the posts into her pierced lobes and when the jewels were in place they looked smashing. Connie knew it and glowed.

Up to that moment the evening had been

pleasurable and continued so. But when our green Chartreuse was brought an incident occurred which gave our dinner an added significance. We raised glasses to each other in a silent toast and I experienced a startling epiphany.

I do not claim my sudden and unexpected discovery rivaled Sir Isaac getting bopped on the pate by a falling apple or Archimedes yelping "Eureka!" in a hot tub, but I thought it a thing of wonder and good fortune. And what exactly was my serendipitous revelation? Patience! You shall learn shortly. Hint: It concerned the Fabergé ovoid.

"Why are you laughing?" Connie asked me.

"Because I'm happy," I answered, and indeed I was.

We drove home with almost no conversation between us but content all the same. I have long felt a true test of lovers' intimacy is whether or not they can be both silent and pleased while together. I don't mean a silence of a day, week, month, or lifetime, but brief periods when nonstop chatter is unnecessary and unwanted, and shared quiet has its own charm.

We arrived at Connie's condominium, parked, and before leaving the car my light-o'-love again haloed her head with the mistletoe sprig, and this time our embrace and kiss were more impassioned. Then we went up to her apartment.

Connie keeps a liter of Absolut in her freezer for my enjoyment, believing the way to a man's heart is through his liver. We each had a noggin of the icy vodka while we watched a video titled *The Best of Benny Hill* which left us exhausted from laughing. We revived by listening to a tape of Ella Fitzgerald singing "All Through the Night"—so beautiful it leaves one haunted with longing.

Taking the song as our cue we disrobed slowly, smiling at each other.

Connie wore her new earrings to bed.

I won't tell you where she held the mistletoe.

CHAPTER 26

NEED I INFORM you I overslept on Friday morning? (In my own bed I hasten to add.) I awoke to find myself surprisingly clear-headed considering all the wassailing of the previous evening. True, I did seem to be moving slowly, as if a misstep or sudden action might have dire consequences. Fragile! That's the word. I definitely felt fragile. But nothing two cups of black coffee and three Wolferman's crumpets (with apricot spread) couldn't remedy. They did.

I finally arrived at the McNally Building shortly before noon and found on my cluttered desk a message from our receptionist stating Mr. Frederick Clemens had phoned and requested I return his call. I did so and was answered by Felix's toneless, "Clemens Investments. May I help you?"

I identified myself and we exchanged brief holiday greetings. I asked to speak to the panjandrum and was put through immediately. Again salutations were traded and then Clemens explained the reason for his call.

He said, "I wanted very much to speak to you about what we discussed during your recent visit," and I thought I detected something oleaginous in his voice. "I felt it would be best to report my decision to you as soon as possible."

He paused, apparently awaiting a response. The best I could come up with was a tepid, "Of course, Fred."

"However," he continued, "it is not a subject I care to talk about on the phone. It really is a private matter, and I hoped to see you today and tell you what I have decided and explain the reasons for it. But unfortunately a critical business meeting in Boca Raton requires my personal attention and presence and so I will be unable to meet with you. I apologize. I am hoping you will be willing to have a one-on-one with Felix, my capable assistant and confidant. He has been thoroughly briefed on the situation and will be able to relay everything I planned to say as well as answering any questions you might have. What do you say, Archy? Will you allow Felix to sub for me?"

I had several instant reactions to his request. *Primero,* the two men were obviously closer partners than I had suspected. *Segundo,* his tale of "a critical business meeting in Boca Raton" was complete horsefeathers. *Tercero,* he probably had another activity scheduled, possibly an assignation with Helen Westmore. And *cuarto,* the substitution of Felix would slightly alter but not cancel the scheme I had devised after my inspiration at the Ritz during my dinner with Connie.

"I have no objection to meeting with Felix," I told Clemens, "providing you can vouch for his discretion."

"One hundred percent!" he said heartily. "I guarantee it! And I want to apologize again for my unavoidable absence and thank you for your understanding cooperation. Now I'll put Felix back on the line and the two of you can arrange where and when you'll meet."

I had a brief and satisfactory conversation with Felix. I explained I had a luncheon appointment at the Pelican Club but if he could join me there at—oh, say two-thirty, the place would be relatively quiet, we could sit at the bar and have a drink or two while we talked. He immediately agreed and I gave him the address and told him how to find the Pelican.

"It's not a fancy joint," I warned.

"I'm sure I've been in worse," he said politely. He had a sibilance in his speech which reminded me of Humphrey Bogart.

I tore (literally) through a stack of junk mail accumulated during the past week, deep-sixed everything, and hustled down to the garage. I arrived at the Pelican Club about one-thirty and was happy to see midday diners were already departing. I had two chili dogs and a brew at the bar, ate slowly, and by the time I finished my calorific lunch there was only one couple left in the dining area and I was alone at the bar. Perfect.

I made certain Priscilla removed all evidence I had lunched alone. Then I motioned Simon Pettibone closer and slid a fifty-dollar bill across the mahogany.

"Paying your tab, Mr. McNally?" he asked.

"No, Mr. Pettibone. It's for you."

He stared at the bill. "I wonder what General Grant would look like without a beard," he said. "Probably like Mrs. Grant. Well, I thank you very much for your generosity but who do I have to kill?"

"No mayhem," I said. "Just a little job for me."

"Legal?"

"Eminently. Let me explain."

"I think you better," he said.

I told him exactly what I wanted him to do. It wasn't difficult but it had to be done easily, nonchalantly, as if it were routine.

"He's a bad man," he said—more of a statement than a question.

"I think he's bad, Mr. Pettibone. This is one way to find out."

He stared at me a moment. "All right," he said finally.

I ordered a vodka and tonic in a tall glass. I had taken only a few small sips when Felix Katz came through the door, paused, looked around. He saw me and sauntered toward the bar. I admired the slinky way he moved,

237

with an almost feline grace. He was wearing black suit, white shirt, black tie, and I wondered what he had against colors.

I slid off my barstool and stood just long enough to shake hands. His four-fingered grip felt odd. Then we sat side by side, and Mr. Pettibone came over to us.

"What will you have, Felix?" I asked him.

"Chivas Regal, please," he said. Then to Pettibone: "Do you have any Pellegrino?"

"No, sir," the bartender said. "But we have Perrier."

"That'll do fine. In a tall glass, thank you."

Quite mannerly, our boy, but his politesse was as cold and lifeless as his voice. His courtesies sounded like phrases from a foreign language.

"I don't want to rush you," he said, "but I'd like to get back to the office as soon as I can. As Fred told you, he'll be away and I'll have to hold the fort."

"I understand," I said, and waited while Mr. Pettibone carefully placed the highball on the bar. Katz picked up the glass in his right hand with no fumbling and tasted it.

"Satisfactory?" I asked him.

"Just right, thank you."

"What have you decided about my proposition, Felix?"

I put it that way deliberately, wanting to see if he'd correct me by saying, *"Fred* decided..." But he accepted my wording.

"We decided to pass," he said after taking a gulp of his drink. "I don't need to tell you it was a very tempting offer. But after considering all the angles I'm afraid it's a no-go."

"I'm disappointed," I said, although I had expected their verdict.

He swung around to face me directly. It was the first time I realized, almost with a shock, what a cadaverous face he had. "You're disappointed?" he repeated. "Not as much as we are. Mrs. Westmore is not the easiest client to handle, and those children of hers are off the wall. But we've made a commitment to her. If we dump her now, our reputation tanks. Not only would she pull her account but all her friends who are clients would yank theirs as well. We can't risk that. We've worked too hard to build our rep as an outfit to be trusted."

"Uh-huh," I said, bored because he was just parroting the mendacious excuses Clemens had already used. I drained my drink. "Let's have another," I suggested.

"I'm fine, thank you."

"Just one more," I urged.

"All right," he said. "One more. Then I've got to split." He finished his highball.

Mr. Pettibone took our empty glasses and placed them in the stainless-steel sink under the bar. He brought us refills in fresh glasses, and Felix and I began sipping again.

"Look," I said, "I can understand how you and Fred feel. It makes sense. But what if Mrs. Westmore pulls out of the deal voluntarily, on her own. If that happens do I get first chance at buying the Fabergé egg?"

He looked at me directly again, not blinking. "Absolutely," he said. "You have my personal guarantee."

"Glad to hear it," I said. "Makes me feel a little better. I'd really like to get in on it."

"Don't blame you; it's a sweetheart deal. If Fred and I had the liquidity we'd swing it ourselves. But right now we're tied up in other things."

"How long have you and Fred worked together?" I asked, hoping it sounded like a casual inquiry.

"Years," he said. "We met in Denver a long time ago. It was at a convention of security dealers and we hit it off right away. We decided to have our own company someday, catering to a limited number of clients looking for unusual and profitable investment opportunities. It took us a while to get rolling. Long hours and lots of black coffee and Tylenol."

"But you're successful now?"

"We're doing okay but not as well as we could. We've been discussing opening branches in other cities."

"I'm impressed," I said. "Keep growing and one of these days you might be going public."

"Could be," he said. He finished his drink in three deep swallows and stood up. "I have to get back to the office. Glad I had a chance to talk to you and I thank you very much for the drinks."

"I'll walk you to your car," I offered.

I thought he might object but he didn't. We went out to the parking area, where the maroon Bentley was pulled in alongside my convertible. I wondered how Fred Clemens would get to his critical business meeting in Boca—walk?

"Great car," I said to Felix.

"Thank you," he said. "I would have preferred something with a little more zing but Fred feels this projects a better image."

"He's more conservative than you?" I suggested.

"You might say that," he agreed, totally deadpan.

We shook hands; he slid into the Bentley, and pulled away. I stood there until I was certain he was well gone. Then I went back inside. Mr. Pettibone had Felix's two empty highball glasses ready for me, loosely swathed in paper napkins.

"Beautiful," I said. "Thank you for a professional job."

"You may find my prints down near the base," he said. "But the others are his. I lifted the empty glasses by spreading my fingers inside."

"I think it's going to work, Mr. Pettibone."

"Let me know what happens," he said, then added, "I don't much like his looks. He's got the kind of face you see on a post office wall."

"I know what you mean," I said. "And you're right."

"Has he ever done time?"

"I have no idea. Why do you ask?"

"He talks without moving his lips. Didn't you notice?"

"No," I confessed, "I didn't."

I went to the public phone at the rear of the bar area and called Sgt. Al Rogoff at headquarters.

"I have the fingerprints of Felix Katz," I reported.

"Yeah?" he said. "How did you finagle that?"

I told him and he laughed.

"What a sly lad you are," he said. "Well, it just might work. Bring in the glasses and we shall see what we shall see."

"Brilliant," I said. "And have you heard the one about what you don't know won't hurt you?"

"Go to hell," he said cheerfully, and hung up.

I handled the glasses with TLC and delivered them to Rogoff about half an hour later. While I was in his office I dictated a statement detailing my discovery of the body of Sydney Smythe. It was recorded and the sergeant told me to stop by in a day or two and sign the transcript.

"Let me know what happens with the fingerprints, Al."

"Sure," he said. "If we can lift anything usable I'll start a trace right away. But don't expect overnight results; it's going to take time. Meanwhile see if you can pull the same trick with Clemens. By the way, to save me time give me their address and telephone number."

He wrote the information in his pocket notebook, so stuffed with scraps of paper it had to be closed with a thick rubber band.

"How about a telephone tap?" I suggested.

"On Clemens Investments."

He shook his head. "No can do. Not yet. We just don't have enough to take to a judge. Listen, old buddy, don't forget what I told you about watching your back."

I nodded and left headquarters. Rogoff's final admonition spurred some unpleasant thoughts.

I had assumed—quite logically I believed—Clemens and Katz had rejected my proposal to take over the Fabergé egg deal because my stipulations would destroy their con. They didn't want a prospective victim flying to Paris to examine the merchandise and having it appraised by an independent expert. And they certainly didn't want the pigeon paying the seller directly. By setting those conditions I had included myself out. They wanted a more credulous mark.

It was an understandable reason for refusing to accept my proposition. Another reason—just as valid I had to admit—was they were aware of or suspected my investigation into their activities—and particularly the Fabergé egg investment. In which case they sought to limit my knowledge of their proposed swindle and so put the kibosh on my cute attempt to bribe my way into participation.

And if they were cognizant of my inquiry perhaps their realization of the danger I represented drove them to employ Droopy to end my snooping. If that was true it was reasonable to assume their desire to get rid of me didn't end with Droopy's failure. They would try again.

Sgt. Rogoff was correct; I must watch my back.

It didn't mean I had to hide in a closet of course. Late in the afternoon I did something I had skipped for days and days: I went swimming in the ocean. During the warm-weather months I try to swim two miles three or four times a week. But Christmas was just around the corner and a winter dunk in a chill and choppy sea isn't quite as tempting.

But I tried it that afternoon and the water was cold, no doubt of it, but endurable. I did perhaps one mile, wallowing parallel to the shore, and when I emerged my choppers weren't clacking but I wasted no time getting back to the house and under a hot shower.

During the family cocktail hour something occurred which was to have a significant effect on my Discreet Inquiry. We were enjoying our martinis when mother asked an innocent question.

"Archy," she said, "have you learned anything more about the Fabergé egg Edythe Westmore wants to buy?"

"Very little," I said. "My investigation is progressing—but slowly."

"I'm curious about what the egg is actually worth. Edythe said it was going to be appraised by an expert."

"So I understand," I said, and then realized this was a detail I had neglected. "Mother, how would you like to play detective?"

"Oh, I'd love to. Do I get to carry a big magnifying glass and wear one of those funny caps with earflaps?"

"A deerstalker." I said. "No, you don't have to dress up. Just phone Edythe Westmore and ask her the name of the expert who's going to appraise her Fabergé egg."

"Won't she think it a rather strange request?"

"Possibly, but you might explain you have some heirloom jewelry you'd like appraised and need the name of a good man. I'd phone Edythe myself but I'm afraid she might mention my call to her investment adviser and I'd prefer to avoid that."

"All right, Archy, I'll phone her tomorrow."

Father had been listening to our conversation with increasing interest and now he spoke up: "Why don't you give Edythe a call right now, mother."

(My septuagenarian father frequently addresses his sexagenarian spouse as "mother" and she never objects. But when she addresses him as "father" he bridles. Go figure it.)

Anyway, mother made the call immediately, using the phone on her sitting room desk. Father and I, finishing our drinks, could not hear her part of the conversation. But after she hung up she came back to us looking perplexed.

"Isn't that odd?" she asked no one in particular.

"What's odd?" the lord of the manor demanded impatiently.

"Well, Edythe said Fred Clemens, her financial adviser, is looking for a new appraiser to value the Fabergé egg. The original expert he had hired was Sydney Smythe, the antique dealer on Worth Avenue who was killed in his shop a few days ago."

Father and I stared at each other.

CHAPTER 27

DINNER WAS A sockdolager (baked scallops with tangerine fritters) but I could hardly wait to get upstairs. I wanted to make certain my memory was still chugging along on all two cylinders.

It was. Within moments I found the journal entry I had recalled: a précis of my first conversation with Sydney Smythe. I had asked him to value the imaginary Fabergé egg I had conjured up and he declined. He stated he was not an expert but could recommend an experienced appraiser if I so desired. And this was the man reportedly employed by Fred Clemens to put a price tag on Mrs. Westmore's investment!

Of course it was possible Smythe, desperate for money, had conned Clemens into thinking he was dealing with the world's foremost maven on bejeweled eggs. I didn't believe that for a minute. I reckoned Clemens, Katz & Co. had sought and found the perfect man to provide legitimacy for their scam: a fogyish antique dealer, well known to locals, who was so hungry for a buck he was willing to cooperate in what he must have recognized was an arrant swindle.

I tried to put myself in Mr. Smythe's place and could understand why he was easily corrupted. Up to the time of his death he had committed no crime nor had he been asked to. He had not seen the Fabergé egg in question; he could hardly appraise it. Perhaps he had good reason to know or suspect the egg simply did not exist. If that was true then all he was doing was lending his name for a fee vital to his survival.

But if Smythe's role in the con game was so minor, why was he killed? Because he had a change of heart and threatened to report a crime-in-progress to the police? I didn't think so. I still believed the reasons for his murder I had given to Sgt. Al Rogoff were sound and convincing. But I had an unshakable suspicion there was an additional motive for Smythe's slaying. What it might be was a puzzle frustrating enough to drive a man to drink. And so it did.

I had only one brandy, I swear, but it helped me sleep after I gave up trying to guess the whys and wherefores of an old man's quietus. I resolutely turned my thoughts to a fond remembrance of Rita Hayworth in *Gilda,* singing "Put the Blame on Mame." Ahh!

I awoke Saturday to a socked-in world. Radio forecasters had predicted the weekend would be miserable—and so it was. There was no rain but the air seemed supersaturated; a clammy fog hung low and I hoped Santa Claus had a workable windshield wiper on his sleigh.

Usually I like to adopt the role of a Palm Beach drone on weekends. I might play a little golf or tennis, go out to Wellington to watch polo, visit the Pelican Club to toss darts, perhaps join a poker session with like-minded parasites. In other words, for two days we try to make ourselves useless.

The doomy weather made outdoor games a chore rather than a joy, and I found myself in such a restive mood I decided I might as well do some work. I doubted if Clemens and Katz were lazing about. They were probably busy concocting new cons and if I expected to thwart their plans I had to be just as active and wilier.

I dug from my wallet the newspaper clipping recounting the murder of Sydney Smythe, took note of the name and address of the motel where he had resided, and started out. I wore a nylon golf jacket and a yellow oilskin cap—not exactly swank attire but it kept me reasonably dry.

It took me almost an hour to locate Smythe's motel. It was way to hell and gone, west of the Turnpike and right in the middle of nowhere. I figured there was no way a motel could exist in that wilderness unless it was a hot-pillow joint, although it was difficult to believe any amorous couple would journey so far to slake their passion.

The place itself had a sad, eroded look and

I wondered if the mattresses were stuffed with cornhusks. There was only one car in the parking area: an ancient Chevy originally blue but now faded to a streaky purple by the Florida sun. I walked slowly around the one-story building looking for a sign of life and found it, sort of, on the west side where an old geezer in overalls sat in a caned rocking chair moving back and forth so energetically I expected him to be catapulted out at any moment. He watched me approach with no interest whatsoever.

When I was close enough to see the grayish stubble on his chin he demanded, "You married?"

I was startled by his query and imagined he was the owner, who thought I had arrived accompanied by a complaisant female and he wanted to verify my connubial status.

"No, sir," I said. "I am not married. And I am alone."

He was the owner all right but his question turned out to be of a rhetorical nature. He really didn't care a fig about my conjugal state; he wanted to tell me about his.

"Well, *I'm* married," he declared. "I'm an S.I.S. husband. You know what it is?"

"No, sir, I do not." It was difficult to converse with him, he was rocking so rapidly.

"Suffer In Silence," he said with a ghastly grin revealing several gaps in his dentition. "It's the kind of husband I am. For more'n forty years. How would *you* like a wife who tries to take off her fingernail polish with your gin?"

"When did she do that?" I asked.

"Oh, I don't know," he said vaguely. "Five or ten years ago."

I thought it a fascinating conversation but definitely unproductive. "I understand Sydney Smythe used to live here," I said, trying to get back on track. "The antique dealer who was killed in Palm Beach."

"Read about it in the paper, huh?" he said. "Yeah, he lived here. The cops was out for a couple of days but they stopped coming. Had some sightseers but none of them rented. I was hoping the TV would show up but they never came. I figured the publicity would help."

"I understand you're selling his belongings?"

"Yeah?" he said. "Where did you hear that?"

"I met Smythe's cousin at church and she said she had taken a few personal effects but the rest of his possessions would be sold to pay his back rent."

"Yeah, that's right. As soon as I get to it I'm going to clean out his room and have a lawn sale."

I was tempted to say, "What lawn?" since the place was located in a desert, but instead I asked, "Do you mind if I take a look at his stuff. Maybe there's something I can use."

"Go ahead," he said. "If you find anything you want I'll give you a good price. Inside, down the hall, on your right, suite four."

"Thank you," I said. "I won't be long."

I opened a torn screen door, stepped inside,

and became an instant candidate for CPR. It was hardly a warm day but the inside of the motel was so stifling it must have contained the stored-up heat of summer. I looked about and saw no indication of air conditioning. And the aroma was not something you'd care to spray behind your ears.

The late Sydney Smythe's apartment was a dungeon. Terming such a cramped chamber a "suite" was akin to calling a drainage ditch the Grand Canyon. It was one small room with a kitchenette alcove and a tiny attached loo of cracked tiles. The whole conveyed such an impression of decay and despair I almost wept from the vision of the would-be dandy spending his final days in such a miasmic sty.

His pitiful belongings had obviously been pawed over, perhaps several times. They were a jumble of thready clothing, a few dented kitchen utensils, old letters and magazines, yellowed newspapers, a can of roach spray, and bits and pieces of things I simply could not identify. I saw only one book although I had hoped to find more.

I picked it gingerly from the pile of trash and examined it. It had been published in Nantes in 1826 and my French was sufficient to translate the title: "Illustrated History of the Pistol." The leather binding was split and shredding away but as I slowly turned the brittle pages I saw many fine old engravings of antique handguns.

I was happy to emerge from the fetid atmosphere and take a deep breath of fog. The old man was still rocking steadily. I held up the tattered volume I had salvaged.

"This is the only thing I want," I said.

He scarcely glanced at it. "Ten bucks," he said.

I took out my wallet and paid him without demur. He looked longer at the wallet than he had at my purchase.

"I was hoping he'd have more books," I mentioned.

"Did have when he moved in," the gaffer said. "Had a whole danged library. Filled his suite. But he must have sold most of them off. And his cousin took four of what was left."

"Perhaps he gave some of his books to his friends," I suggested, finally getting to the purpose of my visit.

"Didn't have no friends."

"No friends at all?" I said, trying to appear astonished.

"Nope. And no visitors."

"I find it hard to believe."

He shrugged. "That's what I told the cops. You can ask them."

I thought there were three possible reasons for his reticence: he didn't want to get involved; he had been paid to keep his mouth shut; he had been threatened with violence unless he kept silent. The second of these seemed to me the most likely.

"What you told the cops is one thing," I said boldly. "The truth is another."

I took two twenty-dollar bills from my wal-

let and dangled them before him. The rocking became more rapid; he couldn't take his
eyes from the fluttering bills.

"Now then," I said, "did Sydney Smythe have
any friends or visitors?"

"You trying to bribe me?" he demanded.

"Yes," I said, "that's what I'm trying to
do."

He ruminated a long moment. "It ain't
exactly a bribe," he said at last. "It's like I got
a product to sell. Merchandise, you know. Only
in this case it's information. I'm the seller;
you're the buyer."

"You're quite right," I assured him. "It's cap-
italism. A free and open market. It makes
sense to maximize your profit."

Again he pondered while I waited patiently.

"Nope," he muttered, "I ain't talking."

The devious McNally brain went into over-
drive. "You don't have to talk," I told him. "I'll
describe Smythe's visitors to you. If I'm right
you just stop rocking and you get the forty. You
don't have to say a word."

He looked at me. "Honest?"

"Honest."

"Make it fifty," he said hoarsely.

I added a sawbuck to the twenties.

"Okay," he said, "let's hear it."

"Smythe was visited on more than one
occasion by two men in a large maroon car.
They went directly to Smythe's apartment
and stayed awhile. Probably less than an
hour. The door was closed and you couldn't

253

hear what they were talking about, though you tried. Both visitors were tall. One man was dark, slender, and usually dressed in black and white. The other was heavier, fair-haired, and usually wore a vest with his suit. Had an expensive wristwatch. Both men looked prosperous."

But before I finished speaking the oldster had stopped rocking. He was staring at me, his mouth half open. I handed over the fifty, gave him a nod, a smile, a farewell hand flap. Did I trust him to be truthful? I did. I had once been told never to trust a man you can't bribe. The obverse is just as logically correct.

It was an amateurish investigative ploy, I admit, and hardly constituted proof. What I hadn't mentioned to my informant was the possibility of his being subpoenaed to testify under oath in a court of law. And I didn't think he'd find a rocking chair in the witness box. But I was satisfied I had established a firmer link between Smythe and the subjects of my inquiry. Not conclusive of course but strong enough to add credence to my theory of what had happened and was happening.

I used my cellular phone to call Sgt. Al Rogoff at headquarters. He wasn't there and they wouldn't tell me his whereabouts. I tried him at his home and caught him as he was going out to buy five pounds of sliced bologna.

"This will take just a minute, Al," I told him. "I know how important the bologna is to you. But I've changed my mind about meeting

Sydney Smythe's English cousin. I really should express my condolences—don't you agree?"

"It's your call," he said.

"Is she still in town?"

"Well, she is and she isn't. She's staying at the Dover in West Palm but she's gone up to Disney World for the weekend. Said she wants to have her photo taken with Mickey Mouse."

"Doesn't sound like she's prostrated with grief."

"She's coping. Stiff upper lip and all that."

"Is she burying Smythe here?"

"Nope. Going to have him cremated and take the ashes back to England. There's a village graveyard where most of the family's dead are buried."

"When is she returning from Orlando—did she say?"

"Thought she'd be back on Monday but wasn't sure. We're not rushing her. Smythe is in the refrigerator. He'll keep."

"I admire your delicacy of expression. If you get anything on Katz's fingerprints give me a shout."

"Sure. You got anything new for me?"

If I wanted to learn about the fingerprint trace I thought I better offer something in return.

"Yes, I have something," I told Rogoff. "Clemens and Katz had several confabs with Smythe at his motel."

Brief silence. Then: "Where the hell did you get that?"

"From the motel owner."

"He told us Smythe had no visitors."

"He was lying."

"The cretin! I'll have his gizzard!"

"Please, Al, don't lean on him. Leave him to me. Okay?"

"All right," he said grudgingly. "For now. But eventually we may need his testimony."

"You'll get it; he's not going anyplace."

"All right," Rogoff said again. "We'll play it your way for the time being."

We disconnected and I continued homeward. Was I thinking of the murder of Sydney Smythe and the apparent swindle of Mrs. Edythe Westmore? I was not. I was thinking about what I might have for lunch. First things first.

CHAPTER 28

THE REMAINDER OF the day yielded zip as far as my Discreet Inquiry was concerned and I suspected the second half of the weekend would be more of the same. But then, shortly after Sunday dinner, something occurred which almost brought my entire investigation to a whinnying whoa.

I was at my upstairs desk, browsing through my journal in hopes of finding a clue hitherto ignored, when a phone call interrupted my search. It was Walter Westmore—with attitude.

"Archy," he said—almost barked as a matter of fact, "it is very important Natalie and

I see you as soon as possible. Can you come over now?"

The weather was still as dismal as it had been on Saturday and I wasn't eager to leave the dry, warm snugness of my sanctuary. I said, "Can't it wait until tomorrow, Walter? The sun may be shining and—"

"No," he said sharply. "This matter must be settled immediately."

I didn't ask what he meant by "matter"; I assumed he was referring to the stalking of Fred Clemens. "Very well," I said, making no effort to sound cordial. "Where do you wish to meet?"

"Nettie's studio," he said, and repeated, "As soon as possible." I was getting awfully bored with that phrase. I had used it too many times myself.

So I pulled on my foul-weather gear again and went out into the late-afternoon gloom reflecting that dealing with the Westmore siblings really should qualify me for combat pay.

Walter and Natalie were waiting in her timbered hut. The big electric lantern had been switched on; the bright light it dispersed was so glaring I felt I was in a dystopian interrogation chamber. It was an impression heightened by the ensuing conversation.

"Archy," Natalie started, "have you discovered anything to prove Frederick Clemens and his icky sidekick are crooks?"

"Nothing definite, no," I said. "But I hope within a week to have—"

"We can't wait a week!" she wailed. "Don't you understand? We need action right now!"

Walter chimed in on a slightly calmer note. "At dinner this afternoon mother announced she was selling some of her Treasury bonds. She needs the cash to pay for a half-million-dollar bank check."

"Which she's going to sign over to Clemens," Natalie said wrathfully. "Probably by Wednesday or Thursday. Then it's gone. Half a million dollars! That's why we can't wait for you to complete your investigation."

"If we're going to stop mother," Walter said, "we must act at once. We appreciate all you've done but—"

"We're going to hire someone else," his sister broke in. "A professional investigator."

Was I hurt? My pride wounded? You betcha. A "professional investigator" indeed! Who did they take me for—Inspector Clouseau?

"It is certainly your prerogative to replace me," I said, squelching a maniacal desire to recommend Binky Watrous as my successor. "But what do you expect a new detective to accomplish in a day or two? It would take anyone a week or so to acquaint himself with the situation and begin preliminary inquiries."

"We need someone nasty," Natalie said savagely. "Someone rough enough to take Clemens by the throat and choke the truth out of him."

I think even her brother was taken aback by her suggestion of a violent solution to their problem. I know I was.

"I'm not sure we want to go that far," he said hesitantly. "But a confrontation with Clemens is certainly one option. There are other ways to resolve this crisis. But whatever we do must be done at once. We've tried logical arguments and moral suasion but mother just won't listen. All she can think of is the enormous profit Clemens has promised. So direct action is the only way left to bring her to her senses."

The two glanced at each other and I reckoned they had already discussed possible "direct actions." I didn't want to know what they were, for I feared they might be illegal. As a representative of McNally & Son I didn't relish being an accessory before the fact, a charge I had suggested to Binky he'd be wise to avoid.

I was now more convinced kookiness was a Westmore family trait and their current brouhaha had pushed Natalie and Walter into the realm of utter irrationality. In a way I was happy at being relieved of my duties to them. I mean it's no fun and somewhat scary working for a couple of befuddled fruitcakes.

"All I can do," I said carefully, "is to wish you good luck in whatever course of action you decide to take."

But they were both too deeply engrossed in their problem to make any response to my remark. I then departed, wondering if the next time I saw them they might be behind bars charged with assault on Frederick Clemens and Felix Katz. It was possible. In their present mood I thought them quite capable of mayhem.

I drove home, garaged the Miata, and stopped at Hobo's house to peer within. He stood up, flicked his tail, and nibbled my fingers when I reached in to pat him. Smart terrier; he wasn't about to come out into the persistent mist.

Before going upstairs I knocked on the closed door of my father's study and didn't enter until I heard his, "Come in." He was seated behind his desk smoking one of his silver-banded James Upshall pipes and doughtily reading his way through the Sunday *New York Times*.

"Yes, Archy?" he said, a mite peckish at being interrupted.

"I've been fired," I announced, and when one of his eyebrows took an interrogative lift I told him about my most recent conversation with Natalie and Walter Westmore, repeating our trialogue as accurately as I could. I finished and awaited his reaction.

"Damned idiots!" he growled, which surprised me since he rarely uses even the mildest of oaths. "Did they tell you the nature of the 'direct actions' they contemplate?"

"No, sir. And I thought it best not to ask."

"Quite right. Let's not get involved in their tricks. As Lincoln said, 'Ignorance is preferable to error.' "

"I believe it was Thomas Jefferson, father."

He glared at me.

"What are my marching orders, sir?" I

asked hurriedly. "The children have downsized me. Does that mean my Discreet Inquiry should cease?"

"Not at all," he said promptly. "Our foremost duty is to protect the interests of our client, Mrs. Edythe Westmore. The approval of your investigation by her children was welcome but not essential to your task. Continue your inquiry and try to conclude this vexing matter as—"

"I know," I said, laughing. "As soon as possible. It seems to be everyone's favorite expression these days—mine included."

He looked at me sternly. "I was about to say as rapidly as prudence and discretion permit."

"I beg your pardon, sir," I said humbly, and made a chastened withdrawal.

Connie Garcia phoned from Miami on Sunday evening and our hour-long chat was a pleasant buck-up after my travails with the Westmores. Connie said the sun had been shining gloriously on Miami and I asked her to send the benediction our way.

"Have you been behaving yourself?" she demanded.

"I have indeed," I said with no prevarication. "I am hoarding all my pent-up passions to await your return."

"See that you do. I want to receive a good report on your conduct from my spies."

"I haven't lollied a single gag," I vowed. "I miss you, Connie."

"That's nice," she said.

The next morning brought a new world. Miami was sharing its sunshine with us, birds were tweeting, the sea was plashing, and I should have felt like Hannibal heading for Rome astride a pachyderm. But I didn't.

My ego had suffered such a grievous injury from my being canned by the Westmore kiddies I hadn't fully recognized the import of what they had told me: their mother intended to consummate the Fabergé egg deal by Wednesday or Thursday. It meant I had only two or three days to prevent her from being bamboozled. At the moment I had absolutely no conception of how I might accomplish it. I began to feel a grudging sympathy for Natalie and Walter's decision to take direct action to defeat Señor Clemens. But what action?

And so instead of enjoying a bloomy morn I suffered a junior anxiety attack and urged myself to *do* something, anything, no matter how outlandish or likely to prove resultless. My first act was to phone Sgt. Al Rogoff, not caring if he had a hissy because of my importunity. Surprisingly I found him in a chipper mood and the reason for it soon became apparent.

"Did you receive any skinny on Katz's fingerprints?" I asked.

"Oh yeah," he said happily. "A preliminary fax with more detailed info to follow. His real name is Luther Bradbury and he's got a rap sheet longer than a roll of toilet paper. He's originally from Dallas and started out touring as a pool hall hustler. Then he graduated to running crooked crap games. It's how he lost a finger; two Chicago bentnoses caught him using loaded dice and chopped it off."

"Nice," I said. "Has he done time?"

"Three stretches, none more than eighteen months. What's interesting is how the crimes he's been charged with have become more violent: felonious assault, attempted rape, robbery—strong-arm stuff like that. He's been lucky to get off with probation or short sentences."

"Married?"

"Four times and dumped by the wife every time. He's a sweetheart, huh?"

"Any mention of a connection with Frederick Clemens?"

"Nothing yet but I've got urgent queries out to Dallas, Detroit, L.A., Frisco, Denver, Boston, and New York. This guy is a traveling nogoodnik; he must have a lot of frequent-flier miles."

"Al, do you mind if I check with you later today?"

"Be my guest. I've put a twenty-four-hour watch on Katz and maybe I'll have more goodies to pass along."

He hung up, leaving me at once pleased and puzzled. I was glad to hear my suspicions about Katz had been confirmed. But I couldn't understand Rogoff's motive in establishing round-the-clock surveillance. Katz had committed no crimes in our area of which I was aware but the sergeant seemed intent on keeping him under observation. Perhaps, I thought, Al knew something he hadn't told me and wouldn't until his caution proved productive.

The phone call to headquarters had been made from home while I was still in PJ's. I shucked them and went through the usual morning drill of showering and shaving. Then I dressed, including a lilac sport jacket of wool crepe with sand-colored slacks. The headgear I selected was a tweed cap in a cheerful glen plaid. McNally's Rule: When facing a desperate situation dress with dash.

I was too tardy to breakfast with my parents but Ursi poached a couple of eggs and slid them onto buttered w.w. toast. She also blessed me with two cups of her special coffee laced with chicory. That'll get your corpuscles moshing.

I arrived at my office in time to field a phone call from Mrs. Lenore Crittenden.

"Archy," she said, "I finally received a possibly significant response to inquiries on the man you asked me to check out. It came from an agency in Denver specializing in nabbing crooks who manipulate penny stocks. They have no Frederick Clemens in their files but about five years ago the law clamped down on a guy peddling shares in a blind corporation with zilch in assets. He was fined and made restitution, thus avoiding a forced vacation in the jug. His name was Frank Clement. Close enough?"

"I'd say so," I told her. "You know when a white-collar rogue changes his name he usually selects an alias with the same initials so he doesn't have to discard his monogrammed shirts, cuff links, and attaché case. I'm betting Frederick Clemens and Frank Clement are one and the same. Thanks for your help, Lennie."

I hung up happy with the info and wondering how many other F.C. names the knave had used in his larcenous career.

Still driven by a compulsion to act, I looked up the number of the Hotel Dover in West Palm. It was, you'll recall, the temporary residence of Penelope Blakely-Jones, the English cousin of Sydney Smythe. I begged fate to sanction the lady's return from Disney World and fate gave me a pat on the head—sort of. She was not present but was expected to return from Orlando soon after noon.

I calmed down by spending the remainder of the morning addressing and signing a stack of Christmas cards I should have mailed a week ago. There were more than fifty and I wondered how barbarous it would be to run them through the company's meter rather than purchase stamps. I finally decided a metered Xmas card was simply too gauche.

I went out for a quick lunch, bought self-adhesive stamps, mailed my cards, and treated myself to a vodka gimlet as a reward for donkeywork completed. I then returned to my office, phoned the Dover again, and this time fate definitely cuddled me. Smythe's next of kin was present and came on the line.

"Ma'am," I said, "my name is Archibald McNally and I was acquainted with your late cousin. I'd like to express my condolences."

"Thank you," she said. Strong voice. "It was nice of you to call."

"I was hoping I might have the opportunity of meeting you personally before you return to England. Perhaps we could have a drink together."

"Well, I'm quite busy, Mr. McNally—so much to do. I really shouldn't have gone up to Disney World but my youngest daughter—she's only seven—insisted I bring her a snap of me with Mickey Mouse."

"And did you get it?"

"I did indeed. A lovely color Polaroid. Tell me, how did you know I'm at the Dover?"

"A friend of mine, a local bobby, told me."

"Bobby? Are you a Brit, Mr. McNally?"

"No, ma'am, I am not. But I am an Anglophile and occasionally use Briticisms. It's an affectation and I hope you forgive me."

"Nothing to forgive," she said stoutly. "And who is your favorite English actor?"

I think she expected me to name Olivier, Richardson, or Gielgud. I said, "Benny Hill," and she laughed.

"I think I would enjoy having a drink with you," she said. "Could we meet at the Dover bar at, say, three o'clock—or is that too soon?"

"Three is fine," I assured her. "You'll easily identify me. I'm wearing a lilac jacket."

"Oh my," she said.

CHAPTER 29

I HAD ABOUT an hour to spend and didn't want to waste it counting the walls so I phoned Rogoff again and asked if he had received any recent information about Felix Katz né Luther Bradbury.

"Sure have," he said, sounding exultant, "and it gets dirtier and dirtier. A detective in Detroit saw my fax and gave me a call. He's still teed off because Katz beat a manslaughter rap. The cop who called handled the case and he says Katz was as guilty as Lee Harvey Oswald. Apparently our boy was acting as muscle for a con man. One of the shark's victims threatened to take him to court and Felix dissuaded him with brass knucks. On the street in broad daylight yet! The poor dupe was knocked down, hit his head on the curb and died. A dumb jury decided it was all a sad accident. Can you believe it? The detective who called is still steaming after three years. He says Katz is a mean and dangerous punk."

"Did he happen to mention the name of the con man Felix was working for?"

"He told me. I have it in my notes. Wait a minute.... Yeah. Here it is. The swindler's name was Floyd Clifford."

"Banzai!" I shouted. "Another F.C.!"

I repeated to Rogoff what Mrs. Crittenden had told me about Frank Clement, and he agreed the chances were good Clemens, Clement, and Clifford were the same scurvy character. He promised to try an alias trace on all three names and determine if there were other instances of Clemens and Katz working together.

"By the way," he said, "a few minutes ago I heard from the guy tailing Katz. You know where the shtarker is now?"

"Where?"

"Shacked up in a no-tell motel with a zaftig bimbo. They arrived in a lavender Riviera. Got any idea who she might be? Hello?... Archy?... You on the line?"

"Still here," I said, "but I've been busy kicking myself. Mrs. Helen Westmore drives a lavender Riviera and I could have sworn she was playing games with Clemens. Why on earth is she consorting with a public enemy like Felix?"

"Maybe the danger turns her on," Rogoff said sagely. "It happens sometimes. Keep in touch."

I wondered if Walter was aware of his wife's extramarital frolics and thought it likely Natalie had told him of her suspicions. I began to see sister and brother as a cabal of two united against Edythe and Helen. Just your average clean-cut American family—but not quite The Brady Bunch.

At the moment I was more concerned with meeting Penelope Blakely-Jones at the Hotel

Dover. I resolved not to tell her I was the one who discovered her cousin's body. Nor would I mention his final phone call to me. I felt both revelations might evoke questions and what I needed were answers. By the time I started out I had devised a bare-bones scenario I hoped would inveigle Ms. B.-J. into telling me what I wanted.

I had been to the Dover a few times in the past. It is a pleasant hostelry, slightly shabby but boasting a friendly staff and moderate rates for its less than posh rooms and suites.

The lounge was sparsely peopled when I entered a few minutes after three. I removed my cap and looked about. A woman seated alone at a corner table raised her hand and I walked toward her wondering why my initial impression was "motherly type" when she was not, I judged, more than forty. Well, perhaps forty-five, but with an air of alertness and a marvelous complexion.

"Ma'am," I said, "I am Archibald McNally."

"Had to be," she said, laughing. "Surely there can't be two men in America with the swagger to wear a jacket in that shade. And yes, I am Mrs. Penelope Blakely-Jones, but it's such a mouthful I think it would be simpler if you called me Penny. I'd prefer it to 'ma'am.' "

"That makes me Archy," I said, delighted with her informality. "Penny, I see your glass is almost empty. Before I sit down please let me fetch you a refill. What are you drinking?"

"Gin and tonic, thank you." she said. "And do ask the barkeep to lighten up on the ice. A cube or two is quite enough."

I returned from the bar with two gin and tonics, both prepared in the manner she had requested. I sampled mine and found it too warm.

I sat opposite and as she sipped I had an opportunity to observe her more closely. If she was indeed forty or forty-five the years had treated her gently. She had sparkly eyes, thick well-brushed hair, smile lines at the corners of a wide mouth. I found her lack of starchiness a comfort and guessed she was a physically passionate woman. She was wearing a lightweight tweed suit with a white jabot and had an old cameo pinned to her lapel. No frippery or flash; more style than fashion.

"Penny," I said, "I want first to thank you for seeing me on such short notice. I must also confess I find it difficult to think of you and the late Sydney Smythe as cousins. I mean the disparity in your ages. He seemed so ancient."

"It is odd, isn't it. But it's the way it worked out in our rather large family. You know I only saw Syd three or four times in my life. When I first met him I was just a tyke and he seemed fearfully old to me even then. I thought this old man cannot possibly be my cousin; he must be an uncle at least or someone's grandfather."

"I can't claim to have been a close friend—I don't believe he had any—but I bought several things—mostly antique jewelry—in his shop and stopped by occasionally just to chat. I found him good company: friendly, witty, and obviously well educated."

"Yes, he was all that. I can't tell you how shocked and depressed I was when I saw his shop and the horrid hovel where he lived. We exchanged letters three or four times a year and he never once wrote how badly things were going for him."

"Didn't ask for financial assistance?"

"Never! His letters were always cheerful, with funny stories about some of his customers. He remembered my children's birthdays and always sent them little gifts: unusual things from his stock which delighted them."

"Like you I was surprised to learn of his poverty. I had just assumed he was doing well. Not amassing a fortune, you understand, but getting along. After all, he was on Worth Avenue you know."

"What a horrible crime," she said, and shuddered. "Why would anyone kill an old man like Syd? The police seem to have no leads."

"They're very competent," I told her. "I'm sure sooner or later they'll find who did it. Penny, your cousin never spoke of his past, what he did before he came to America, and how he ended up with an antique shop in Palm Beach. I'd be grateful for anything you can tell me about him."

She took a deep swallow of her drink and then stared over my head for a long silent moment.

"I can't see where it would do any harm,"

she said finally. "But I must tell you, most of what I know about Syd was told to me by my mum because I wasn't even born when much of it happened."

"He had an eventful life?" I suggested, eager to keep her talking.

"Two lives actually. He was, as you said, well educated. He wanted to be an art historian and after he took his degree at Balliol began to write monographs on Celtic art which were very well received. But of course one can't become wealthy doing that kind of work. Syd had inherited a small sum and that enabled him to get by. He married a young woman who worked as a typist and her income helped. About a year after their marriage she had a son who died in childbirth. Apparently it devastated them. I can understand that; it happened to me too."

She drained her glass and, without asking, I went to the bar to get us refills. This time I asked for more ice in mine. When I returned to the table she said, "Thank you. I better stop with this one or I'll get tiddly." Her smile was enchanting.

"About Sydney..." I prompted.

"Oh yes," she said, and took up her story again. "Well, then the war came along and Syd signed up. And you know, he became a hero, he really did—that slight, mild darling. He fought in Africa, Italy, and France. Wounded three times. Won a chestful of medals. Mum kept all the newspaper stories about him. After the war was over he came home to more honors. But his wife had been killed in one of the air raids."

"Good lord," I said, "he had his share of sorrows."

"He did," she said, nodding. "And they changed him. The deaths of his son and wife and what he had endured in battle, all made him a different man. He never wrote another monograph but he opened an antique shop on Bond Street and it was an immediate success. Mum says he became obsessed with making money."

"Why do you suppose that was?" I asked her.

"Oh Archy, no one acts from a single motive. It only happens in Russian novels. But I think he had lost his faith in religion, his country, the future. The only thing real for him was money and the power it bought. I'm sure there were other reasons as well but he did become money-hungry, almost pathologically so. And he did make a lot. He had marvelous taste, you know, and his shop became the *in* place to find lovely things, rare things: jewelry, furniture, art, and even antiquities. Syd became so wealthy he was able to buy a town house in Mayfair. He was simply swimming in filthy lucre, buying big cars and small cars, bespoke clothing without end, even a yacht, champagne dinners and all that. The lush life. And he was very generous to family members I must say. But then he was arrested."

I was about to take a sip of my drink but set the glass down. "Arrested?" I said, astonished. "What on earth for?"

273

"I was old enough by then to read newspapers and watch the telly, so I learned firsthand of what happened. He was arrested for being a fence. The police said many of those beautiful things he sold had been stolen. Apparently Syd had been buying thieves' loot for pence and selling it for pounds. Hundreds of pounds."

"Incredible."

"But that wasn't the worst of it. He was also accused of blackmail. In the privacy of the shop's back room he would tell a potential customer the art object or antique wanted had been purloined and would have to be kept in the privacy of his home, shown only to trustworthy friends, and never loaned for exhibition. You'd be surprised at how many people accepted those conditions and bought stolen items. Several buyers were well-known, reputable men and women in government, law, banking, and so forth."

"Where does the blackmail come in?"

"While Syd was telling them the truth about what was for sale he was secretly recording the conversation on tape. Then if they bought— and most of them did—he had evidence of their complicity and blackmailed them later. The majority paid up. They were famous, you see, and wanted to avoid a scandal at all costs. But one, a theatrical producer, was outraged by the attempted extortion and went to the police. They investigated and Syd was finished."

Then I took a deep swallow of my drink. "Astonishing," I said. "Did he do time?"

"No, but he was wiped out. Forced to make restitution and pay horrendous fines. I think the only reason he wasn't imprisoned was because of his war record. He had been a genuine hero, you know, and that counted for something. So he wasn't jailed but I suspect the authorities told him they'd be happy if he chose to emigrate—which he did."

"And ended up dead in Palm Beach," I said. "What a story! And what a picaresque life he had."

"Yes," Penny agreed. "And the amazing thing was to all appearances he was a meek little man, giving the impression of being weak-willed. But he was far from that. Well, I think I've talked quite enough for one afternoon. You must think me a frightful chatterbox."

"Most certainly not," I said. "I am fascinated by what you've told me and I thank you for it."

"I think my drink is gone and so must I be," she said. "I hope to leave in a few days, and still have to make final arrangements for Syd's cremation. It's been so nice meeting you, Archy."

My opportunity was slipping away and almost desperately I grabbed for it. I ignored her farewell remark and said, "You know, Mr. Smythe occasionally mentioned art books he owned, and on Saturday I drove out to his motel hoping to find and buy anything he had on antique jewelry, which is of particular interest to me. But all I found was an old history of pistols."

"I know," she said sadly. "Apparently he was

forced to sell off most of his library just to subsist. I took four books only because they're illustrated and I thought my daughter might like
to clip some of the pictures to make an album
on antiques. She already has albums on cars,
castles, and rock stars."

"Really?" I said, trying not to seem too
eager. "What are the subjects of the books you
have?"

"Two on furniture: Victorian and
Hepplewhite. One on Greek coins. And yes, the
fourth is on jewelry. I leafed through it. Royal
crowns, gold from Tut's tomb, and similar
things. Is that what you were looking for?"

"It may be," I said. "Would it be pre-
sumptuous to ask if I might take a look at it?"

"I'll do better than that," Penny said. "You
may have the book—a small gift for your having been such an attentive listener."

"Oh no," I protested. "It's very kind of
you but I couldn't possibly accept it. After all,
it's one of your few remembrances of your
cousin. But if you would be willing to lend the
book to me for a short time I promise to
return it to you in person if you are still here
or by airmail to your home in England."

"A good idea," she said. "I'll just pop up to
my room and bring it down. Thank you again
for the drinks, Archy."

"I'll wait for you in the lobby."

Fifteen minutes later, having bid Penelope
Blakely-Jones good-bye, I was driving homeward
with an oversized art book on the seat beside
me. The thick volume was *Fantastic Jewelry*

of Royalty. The title dismayed me until I recalled Fabergé Imperial eggs had been made for the Romanovs. And my scheming to obtain the book had not been entirely a blue-sky venture. I'm sure you remember Smythe offering to check out my imaginary "surprise" in his library.

When I arrived home I was in such a hurry to get upstairs I didn't even pause to tip my cap to Hobo. Nor did I bother removing cap or lilac jacket when I sat at my desk and slipped on my reading specs to examine my treasure. I softly sang, "Luck, be a lady tonight..." as I turned first to the index. I was disappointed to find only two pages devoted to Fabergé eggs, but even a little something is better than a big nothing. I flipped hurriedly to the designated pages—and there it was!

I saw a full-page color photo exactly like the one Natalie Westmore had shown me, exactly like the one she had filched from her mother's desk, exactly like the one given to Edythe by Frederick Clemens, who claimed it was the Fabergé Imperial egg in Paris awaiting her purchase.

The brief inscription on the facing page stated the jeweled ovoid pictured was called the Coronation Egg and was a masterpiece of the Forbes Magazine Collection.

Game, set, and match!

CHAPTER 30

I READ THE copy hastily and learned the Coronation Egg had been given to Alexandra by Czar Nicholas II in 1897. But that became of peripheral interest when I closely examined the color photo of the egg itself. I discovered the page on which it was printed had been oh so carefully cut from the book, probably with a single-edge razor blade, and then just as carefully reinserted into the book and reattached with a narrow strip of transparent Scotch tape.

It was as obvious to me as I trust it is to you what had happened. The page bearing the image of the Coronation Egg had been neatly sliced from the book and a color copy made at a photo shop. The original had been taped back into the book. The exact reproduction had been given to Mrs. Edythe Westmore as "proof" the egg she was being gulled into buying actually existed. It was an elegant con, breathtaking in its simplicity, as effective and convincing as a goldbrick (an ingot of lead covered with gold leaf).

I phoned Sgt. Al Rogoff immediately to tell him what I had found but was informed he was busy and couldn't come to the phone. I left a message asking him to call me back when he had a free moment. Then I took off cap and jacket and donned suitable duds for the family cocktail hour and dinner. My father is offended by my more daring sartorial selections. But what do you expect from a man who wears garters?

I refrained from phoning Rogoff again that evening, not wanting to be thought a nudge— or as they say in New York, a noodge. I worked steadily on my journal and eventually Al called a little after nine o'clock. He sounded weary.

"What a day," he said. "I haven't stopped for twelve hours. I'm ready for the sack."

"Can you stop by before you go home?" I asked. "I want to hear the latest and I have something to show you."

"Can't it wait?" he pleaded. "I'm wiped out."

"I hate to use the old chestnut 'Time is of the essence,' " I said, "but time is of the essence. Al, the swindle has to be stopped before Wednesday or Mrs. Westmore is out half a mil and Clemens and Katz disappear back in the woodwork."

"All right," he said, sighing heavily, "I'll stop by for a few minutes. Do I have to bring my own beer?"

"I don't think it'll be necessary," I told him. "There's a six-pack of Coors Light in the fridge."

"A good start," he said. "See you soon."

By the time his pickup skidded to a stop on our graveled turnaround I was in the kitchen with beer and glasses ready. I had also brought down the art book borrowed from Penelope Blakely-Jones.

Rogoff clumped in, removed his gun belt, and collapsed onto a chair at the enameled kitchen table. He looked drained.

"Hungry?" I asked him.

"Nah. I had a couple of chili burgers about an hour ago. Maybe that's why I'm so thirsty."

We poured glasses of cold beer and he went to work on his at once.

"Anything new on Clemens and Katz?" I asked him.

He nodded. "A lot. They're not full-time partners but they've teamed up on several capers in the past. Clemens is always the front man, a smoothy who deals directly with the marks. Katz provides muscle if it's needed and acts as collector. Now listen to this one; it's a doozy. Last year, before they came to Florida, they're in L.A. and they buy a dinky two-by-nothing store selling cameras, radios, TVs, and stuff like that. I didn't get the name of the place. Call it XYZ Electronics. The store is just a front for Clemens and Katz, so all their out-of-pocket is the down payment. The reason they want this joint is because it's been okayed by credit card companies and can accept all kinds of plastic."

He paused to open a second beer and loosen the waistband of his trousers. Al is getting quite a paunch; every time I see him I vow to start a diet—soon.

"All right," he continued, "so now our

villains own a store which can accept credit cards. You know a lot of guys in L.A.—and elsewhere of course—go to bordellos or patronize call girls. And many of the johns use plastic to pay because they don't want to carry cash. The madams and the call girls—even streetwalkers—will take a credit card rather than lose a sale. The crunch comes when the stud's credit card bill arrives. He doesn't want it to show he paid X dollars to the Whoopie Club or to some unidentified woman, in case his wife or boss sees the bill and asks questions."

"I'm beginning to get it," I said.

"Sure," Rogoff said. "Clemens and Katz went to all the madams and call girls and said look, do all your credit card billing through XYZ Electronics. And if you haven't got a credit card machine we'll get you one. We'll take ten percent off the top and return to you ninety percent of the cash received from the credit card companies. We'll keep records you can inspect anytime you want to be sure we're playing straight. And you can raise your rates to cover the surcharge. The johns won't object because their bills will show they made a purchase at XYZ Electronics."

"And it worked?"

"Like a charm. They must have signed up every bawd in L.A. These two guys hit it big. You could write a book about them."

"I intend to," I said. "What ended their bonanza?"

"The IRS. They did an audit, checked the

credit card receipts of XYZ Electronics, and levied a big tax plus interest and penalties. So Clemens and Katz, who were using phony names for the scam, skedaddled and came to Florida."

"Beautiful," I said. "But I've got a story that almost matches it. Listen to this...."

And I gave him a condensed account of what Mrs. Blakely-Jones had told me of the past history of Sydney Smythe, war hero and blackmailer. When I finished, Sgt. Rogoff shook his head in wonderment. "As you like to say, Archy, one never knows, do one?"

"You know what I'm thinking, Al?"

"Sure," he said. "I'm thinking the same thing. If Smythe was a blackmailer in England he might have tried the same stunt over here by putting the screws on Clemens and Katz. More money in return for his silence."

"Right. Which would give them another reason for putting him down. He just didn't realize how vicious they are."

"Well, I don't like to hear the murder victim was a wrongo but it doesn't change my job."

"Here's something else you should know," I said. I told him about borrowing the art book from Penny. I showed him how the page with the color photo of the Coronation Egg had been carefully excised. I explained I thought it had been copied and the reproduction given to Edythe Westmore to convince her the egg she was being urged to purchase actually existed and was a glorious objet d'art.

"I think you're right on," Al said. "It's just

the way Clemens and Katz would work. Those pirates know every crooked trick there is. And if they can't use an old one they come up with a new one."

"Well, I'm going to take the book to Mrs. Westmore tomorrow and show her the egg she plans to buy is really part of the Forbes Magazine Collection. That'll be the end of Clemens's scam."

"No," Sgt. Rogoff said sharply. "Don't do that. Don't blow the whistle. Not yet."

"Why not?" I said indignantly.

"Look, buster, you and I have been working two different cases, haven't we? You're trying to prevent a swindle and I'm trying to clear a homicide. Am I right?"

I nodded.

"The swindle isn't my business because no crime has been committed yet. If Mrs. Westmore had paid Clemens the half-million, then we could rack him up on fraud charges. But not at this moment. So it really isn't my worry. But it doesn't mean I can't help you. I have helped, haven't I?"

"You have indeed, Al. A great deal."

"Ever wonder why I was acting like a true-blue chum and putting in long hours to make your Discreet Inquiry easier?"

I looked at him narrowly. "The thought had occurred to me you knew something you weren't telling me. When I was at your place—the first time I told you about Clemens and Katz—you switched gears on me suddenly. One minute you weren't particularly interested and the next minute you seemed totally involved and eager to cooperate. I couldn't figure why you changed so abruptly."

He laughed. "I should have known you'd notice. I flipped when you said Felix Katz is missing the forefinger of his right hand."

"What's that got to do with it?"

"Remember I told you we took prints off the handle of the bayonet shoved into Sydney Smythe. It was determined they were made by someone wearing pigskin gloves. The odd thing was we got good prints of the thumb and three fingers. But no print of the index finger. There was a gap where that finger should have left a print when the bayonet handle was gripped."

I stared at him. "Katz," I said.

"Still not proved," Rogoff said. "But it's the best lead we've got. Sure, I've been helping you on the attempted swindle because I'm trying to learn more about Katz, hoping to find something, anything that'll help pin him."

"I follow all that, Al, and it makes sense. But I still don't understand why I can't take this book to Mrs. Westmore and prove to her Clemens is a phony."

"Because once you do that she'll contact Clemens, tell him what she's learned, and he'll vamoose. Along with Katz. Archy, I think Fred is the weak sister of the Clemens-Katz combo. I'm guessing if push comes to shove he'll rat to save his skin. It's my only chance of nailing Katz for the killing. But to persuade Clemens to squeal I need to have him around. If he takes off I'm finished."

I was silent. I could appreciate his problem but I had my own. If I didn't halt the Fabergé egg con within the next two days Mrs. Westmore would be fleeced—and I could imagine my father's reaction. I explained this to Rogoff and he agreed neither of us had much time.

"Just give me another day," he urged. "I still have a few cards up my sleeve and maybe they'll prove to be aces. Meanwhile I'd like to take this book along for a day or so. Okay?"

I wasn't happy about it but I owed him. "Will the book help put Katz away?"

"It may," he said.

"Then take it," I said. "But if you don't return it to me you get fifty lashes with a wet noodle."

A sad attempt at humor, I admit, but Al knew what I meant. After he left, taking my evidence with him, I cleaned the kitchen and then trudged up to my quarters.

I found myself in a forlorn mood with no intention of working on my journal and no desire to listen to jazz, inhale a brandy, or puff a coffin nail. I tried to determine the cause of my desolation and finally decided it sprang from my repeating to Rogoff the life story of Sydney Smythe as related by Mrs. Blakely-Jones.

Since discovering the corpse of the antique dealer I had thought of him only as a murder victim, a thing rather than a dead human being. But Penny had brought him to life, making me share all the triumphs and tragedies of a man who actually existed, who had virtues and vices, exhibited uncommon valor and moral frailty.

I went to bed that night wondering if my own life would prove to be as strange and unpredictable as his.

Sleep was an antidote for my dejection and I awoke Tuesday morning with energy restored, resolve strengthened, and the firm belief I could, if called upon, discover who really took a hatchet to Mr. and Mrs. Andrew J. Borden. But then I went down to breakfast and couldn't decide whether I wanted honey or orange marmalade on my toasted muffin.

I had a few odds and ends of Christmas shopping to finish and didn't get to my office until eleven o'clock. I found two messages stating Sgt. Al Rogoff had phoned and wanted me to call him ASAP.

"Where you been?" he demanded. "I tried you at both your home and office."

"Christmas shopping," I explained. "I'm giving you a salami as big as the Ritz."

"I can use it," he said. "Listen, I'm going over to Clemens's place. Want to be in on the action?"

I was surprised. "Have you decided to arrest him, Al?"

"Not unless I have to. But I've got a search warrant. It should be fun."

"I want to be there," I said firmly.

"Meet me outside his condo in half an

hour. Don't go inside before I get there. Understood?"

"Yes, *sir,*" I said, hung up, grabbed my hat (a pearl-gray trilby), and ran. I was first to arrive outside Clemens's building. A few moments later two police cars pulled up. Al was in the first with a driver. Two uniformed officers were in the other car. The sergeant came over to me. He was carrying the big art book I had borrowed from Penny.

"You talk to him on the intercom," he instructed. "Make it sound important. When you get in we'll be right behind you."

"Now I know why you invited me," I said. "I'm the bait."

"You've got it. It's easier than breaking down the door. Let's go."

The five of us crowded into the smallish outer lobby and I dialed the intercom. I was answered with a caroled, "Clemens Investments. Good morning." There was no mistaking the voice.

"Fred," I said, trying to sound distraught, "this is Archy McNally and I must see you at once. It's important."

"Of course," he said calmly. "Come right up."

He buzzed us in; we all jammed into one elevator and rose in silence to his floor. One of the cops smelled of garlic and I wondered if it was Rogoff.

The sergeant motioned me to stand in front of Clemens's door. He and the other officers hid to one side. I pressed the buzzer and the door was opened by a smiling Frederick

Clemens. He was wearing his usual vested suit, this one a double-breasted sharkskin with a lapel drape to the lower button. Sharkskin was the perfect fabric for a predator like him.

"Come on in, Archy," he said genially, and stood aside.

I entered and the four cops pushed in behind me. If Clemens was startled he controlled his shock coolly. His sang outfroided mine. He didn't even say, "What is the meaning of this?" But he did stop smiling.

"Frederick Clemens?" Al asked.

"Yes."

"I am Sergeant Rogoff of the Palm Beach Police Department." He held out his ID but Clemens didn't so much as glance at it.

"And?" he inquired.

"These premises are your residence?"

"They are."

"And your place of business?"

"Correct."

"Are these premises also the residence of Felix Katz?"

"Yes."

"Is Mr. Katz here at the moment?"

"No, he is not."

There was a brief pause in the questioning. Clemens did not look at me. I think he was uncertain if I was cooperating with the police or if I was present under duress.

"You're here for what reason?" Fred finally asked. "Am I to be arrested?"

"I hope it won't be necessary, sir," said the sergeant—a beautifully noncommittal statement. "But I have a legal document authorizing a search of these premises. Do you wish to examine it?"

"No, I do not," Clemens said tartly. "If it is not a legal search then it's useless, isn't it?"

Rogoff's smile was cold. "You know the laws of evidence, Mr. Clemens, and you're right."

"What are you looking for?" Fred demanded. "All my records, correspondence, licenses, and legal documents are in unlocked file drawers. It would save time and trouble if you will specify exactly what you hope to find."

Al stared at him. "Not your business records, sir," he said grimly. "We hope to find a pair of pigskin gloves."

CHAPTER 31

FINALLY, FINALLY FRED Clemens was shaken. Instead of growing pale his face suddenly flushed, shoulders slumped, fists were clenched to conceal the tremor of his fingers. He seemed to me more deflated than defeated but it was obvious he had been rattled. Rogoff noted it; his questions became more rapid.

"Is the name Frank Clement familiar to you?" he asked.

"No," Clemens said.

"Floyd Clifford?"

"I don't have to answer your questions."

"That's right; you don't," Al said reasonably. "But you're not under oath so what harm can it do?"

"Well, I never heard of Floyd Clifford."

"Do you know Mrs. Edythe Westmore of Palm Beach?"

Then Clemens glanced at me before replying. "Yes, I know Mrs. Westmore. She is a client of mine."

"And you're trying to sell her a Fabergé egg?"

"I'm not trying to sell her anything. I'm merely advising her to purchase a Fabergé egg from a French seller as an investment with a large profit potential."

"Uh-huh. Is this a picture of the egg in question?"

The sergeant opened the art book and held it out. Clemens looked down at the color photo of the Coronation Egg. *Then* he paled.

"It appears to be the egg, yes," Fred said in a voice now flat and toneless, totally lacking resonance.

"You gave an identical photo to Mrs. Westmore?"

Clemens hesitated just long enough to realize he could not deny it. "I did," he said. "The photo I gave Mrs. Westmore was sent to me by the egg's present owner in Paris."

"This particular egg is part of the Forbes Magazine Collection in New York," Al said. "I verified it by phone this morning."

Clemens gave an excellent imitation of horrified amazement. "You mean I've been duped?" he gasped.

Rogoff laughed. "You're good," he said.

"Really good. This page of this book was cut out and later taped back in place after it had been copied at a local photo shop. It was the copy you gave Mrs. Westmore as part of an intended swindle."

"Ridiculous," Clemens said, "I did no such thing."

Al addressed one of the cops: "Tom, how long did it take you? An hour?"

"Less than that, sarge."

Rogoff turned back to Clemens. "Tom here went out this morning to find the photo shop which made the copy. It didn't take him long because he started with the place nearest this address. The clerk in the photo shop recognized the shot of the Coronation Egg and remembers the customer who brought it in to have it copied. He remembers because the customer was missing the trigger finger of his right hand. Felix Katz has an index finger gone, doesn't he?"

"Yes," Clemens said tightly. "So do a lot of other men."

"Oh sure. But this man paid for the copying job with a Clemens Investments credit card. Smart, huh?"

"Our corporate credit card was stolen several weeks ago," Fred said quickly.

Rogoff's smile was bleak. "That's the first dumb thing you've said. The credit charge was signed by Felix Katz. The photo shop has a copy of the bill and so does the credit card company. That partner of yours may be a muscle but it's mostly between his ears."

Clemens's face had become increasingly stricken as he heard the sergeant detail the evidence of his culpability. But then I saw him recover. His spine stiffened, chin lifted. No pushover he.

"Katz is merely an employee," he said. "He is not my partner."

"No?" Al said. "Glad to hear it. Because if he was you'd be in the pasta fazool as deep as he is, wouldn't you? Mr. Clemens, I'm going to ask you to do something that'll benefit you as much as me."

"What?"

"Come with me to headquarters voluntarily. I would prefer not to arrest you. If you come in voluntarily it will count in your favor. I just want to talk with you while a rep from the State Attorney is there. And you can call in your own lawyer if you like. All I want to do is discuss the situation with you and see if we can work something out. What do you say? Will you come in voluntarily?"

Clemens didn't reply.

"Save yourself," Rogoff said softly. "Save yourself."

There was a long quiet while we all just stood there awaiting the decision. I could guess what was going through Fred's mind: a hurried weighing of pros and cons, knowledge of the evidence against him and fear of more he hadn't been told of. And there was his relationship with Katz to consider. What bargaining chips did he have? None but the fate of his ally. And his own future depended on that.

Finally Clemens drew a deep breath, adjusted his cuffs, made certain the knot of his cravat was in place. "All right," he said.

The sergeant moved swiftly. Two officers were detailed to search the apartment. Clemens, Rogoff, his driver, and I descended to the street. Fred was conducted to a police car but not before he looked at me sadly and said, "I'm disappointed in you, Archy." I could live with that.

Rogoff took me aside before we went our separate ways. "I'd like to keep the art book till tomorrow," he said. "I want to show it to the legal eagles."

"Only until tomorrow," I agreed. "Then I've got to play Mr. Fix-It. Al, why did you ask him if Katz was there? I thought you had a tail on the guy."

"We did but we lost him last night. Who knows where he is now or what he's up to."

"Well, their maroon Bentley is parked over there next to my buggy. If Katz is wheeling around it's probably in Helen Westmore's lavender Riviera."

"Could be. Keep watching your back, kiddo."

"I will," I said. "One more thing: Did you have a warrant for Clemens's arrest?"

"Nope," he said, grinning cheerfully. "But he thought I did. I conned the con man."

I watched the police car pull away and then I swung aboard my own scooter and drove to the Pelican Club for lunch. The joint was wall-to-wall celebrants since two companies were having early Christmas parties. McNally & Son was planning a brief and sober gathering in our cafeteria on the afternoon of Christmas Eve. All employees would be certain to attend, not for the cherry Kool-Aid and oatmeal cookies but because it was the occasion when annual bonuses were distributed.

I had a hasty burger and then fled the noise and confusion for the quiet serenity of my own miniature hideaway. I settled down with an English Oval and thought of how Rogoff had manipulated Clemens, massaging the man's ego, being stern and unforgiving when he had to be, and concluding by appealing to the swindler's instinct for self-preservation and deep-seated desire to avoid a stay at the resort community of Durance Vile.

I had little doubt Clemens-Clement-Clifford would eventually be allowed to walk with perhaps a slap on the wrist. But in return for his freedom he would condemn Felix Katz for the murder of Sydney Smythe and provide enough hard evidence to convict the thug and guarantee his long incarceration. I didn't think the prosecutor would seek the death penalty; it was an iffy proposition when the main witness (Clemens) was something less than an upright citizen.

I could accept it. It wasn't perfect but since when has justice been perfect? As for Clemens's perfidy in ratting on his associate—pooh! We all know there is as much honor amongst thieves as honesty amongst politicians.

My ruminations were reaved by a phone call from Mrs. Trelawney informing me the seignior demanded my presence forthwith. Miffed at having my reverie shattered and wondering why I was being so imperiously summoned, I climbed the back stairs to my father's archaic throne room. I found him standing erect at his antique desk, frowning with what I initially thought was anger but turned out to be puzzlement and concern.

"Mrs. Edythe Westmore phoned a few moments ago," he said, forgoing a greeting. "She sounded hysterical and it was only after a rather disjointed conversation that I was able to grasp what she was saying. She believes her son Walter has been kidnapped."

"Kidnapped?!" I said. "Walter? What details did she give?"

"Apparently he has not been seen since late yesterday afternoon. He didn't appear for dinner and his bed was not slept in last night. Mrs. Westmore claims she received a ransom demand by telephone about an hour ago. A woman with what Mrs. Westmore described as a foreign accent insisted on a payment of five hundred thousand dollars if Walter is to be released unharmed. And that, *in toto,* is all I was able to learn of the matter."

"Bewildering," I commented.

"It is indeed," he agreed. "Mrs. Westmore called to request counsel and assistance. I suggest you proceed at once to the Westmore home and determine exactly what is happening."

"Of course, father," I said. "I'll leave at once. If I feel it necessary, I'll phone you from the Westmores'. If not, I'll report to you this evening at home."

"Satisfactory," he said, nodding. "If you believe a kidnapping is actually in progress—and Edythe Westmore acquiesces—the proper law enforcement agencies should be notified."

"Yes, sir," I said, and departed hurriedly.

Minutes later I found myself zipping along Ocean Boulevard at an illegal rate. I slowed when I realized there was little point in rushing. And being stopped and ticketed by a trooper would be even more unnecessary. So I continued at a more sedate speed and eventually pulled into the Westmores' driveway and parked behind Natalie's battered Corolla, the first time I had seen that heap out of the garage.

The drive southward had given me time to reflect on what my father had told me. If it was true Walter had been kidnapped, who might be responsible for such a heinous crime? My first candidate was the "mean and dangerous punk" Felix Katz. Perhaps he, having learned of Clemens being taken into custody and the collapse of their larcenous scheme, had resolved to recoup by abducting Walter and demanding ransom. It was certainly a remarkable coincidence the kidnappers wanted half a million dollars—the identical sum Clemens and Katz had planned to mulct from Edythe.

But the bracing December air cooled my perfervid imagination; I realized my scenario was ridiculous. Clemens had been led away only a few hours previously. Katz could surely not be aware of it so soon. In any event, Walter apparently disappeared late Monday afternoon. No, Katz in all likelihood had not been involved in the snatch. Then who was next in line as a suspect? I simply didn't know, and recalling the kidnapping of the Franklin boy, wondered if it might be the work of visiting hoodlums.

My ring at the Westmores' door was answered by the lugubrious houseman Algernon Canfield, who obviously had not yet obtained the new job he sought. It seemed to me there was a hint of glee in his expression when he said, "They're in the sitting room, sir." I thought it was possible he was relishing the tribulations of the woman he called Madam Nag.

I found Natalie and Edythe Westmore huddling close on a wicker couch. I noted the missing man's wife was not present. Both mother and daughter appeared agitated and teary, which was understandable. Nettie rose swiftly and rushed to clutch me.

"Walter is gone, Archy!" she wailed. "He's been kidnapped!"

"And they're demanding half a million dollars," Edythe added indignantly. "Oh dear, oh dear, whatever shall we do?"

The first thing, I wanted to say, is to lower your voice, for despite her anxiety she was still braying. I sat down unbidden in an armchair, mostly to escape from Natalie's embrace, and faced the two women with sympathetic interest in their plight.

"Now tell me precisely what has happened," I said. "My father could provide only a few details."

They both began speaking at once and I was forced to shush Natalie and let Edythe relate the sequence of events. She added very little to what *mein papa* had already told me. She did amend her first account by saying the woman who phoned with news of Walter's abduction and demanded ransom had spoken with a southern, not a foreign accent. Whatever additional information I gleaned was elicited from questions answered by both women.

"His bed was not slept in last night?"

Edythe: "No, and his shaving brush was dry. Walter shaves every morning without fail."

"Can you be more specific about the last time he was seen?"

Natalie: "Three o'clock yesterday afternoon. I remember because he came over to the studio to see what I was working on and I asked him the time."

"How was he dressed?"

Natalie: "He was wearing his khaki safari suit with a light sweater under the jacket."

"Edythe, were you at home at three o'clock yesterday afternoon?"

"No, I was at my bridge club. The games were at the home of Mrs. Louis Fortuna on Sea Breeze Avenue."

"Did your houseman or cook see Walter yesterday after three?"

Natalie: "They say no. They say they were

both in the kitchen around that time and didn't see him."

"Did his wife see him at that time or later?"

Natalie: "No. She wasn't home."

Edythe: "And she returned quite late. It was nearly midnight."

"So she wasn't aware Walter was missing?"

Natalie (bitterly): "And she still doesn't know. She left early this morning and hasn't returned yet. Disgusting!"

Edythe: "Nettie, behave yourself."

"I presume Helen was driving the Riviera."

Natalie: "Yes, she was. She acts like it's her car. Walter paid for it."

Edythe: "He bought it for both of them, dear."

Natalie: "But he never gets a chance to use it!"

"Did either of you or your staff see a strange car on the estate at any time yesterday?"

Both: "No."

"Did either of you—"

But I was interrupted by the shrill of the telephone. We all looked at one another.

"It may be the kidnappers," I said quickly. "I want to listen in. Where is the nearest extension?"

"In the hallway," Natalie said. "Just inside the front door."

"Edythe," I said, "you answer and if it's the same woman try to keep her talking. Tell her you want to speak to Walter to make sure he's all right."

I ran out but by the time I found the hall

extension and picked up the receiver deli-
cately, the conversation was well along.

"...the po-lice or the FBI," I heard a woman
say with a molasses accent. "Not if you want
to see him again."

"How do I know he's still alive?" Edythe said
desperately. "Please let me speak to him."

"Okey-doke," the woman said.

Within a moment Walter came on the line.
He sounded almost cheery. "I'm fine, mother," he said. "They're feeding me. Do what
they say and everything will be all right. Try
not to worry."

Then there was a shuffling sound as if the
phone had changed hands. The woman with
the syrupy voice came back on.

"You remember now," she warned. "No
cops or your son is a goner. You get the cash
together—half a million, no bills bigger'n a
twenty. We'll call again and tell you how and
when to deliver. 'Bye now."

She disconnected and I hung up thinking half
a million dollars in twenties would have to be
delivered in a U-Haul truck. I went back into
the sitting room, where Edythe was weeping
and Natalie was trying to console her, one arm
about her mother's shoulders. I thought Nettie
looked devastated, not by her own fear but by
her mother's grief.

"Did you hear?" Edythe asked me between
sobs.

I nodded.

"I'll pay," she said mournfully. "I'll pay anything to get my boy back."

"The police—" I started, but Natalie broke in.

"No!" she said sharply. "Absolutely not! You heard what the woman said. No police and no FBI if we want to see Walter again. Don't you agree, mother?"

The despairing woman bobbed her head up and down.

"It's your decision," I said. "I won't attempt to advise you what to do. Edythe, if you need assistance obtaining the cash or making the delivery, please contact my father or me. We'll do all we can to help."

"Thank you, Archy," she said, and at last, finally, her voice was low.

I left the Westmore home in a wrathy mood. I thought I knew what was going on and I didn't like it one whit.

It was a simple task to confirm or negate my suspicion. The moment I arrived home I looked up the number of Barney Newfield in Manalapan and phoned. A woman answered.

"Miz Newfield's residence," she cooed.

"Sorry," I said. "Wrong number." And I hung up.

But it wasn't the wrong number of course. Because the last time I had heard that sugar-coated voice the owner had been asking for half a million in twenty-dollar bills.

CHAPTER 32

WEDNESDAY WOULD BE a day of reckoning, I decided when I awoke. I had to bring my Discreet Inquiry to a successful conclusion—a tidying up, so to speak. It was the only item on my agenda for I had finished my Christmas shopping with gifts for everyone on my list except myself. I couldn't decide which I wanted more: a mulberry fez with a tassel or mauve briefs decorated with flying champagne corks.

I had roused in time to breakfast with my parents, which proved fortunate since Ursi had baked an enormous chicken pie. If you think it an odd dish for a matutinal meal I suggest you try it sometime; you'll be ecstatic.

Father had apparently not informed mother of Walter Westmore's disappearance and so I made no reference to it. Nor did I mention the collapse of the Fabergé egg swindle or the solution of the Sydney Smythe homicide. I knew m'lord would consider it bad form to discuss such matters at the breakfast table. Besides, I was so busy with the chicken pie my conversation was limited to, "May I have a bit more, please."

I waited at home until ten o'clock, when I phoned Sgt. Rogoff. I told him firmly I wanted the art book because I intended to show it to Mrs. Westmore and reveal the scam to which she had almost fallen victim.

"Okay," Al said. "You can have it. The State Attorney's man has seen it and we have a signed statement from Clemens, so it's served its purpose. But I can't get away right now. Can you pick it up?"

"Of course," I said. "Half an hour."

I was on time and Rogoff came out of his office bearing the book. He handed it over.

"I'd ask you in," he said, "but Clemens is there singing his heart out and I don't want to interrupt the flow of his true confessions. And put quotation marks around true. Let's go outside for a minute."

We stood near my car in the bright morning sunlight. Al looked rested and sounded confident. I guessed things were going well with the interrogation of the Master Criminal.

"Has Clemens really confessed?" I asked.

"To everything," Al said. "Only he says he didn't do anything. Felix Katz did it all."

"He's fingering Katz?"

"Yeah. Middle-fingering. He claims the whole schmear was Katz's idea. Felix thought up the Fabergé egg con, contacted Sydney Smythe, cut the photo of the Coronation Egg from the book and had it copied."

"How much did they pay Smythe?"

"Ten grand. But then the dealer learned how much they stood to make—a cool half-million—and demanded fifty thousand more. Like you figured, he took up his old hobby of blackmail again. Katz said he had to be eliminated or he'd keep bleeding them. Also, he had already screwed up on what was inside the egg, feeding them your description of an imaginary 'surprise.' So, according to Clemens, Katz did the dirty deed. He went to Smythe's shop intending to strangle the old man but saw the bayonet handy and decided to use it. He returned to the office and told Clemens what he had done. They then both went out for a spaghetti dinner. A couple of choice beauties, those lads."

"Where is Katz now—do you know?"

"No idea. We've got the cops of three counties looking for him. And by the way, we found his pigskin gloves! The stupid bozo didn't throw them away. Stay tuned."

He returned to his office. I hopped into the Miata and made tracks for the Westmore home. What Rogoff had related was expected but I had no feeling of triumph. And I supposed when they apprehended Katz and detailed the evidence against him, he'd say, "Clemens told me to do it." The Nuremberg defense: "I was just obeying orders."

The only car parked in the Westmore driveway was Edythe's white Cadillac. I peeked into the garage to make certain Natalie's Corolla was gone. It was. The houseman opened the front door for me and I walked back to the sitting room carrying *Fantastic Jewelry of Royalty*.

I found Mrs. Westmore seated at a small wicker desk close to the white phone. She was listlessly turning the pages of a magazine, *Smart Money*, looked up when I entered, and gave me a wan smile.

"I haven't heard anything, Archy," she said. "No one has phoned."

"Everything's going to be all right," I told her. "You'll get your son back unharmed."

"How do you know?"

"Just a hunch. Meanwhile I have something to show you."

I opened the art book and displayed the color photo of the Coronation Egg. I informed her it was part of a famous collection of Fabergé eggs in New York. I explained how the photo had been cut out, copied, and the reproduction given to her as part of a plot by Frederick Clemens to defraud her of half a million dollars. There was no egg in Paris. Clemens was a crook.

Her mouth had fallen open when I showed her the photo and remained ajar during my recital. By the time I finished, her outrage had temporarily banished fears for Walter's safety. Her face had become positively vermilion with fury. She jerked to her feet bristling like an enraged porcupine.

"Why, that's—that's *illegal*!" she roared.

"It is indeed," I agreed.

"I'm going to call Fred Clemens this minute and give him a piece of my mind," she shouted angrily.

"You won't be able to speak to him, Edythe. He's in police custody facing a variety of charges."

"Well, I should think so!" she said. "And if they want me to testify against him I'll be happy to. Archy, does this mean all the money I gave him for other investments is lost?"

"Not necessarily. It depends on how much he has in assets. If they are sufficient and he is forced to make restitution you may recover all or a portion of the sums you invested with him."

"Fred Clemens a scoundrel," she said wonderingly. "I can scarcely believe it. He was so charming."

"His stock-in-trade. I assure you other people were fooled by his manner as well as you. Edythe, you'll probably be hearing from the police about this matter. I know you'll cooperate and, even if it causes you embarrassment, answer their questions fully."

"Will I ever!" she vowed. "That thief deserves to spend the rest of his life behind bars."

"I doubt if he will. But you can console yourself with the thought of having saved half a million by his nick-of-time exposure."

"Half a million dollars," she repeated. "Just what I need to ransom my son."

"Not yet," I said, and with that delphic utterance I left her to reflect on the treachery of charming men.

I was about halfway down to Manalapan when Natalie's Corolla passed me going north at a lively clip. I'm sure she saw me—a fire engine–red Miata is hard to miss—but she didn't even give me a friendly tootle of the horn, nor did I make any similar effort. At the moment I was not harboring any cordial feelings for that young lady.

About an hour later I was parking outside the residence of Barney Newfield. It was a pleasant, two-story house not far from the Waterway. The front lawn was hemmed by a white fence, attractive even though the pickets were vinyl. The landscaping was verdant enough but rather formal for a South Florida home on the water.

I carried the art book up the steps to the porch, noting a well-worn banister undoubtedly used by the vision-impaired owner. (Oh Connie, how well you taught me!) I rang the bell and in a few moments the door was opened by a diminutive, middle-aged woman who wore a pink apron over tight denim slacks and a black T-shirt.

"Yessir," she said softly, and I knew at once she was the possessor of the cloying voice and probably the companion Barney had mentioned at the Westmore cocktail party. I strove mightily to recall her name. Was it Jewel? No. Pearl? No. Ah! I had it.

"Ruby?" I asked.

"Why, yes," she said, puzzled. "We met?"

"Not until this moment. My name is Archy McNally. Would you be kind enough to ask Ms. Newfield if she would be willing to receive me?"

"Jus' a minute now," she said, and closed the door.

It was more than a minute but eventually the

door was opened and Ruby said, "Walk this way, please, sir," and sashayed down a hallway. I followed and called, "I'll never learn to walk that way," and was rewarded with a fleeting smile tossed to me over her shoulder.

Barney Newfield was in a small chamber at the end of the corridor. It seemed to be more a conservatory than a room, for it was only one story high with the ceiling and three walls entirely glass. It had obviously been added after the house was built, for the scanty woodwork was new and burnished while the paneling and floor of the hallway had a patina of many years.

The greenhouse was filled with what appeared to be hundreds of potted plants, large and small. Many of them were flowering and the sweet aroma was almost overpowering. But the blossoms made a lovely rainbow and I thought it sad all this beauty was invisible to the owner. But Walter had said her sense of smell was incredibly acute so perhaps the scent of the plants was pleasure enough.

Barney was seated in a motorized wheelchair, her white cane hooked over one arm. She turned her opaque glasses toward me when I entered. "Archy!" she said. "How nice of you to visit. Forgive me for not rising but I twisted my ankle the other day and I'm temporarily confined to this vehicle." She held out a hand.

I stepped forward to shake it but wasted no time on pleasantries. "Where is he, Barney?" I asked.

And she wasted no time on futile denials. "Upstairs," she said. "I told him it wouldn't work."

"Does he realize his mother is suffering?"

"He knows and it troubles him. But he says it was the only way to keep her from being cheated."

"The fool! Why didn't he leave it to professionals? The man who tried to swindle Mrs. Westmore is now in police custody. She's not going to be cheated and all his stupid fake kidnapping has accomplished is to cause her grief. Was it his idea or his sister's?"

Her handsome, wrinkled face became set. "He says both but I think Natalie heard of a local kidnapping and decided it was the only thing they could do."

I suspected Nettie was inspired by my tale of the Franklin abduction but I didn't mention it to Barney.

"You must realize, Archy," she continued, "Walter's sister has a great deal of influence over him. He can't seem to resist her intensity. She's always been able to convince him to do what she wants, and sometimes what she wants is not in his best interest."

"No excuse," I said angrily. "He's an adult and should have a mind of his own."

"He does," Barney said. "A very good mind. But he is not assertive and in personal relationships he prefers to take the path of least resistance. You may call him wimpish but I prefer to think of him as tractable."

"Well, he's on the wrong tract now," I

said—a lousy pun if ever I heard one. "I'm calling a halt to this cockamamy scheme right now."

She sighed. "Please believe me when I say I'm glad. I didn't want to get involved, knowing how his mother would be affected by his disappearance, but he pleaded and I agreed. I'll always be ashamed of it."

"There's enough blame to go around." I said. "May I speak to him now, please?"

"Ruby!" she called, and when her companion appeared at the doorway she said, "Please ask Walter to come down for a moment." Ruby nodded and left.

"She really made a ridiculous accomplice," I told Barney. "I never heard a vicious criminal say 'Okey-doke' or ' 'Bye now.' "

"Don't make fun of Ruby. She just tried to say what Walter told her to say. He wouldn't let me talk because he feared his mother might recognize my voice. Archy, don't be too hard on him."

"Hah!" I said. "Flaying alive is what I have in mind."

Walter took one step into the conservatory, saw me, and staggered back one step. "Archy," he said in a choky voice.

"You idiot!" I said disgustedly. "Just what kind of a rotten trick do you think you're pulling? Your mother is home weeping. Can't sleep. Going out of her mind with worry. Did you give a single thought to how you're hurting her?"

"Natalie—" he started, then stopped. I was happy he had. He was about to hold his sister responsible for the cruel farce but then he acknowledged his own guilt. Maybe there was hope for him.

"Useless!" I practically shouted at him. "All the stupid plotting by your sister and you was useless. Look at this!" I showed him the color photo of the Coronation Egg. "That's the objet Fred Clemens was trying to sucker your mother into buying. It's owned by the Forbes Magazine Collection in New York. Now Clemens is in the pokey and the swindle is kaput."

He continued to stare at the picture. "Did you discover this?" he asked.

"I did. And went to the police, who took Clemens out of circulation. So your moronic scheme was completely unnecessary."

"Does mother know about it?"

"She does. I told her an hour ago. And you know what her reaction was? She said, 'Oh thank you, lord. Now I have half a million dollars to rescue my dear son.' The purpose of your insane plan, wasn't it?"

"All we wanted was to keep Clemens from stealing it."

"With no consideration whatsoever of how your disappearance would cause your poor mother to suffer."

He hung his head, shuffled his feet. "I'm so ashamed," he said faintly.

"You should be," I said sternly. "What you did was unconscionable. Infamous is not too strong a word."

I was inordinately pleased with myself. I had

never before fully appreciated what a joy it is to excoriate the moral turpitude of others. Preachers must derive great satisfaction from their calling.

"What should I do now, Archy?" Walter asked timidly.

"What you should do," I told him, "is pack up whatever you brought with you. Then I'll drive you back to Palm Beach. I'll let you out a block or two from your home. You will continue on foot, make a triumphant entrance, and tell your mother you managed to escape from your captors by using a clever stratagem I leave to your imagination."

"Will mother believe me?"

"Of course. She is a credulous woman with an inexhaustible capacity for accepting the outlandish as gospel. You may tell Natalie the truth since she was your partner. As for Helen..."

"She won't care one way or another," he said coldly. "Nettie was here earlier this morning and said Helen doesn't even know I've disappeared. The hell with her!"

I didn't know if his rejection of his wife was heartfelt or if his love for her had been corrupted by his sister's venom. He left to gather his belongings and I turned to Barney Newfield.

"I'm sorry your home was the setting for such a nasty scene," I said. "I apologize for my harsh language."

"He deserved it," she said, "and I deserve just as much for agreeing to aid him."

"You acted through friendship. I can't fault you for that."

312

"I hope, Archy, this won't end our relationship. I'd enjoy it if you'd be willing to visit me again."

"It would give me great pleasure," I assured her. "I might even sing an old song for you. I'm certain you've never heard it."

"Oh?" she said. "What is it called?"

" 'My Barney Lies Over the Ocean.' "

"Surely you're joking!"

"Surely I am not."

She was still laughing when Walter and I departed a few moments later.

CHAPTER 33

AFTER DINNER ON Wednesday evening I asked my father if I could speak to him in re my Discreet Inquiry. He agreed and led the way into his study, where he invited me to pour myself a noggin of his second-best cognac. He had a glass of port and I wished him "Salud!" for the case he had recently purchased was definitely corky.

I told him the entire story. Well, perhaps not the *entire* story since I bowdlerized those portions I knew would offend him, such as my merrymaking with Natalie Westmore.

I related the downfall of Clemens Investments and the end of the attempted swindle by Fred and Felix, the former now in custody, the latter being sought by the gendarmerie. I explained how the con game had led to the murder of Sydney Smythe and I detailed the role

I had played in the solution of that brutal crime.

Finally I told him of the false kidnapping engineered by the Westmore siblings and how I had brought it to naught. I must have spoken for almost an hour, interrupted occasionally by his questions. When I finished I waited in silence for his judgment, betting on "Scandalous!" or maybe "Abominable!" But he one-upped me.

"Reprehensible!" he said. "Archy, I never cease to be amazed by the depth of human wickedness and the just plain stupidity of Homo sapiens. It does not bode well for the future, does it?"

"No, sir," I said, finishing my brandy. "But all is not gloom and doom. In this case, as an example, justice has not scored a total victory but it has certainly run up an estimable score against the forces of darkness."

"Yes, of course," he said. "You are quite right and we must constantly strive to look on the bright side. For instance, I assume you kept an accurate record of the billable hours you spent defending the interests of our client, Mrs. Edythe Westmore."

"I did indeed, father. I'll deliver my tally to the Accounting Department tomorrow."

"Excellent," he said. "And my congratulations on a difficult job well done."

"Thank you, sir," I said, and backed from the room since I had read somewhere it is not de rigueur to turn one's dorsal surface to one's sovereign.

I went upstairs intending to add concluding notes to my journal and close out a record which began with the first mention of a Fabergé egg. But the phone was ringing when I entered my suite and I plucked it up hoping Connie was calling from Miami to share an intimate chat.

"Hi, Archy!" Natalie Westmore said brightly.

"Hello, Nettie," I said in the dullest tone I could muster.

"Isn't it wonderful the way everything turned out!" she bubbled on. "I'm just so happy. Listen, Archy, I'd love to see you and thank you personally for all you did."

"Not necessary," I said stiffly. "I've already told Walter how I feel about your—your escapade."

"I know and it's why I must see you. What we did was not as awful as you think. And if I could see you I could explain our motives and I know you'll understand. Please, Archy, can't you come over even for a short time? I won't be able to sleep tonight knowing what you must think and not having a chance to explain. Please?"

"Very well," I said. "I can't see how you can possibly justify your conduct but I don't wish to be adamant. Where are you now?"

"In my studio. Come as soon as you can. And thank you for being such a darling."

She hung up and I combed my hair and dabbed my jowls with a few drops of "Obsession." "Darling" or not I was determined

315

to repeat to her my scathing remarks to Walter. She might be deliriously happy but I would not allow her mood to mollify my denunciation of her shameful behavior. Almost glowing with self-righteousness I danced downstairs, bid Hobo farewell, and started out.

When I entered the grounds of the Westmore estate I slowed to a crawl for I saw the portico of the main house was brilliantly illuminated. The lavender Riviera was drawn up on the driveway close to the steps, and set near the front door were two large suitcases. It did not look like an arrival to me; it looked like a departure.

I parked far back in the semidarkness and made my way on foot to Natalie's studio, gleaming through the foliage. Before I knocked on the closed plank door I glanced again at the lighted porch but saw no signs of activity.

The studio door was flung open and Natalie greeted me with an animated smile. She immediately grabbed my arm, hauled me inside so forcibly I almost tripped over the heavy lantern on the floor.

"Oh Archy," she said, "I'm so glad you're here! We have so much to talk about!"

I was scarcely listening, for my firm resolve to upbraid her received a kick in the gluteus maximus when I saw how fetching she looked. She was wearing her usual raggedy denim cutoffs with a faded blue tank top. Her bare legs had never before seemed so tender, her slender arms so chewable.

But more than her physical appeal caused

my intention to scold to simply drain away. She was vibrant with delight, could not stop smiling, grasped my hands to draw me close. She smelled fresh and young. I could feel my resoluteness weaken and become flaccid as base lust, which seems to lurk in my bloodstream like an inexpugnable virus, gained control.

"You do forgive me, don't you, darling?" she asked softly.

I wasn't quite ready to surrender completely. "What you did was wrong," I said—a very tepid condemnation compared to the accusations I had hurled at her brother.

"I know," she said cheerily. "But we had to do it because there was no other way to rescue mother from Clemens, that oily crook. You do see we were forced to do it, don't you? Archy? You agree?"

I nodded dumbly. When it comes to a violent conflict between my will and my glands, I'll give you one guess as to which usually emerges victorious.

"But everything has turned out just super," she nattered. "Mother has all the money she saved and she is so happy Walter is safe and sound she has agreed to finance a year of exploration in Africa. He'll be leaving in about a month."

I found it difficult to believe. "She's giving him the money, Nettie?"

"Well, not exactly. She's lending it to him at only twelve percent interest."

"Ah," I said, reassured Edythe Westmore had made a quick recovery from her nearly disastrous venture into high finance and had reverted to her penurious ways. "And is Helen going with Walter?"

"To Africa?" Natalie said. "Are you off your rocker? They're getting a divorce. Helen is leaving tonight. Those are her bags on the porch. Good riddance!"

I remembered what Barney Newfield had said about Walter acceding to his sister's wishes and marveled at how her intensity overwhelmed what might be his divergent desires. To be quite honest, I thought Natalie's moral rudder was unhinged and her brother was a fool to let a vixen dictate his behavior.

"Now let's talk about us," Nettie said. "I really do owe you so much, Archy, for what you've done."

"I am happy I was able to be of some assistance," I said haughtily.

"And you must be rewarded!" she cried gaily, stooped, and switched off the lantern. We stood in pitchy darkness for a sec or two. It was obvious she meant to present me with an unexpected Christmas gift. Unwrapped. I considered my options and my proper role in this *opéra comique*.

I cannot to this day fully explain my motives; I can only beg for your sympathy and understanding. To be brutally frank, I rejected the lady's offer. I know it was out of character and even at the time I wondered if I was being a saphead. But if the flesh was willing the spirit was weak. The prospect of strumming the springs of the steel cot was enticing but I could not conquer my fear of resuming an intimate involvement with this perverse and inconstant woman.

"Ah, what a shame," I said as lightly as I could. "But I really must run. I'm already late for choir practice and I promised to sing the baritone solo in *'Stille Nacht, Heilige Nacht.'* So off I go."

I pushed open the door and stepped outside. Natalie followed wailing, "Archy! Archy!" She succeeded in clutching my arm, halting me. At that moment Felix Katz came out of a deeper shadow. He had what appeared to be a huge automatic pistol gripped in his right hand. He moved the muzzle slowly back and forth between Nettie and me.

She was the first to speak. "Who are you?" she demanded.

"Santa Claus," he said laconically. "My reindeer are parked at the gate."

"Well, I'll thank you to get out of here at once," she said fiercely. "If you don't I'll call the police."

"How?" Katz said. "There's no phone in this shack."

"Then I'll start screaming," she threatened.

"Go ahead," he said. "And get a slug in your belly."

"You wouldn't dare!"

"Oh, shut your yap!" he said.

"Shut my yap?" Natalie repeated, and was so outraged she stamped her foot. I had read of people doing that from anger or frustration but had never seen it actually done. I was impressed.

Natalie whirled, went back into the studio, slammed the door. Katz laughed, I had listened to their exchange with fear for our safety and awe at her courage. What a feisty woman she was!

"Hey," Felix said to me, "that's some twist. She's got fire. And I'd like to put it out."

I sought to divert his mind from Natalie. "Your weapon looks more effective than Droopy's," I said.

"Droopy? Who's he?"

"Your emissary at the restaurant parking lot."

"Oh, that loser," he said. "I met him in the clink and he showed up a few weeks ago looking for a handout. So I gave him the job. But I guess he didn't have the moxie for it. I have. Now here's what we do: You walk to the gate with me right behind you ready to blast your spine if you try any tricks. The Riviera is there with Helen behind the wheel. You and me will get in the back seat and then we'll all go for a little trip. Short for you, long for us."

"Does Helen know I'm going to accompany you?" I asked.

"Nah," he said. "But that tramp will do what I tell her to do."

"You're not speaking as politely as you did at the Pelican Club," I commented.

"I was playing a part then," he said. "Not bad, huh? Now move!"

He had maneuvered behind me and we

both had taken only a step or two when it happened. The studio door crashed open and Natalie came out like a whirlwind. She was carrying the heavy lantern by the steel loop handle and with a mighty overhand heave she swung it at the head of Felix Katz.

He had started to whirl when the door banged open, and when he caught a glimpse of the descending lantern he tried to dodge, but it was too late. It crunched into his crown with the sound of an ax splitting an oak stump. He went down as if his legs had suddenly been amputated. I thought it likely his skull had been crushed.

Natalie was preparing to take another swing at the fallen thug when I caught her arm and took the lantern from her grip, prying her fingers loose to do it. "Enough," I said. "He won't revive for a while. Now you run to a phone and call nine-one-one. Tell them to send the police to pick up a killer they've been looking for. His name is Felix Katz. And ask them to inform Sergeant Rogoff. Got all that?"

She nodded and began sprinting toward the main house. I watched her go, admiring the way she moved: a graceful loping gait with no elbow-flapping. Then I lighted the lantern (dented but still working) and crouched to examine Katz. His mouth was open and he seemed to be breathing shallowly. There was less blood than I expected. I stood and nudged the automatic farther away from his body with the toe of my shoe. Then I lighted a cigarette. My hands weren't trembling but my knees had all the tensile strength of tapioca pudding.

The following hour was a period of organized confusion. Two police cars showed up first, soon followed by two more, an ambulance, a fire-rescue truck, and finally Sgt. Rogoff in his pickup. Meanwhile the audience had been increased by Edythe, Walter, the houseman, and the cook.

Natalie and I repeated our stories at least three times to the police and family members. Felix Katz was hauled away still unconscious and the lantern was temporarily confiscated by the officers. Everyone congratulated Nettie and me on our narrow escape and I was unstinting in my praise of her bravery and fearless attack upon an armed hoodlum. Al Rogoff winked at me and murmured, "Happy Holiday."

Oh, one other thing happened you may find as amusing as I did. Helen Westmore apparently learned of the bludgeoning and capture of her criminal paramour, for the Riviera returned to park in front of the Westmore home. I watched as the car door was opened, Helen extracted her two suitcases and lugged them back into the house. A very practical lady. Would she smooth things over with Walter and the two of them be reconciled? I didn't know and didn't much care.

Finally Natalie and I were left alone in the studio with no illumination. I would, I knew, be an unfeeling and ungrateful brute if I deserted her now. I owed her, did I not, and my dear parents have impressed upon me the importance of paying my debts promptly when due. And so I did.

In addition, it was only three days until Christmas.

'Tis the season to be jolly!

If you have enjoyed reading this large print book and you would like more information on how to order a Wheeler Large Print Book, please write to:

Wheeler Publishing, Inc.
P.O. Box 531
Accord, MA 02018-0531

MBal 12-10